A HALF REMEMBERED SONG

Alan Jones

MAPLE
PUBLISHERS

A Half Remembered Song

Author: Alan Jones

Copyright © Alan Jones (2022)

The right of Alan Jones to be identified as author of this work has been asserted by the author in accordance with section 77 and 78 of the Copyright, Designs and Patents Act 1988.

First Published in 2016
Second Edition 2022

ISBN 978-1-915492-22-7 (Paperback)
978-1-915796-47-9 (E-Book)

Book Layout by:
White Magic Studios
www.whitemagicstudios.co.uk

Published by:
Maple Publishers
Fairbourne Drive, Atterbury,
Milton Keynes,
MK10 9RG, UK

www.maplepublishers.com

A CIP catalogue record for this title is available from the British Library.

To my wife Ann

for all her love, patience and support in my search for a voice.

An Garda Síochána meaning "the Guardian of the Peace" and more commonly referred to as the Gardaí or "Guardians", is the police force of The Irish An individual officer is called Garda and the service as a whole is called The Gardai (pronounced Gardee).

Acknowledgement

The author would like to thank all those teachers who helped to make the job so enjoyable.

1

August 24th 1987

The distant shore is shrouded in an early morning mist, just as it had been – two years ago. He could hear cows moving in the stillness.

"Like it used to be! Just me and the cows," he says, a wry smile crossing his lips. It has been a long time since he got up in the morning darkness, and watched the sun come up on his journey to a river or lake for a day's fishing. They had been his special days. Alone on deserted roads and buoyed at the prospect of the challenge ahead. It was like having the whole world to himself.

"Except for the bloody cows!" He says to the open sky.

It swallows the sound, just as he remembered all that time ago. As panic had gripped him then, one word had burst out in uncontrollable repetition, "Glenn! Glenn!"

Then, it was bellowed with all the power he could muster. Now he repeats it in a guttural whisper, born of the despair of the intervening years. He looks about, concerned that anyone should see him standing there talking to the sky, but he knows that he could be alone there for days. Tom Ellison draws in a lung – swelling breath. *He is back here! He has made it!* After today, he might make a new start. His hopes are high – but his expectation less. The stones click beneath his feet as he shifts his weight and the water slips over the toes of his unsuitable shoes. Tom Ellison is back to a place he had dreaded, even to think of, for so long. A place he had tried to scour from his memory, but failed. Nothing could give back all that he used to be, but now he felt more whole, more together, physically and mentally, than he had felt for the past eight years: and it felt good. True, the face that now bore the marks of pain and neglect had once been handsome. The eyes that used to sparkle with a ready openness are now set deep and have a perpetually rheumy look. The youthful freshness of the face, that had been the envy of many, has given way to a puffiness that speaks of years of heavy drinking. But the mouth is firm and the chin has a determined set to it. There is, despite signs of wear, a feeling of renewal about this face. Tom Ellison's nightmare might be coming to an end.

*

It began mundanely enough in May 1987. He had put a notice on the school notice board. FISHING TRIP TO IRELAND. SEE MR. ELLISON. He knew that this cryptic message would be enough and would need no elaboration. It was going to be his holiday too, and he would not overburden himself with a large group, so a low-key announcement was best. Anyway, he had primed the members of the Fishing Club in advance that he intended to employ a "first come, first served" method.

On previous occasions, headmaster Charles Meade had always allowed for Tom's enthusiasms. Theirs was an odd relationship. Neither liked the other very much, nor did they show more than a passing interest in just how the other did his job. Tom had no ambition to taste the day-to-day grind of timetabling, staff substitutions, tiresome paperwork and endless meetings, that seemed to fascinate Meade. For his part Headmaster Meade had little interest in Tom's enthusiasms, but valued their attraction to parents. To put it simply, they used each other unashamedly.

On this occasion his approach to Meade about a trip to Ireland received a cold reaction. A decision to allow this trip was literally "a step too far," for him.

"What about "The Troubles?" It's dangerous," was his immediate response.

"No it's not. Not in the South! Thousands of anglers have been going there for years. I've been three times myself. Not a sign of trouble," reassured Ellison.

"Why would there be? For a fishing trip," he reasoned. It had been his experience that the discord had not touched travellers in the South.

"Try persuading the parents!" Meade said scornfully.

"I have!"

Tom had quietly sounded out likely takers at a recent Parents Evening. His stock was high, and parents needed little persuasion for him to take their young charges off their hands. Besides, refusal would be met by whingeing disappointment from their sons.

"They all liked the idea," he added.

Anger visibly welled up in Meade. "You asked without consulting me!" he thundered, victim once more to a Tom Ellison subterfuge.

"It was only a sounding out. Nothing definite," Tom replied with false meekness.

"You've placed me in an impossible position!" the Head snapped. His face had taken on a pink shade, which looked nearer to red against the grey of his lightweight suit.

"You can always block it," Ellison said disingenuously. "And become the villain!" Meade swivelled in his chair and looked out through the window which overlooked the playing field, turning his back on Ellison. In the silence that followed Tom could sense the weighing up process that Meade was going through. He turned his chair dramatically and pointed an accusing finger at Ellison.

"You're a conman Tom!"

"If you say so," he replied.

"One of these days..," Meade did not finish the sentence. He was deflating like a punctured tyre.

"Why don't you speak to them?"

Tom was ramping up the pressure. This was a master stroke. He knew that he gave, what Meade called, "added value" to the school. It was safe in this knowledge that he took on extra-curricular roles, which made him a popular teacher in the school; and crucially, with parents. Meade hurriedly considered a withdrawal strategy. He wasn't going to be put in the position of dampening parents' enthusiasm.

"I want a letter sent, outlining the details of your proposal," he lent on the word *proposal*. "A fact finder! No promises! I want positive replies from parents, or this thing goes no further,"

A sense of regaining control was reflected in Meade's demeanour.

"I might need some backing from School Fund," Tom added boldly.

"No way! If it doesn't support itself it, doesn't happen. Right?"

"You're the boss!"

"And don't you forget it!" Meade gave him a piercing head teacher look and closed the diary on his desk, to signify that the interview was over. Tom turned to leave.

"And don't forget you'll need someone to go with you. I want a name out front before the letters go out," Meade asserted. This might stop the trip in its tracks, he thought. To his surprise Ellison responded instantly

10

"Righto," he said lightly, just as the lesson bell sounded.

He turned about, his objective achieved. As he closed the door behind him, his fist clenched in triumph, he whispered, "Yes!" Everything was now in place.

He had already inveigled another member of staff to join the trip, to act as his "side gunner". Experience told him that he wouldn't find a kindred fisherman on the staff, but the offer of a free week's holiday in Ireland was too good to miss for an impoverished, underpaid, P.E. teacher, and Dave Cotter took little persuasion to sign up. Of medium height, but muscular throughout and with youthful good looks and wispy blond hair, Dave Cotter was the stereotypical PE teacher. He had a growing reputation in county circles as a quicksilver scrum half. Low gravity, and lighting quick over twenty yards, made him a valuable asset to his club. "Like shit off a shovel," the club president and school governor Ken Collett had said at his interview for the job. Dave was in his second year of teaching, and had been an instant hit with the kids, although some senior colleagues doubted the wisdom of his relaxed attitude. "You're a teacher – not a friend!" was the view from the chessboard in the corner of the staffroom. Tom saw him as a breath of fresh air, and they had quickly set up an easy relationship. He was even persuaded by his young colleague to take up badminton again, despite the gibes of "geriatric!" at the end of longer rallies. Tom was sure that the young sportsman would be a capable lieutenant. A week's full board during the Summer holiday in County Leitrim beckoned; and it was the close season for club rugby. Tom hadn't revealed the depths of his planning, so that part of the head's ultimatum was already met. Dave was a bonus that meant his "fait accompli" was secured.

Tom's mother had always said he had a devious mind in the face of opposition. It was a trait in contrast to his lack of personal ambition. Tom had long since discarded personal ambition to advance further up the teaching ladder. He was content with his life. Career enhancing job applications and the prospect of change were not for him. He had a method for life, and it seemed to work. He had become a trusty fixture in Hillpark School. Working at the school since he started teaching, he had advanced, almost by default, to the heights of second in the English Department. His elevation had been an inducement to keep him there, but he held no special responsibilities in the department. He was happy with that.

Tom Ellison had developed an ambiguous relationship with the rigours of public exams. He tolerated them, and over time Governors and parents knew that the pupils were in safe hands with him. However it was a love of the revealing the knowledge, not the knowledge itself, that motivated Tom Ellison. He believed that his contribution was in the breadth of his involvement, rather than its academic depth. He knew that clever pupils would find that depth as they matured. His mission was not just about making clever children cleverer. In his lessons, questions, sometime awkward, often challenging, were asked and he would answer them as best he could, with honesty and without condescension. His teaching gave everyone permission to be both inquisitive and critical. He could be relied on to respond to pupil enthusiasm for whatever caught their interest at the time. As a bi-product of this approach he was sure that examination results were regarded as good; despite the fact that he felt they had become ever more prescriptive.

Tom had been responsible for starting activities to satisfy a wide variety of young needs, however transient. That, he felt, was his role. Other staff thought he looked foolish in some of his activities, taking part, as he often did, in the latest youthful craze. He accepted that. Children had always shown a fascination in the new, the bizarre and the provocative. For Tom Ellison this would often end up as an out of school event or visit. Tom believed that it was satisfying these interests, which gave his teaching substance. The ability to write a letter and show an interest in the richness of literature, were part of his formal role, but his lessons could be easily derailed by an innocent sounding question from a knowing pupil. Also, for him, what happened outside the classroom was part of being a teacher. Others had different methods and he respected them. It was the plays and musicals that he produced that epitomised his approach. They were ideal vehicles for engaging in extravagant play. They engendered a spirit of collaboration, that he felt could not be bettered in the formative years of a child's life.

So much time spent on these activities, had meant that Tom Ellison's social life might be thought of as being limited. School and fishing. That exemplified Tom's modus operandi. There had been little room for anything else, so at the age of thirty seven Tom was single. Only the occasional skirmish in the battlefield of sexual relationships warmed the lonesome hours. He worried about it at first. Most of his friends were married. It would have been easy to fall into a permanent relationship, or even a marriage, just to become one of The Club. That was too high a price to pay for the loss of freedom to fly off at any tangent that took his fancy. It wasn't that he didn't like women or enjoy sex. It just happened that the two had never come together strongly enough to force an issue of choice, although there had been a brief dalliance with Diane Porter, the school secretary. But for the moment he was happy with his lot.

This was the man who printed out the message "FISHING TRIP TO IRELAND SEE MR ELLISON"

2

He received eight positive responses from parents, much as he had expected. The Fishing Club had been running for five years, and he had sowed the seeds of an expedition to sample the Emerald Isle's fishing, for the last six months. It was in this sort of extra-curricular activity, in the teacher's role, that gave Tom Ellison his greatest satisfaction.

He knew the older boys best. Ben Chamberlain had been to Ireland before with his uncle and would be a stalwart member of the group. Ian Gilbert was a quiet lad, non-academic but with hidden depths that Tom had tried to nurture through fishing, and who was unanimously "elected" to be in charge of bait for the whole group. John Copely had been a regular member of the school fishing team since his first year at the school and was the group's archivist, keeping records of venues fished and fish caught. Gavin Green's father was the secretary of The Kingfishers, a local club that Tom belonged to and was to become Transport Manager on the trip, responsible for the loading and unloading of the minibus. The juniors, all in their first year at the school, were Colin Green, (Gavin's brother), Glenn Wallace, Simon Aylett and Barnaby Coleman (known as "barn man"), as much for his size as his given name.

In addition to week-end visits to local fisheries, Tom used after-school meetings of the group to pay for the trip in instalments. It was also a good way of building up the anticipation and excitement.

Over maps, they discussed the area they would be visiting, and the tactics they would be using. Items of tackle were refurbished; rod rings replaced, nets repaired. Other items were specially made. A rod rest was cut, hammered and bent in the Design block; hand-made floats whittled away around Tom's desk. Tom made a point of talking to the boys about life in Southern Ireland; about its natural beauty, its folk history, its music and of course, its religious tensions. All part of the "Ireland Experience," as someone had grandly entitled it. This pleased Tom Ellison.

Things had been working out just as Tom had planned when, after four weeks, Glenn Wallace brought a note from his mother indicating that he could not make the trip. It was a bald statement, without explanation. Years of school mastering told Tom that there was something behind the message, but it seemed to broach no discussion.

Even in his few dealings with the boy, since he first showed an interest in fishing, Tom's instincts told him that this was a troubled soul. He seemed to have few friends. Even in this small group, he had not been able to start up the relationships that usually developed through fishing. There was a feeling of melancholy about the small tousled haired boy at all times. Even when they discussed fishing, he held back from expressions of over enthusiasm, though Tom knew the trip mattered and he was taking everything in.

He made enquiries about the boy's background, but found out very little, other than he didn't seem to have a father as far as the school records were concerned. This had been hinted at when Tom gave the boys little jobs to do at home, like painting floats. Usually Tom expected to hear that dad had helped. In this case nothing was said, and Tom sensed that the boy had done all the work himself.

"Pity! But that's to his credit," he thought.

As a teacher, it was easy to make judgements on these matters, and Tom knew from experience, that it was a dangerous temptation. His instinct told him that the trip would do this particular boy a great deal of good. The planning and anticipation were factors as important as that of catching fish, and Glenn Wallace had absorbed it all with a veiled interest. It was a deep sense of disappointment that overcame Tom Ellison when the boy sheepishly shuffled close to him at his desk and, as if passing on a secret code, handed him the note from his mother. Without elaboration, it said that the boy could not go on the trip. A resigned shrug of the shoulders was his only response to Tom's question "Why?" It was said with genuine disappointment. It wasn't through any sense of being let down that caused Tom to feel the way he did, but the certain knowledge of the loss that it would be to this solitary boy, who didn't come to the next club meeting. Tom's immediate response was to leave the place open in the hope that there might be a change, knowing full well that finding a late replacement would be very difficult anyway.

Some days later he was on duty outside at break time, when he came across Glenn sitting on the steps leading up to the Art block. As he always did on theses occasions, Tom sat on his haunches and looked directly into the boy's face and saw the same blank, apparently unseeing, look that had concerned him before.

"What's happening Glenn?" he asked brightly.

"Nothing!"

"Been fishing recently?"

"No!"

"I caught a two pound roach at the weekend." A slight lifting of the eyes was the boy's only response.

"Sorry you're not coming to Ireland." It was meant as an expression of his regret, but Tom knew at once that it came out more as an inquisition.

"My mum told you!" It was short of being rude, but a clear sign that the boy wanted an end to the conversation.

"She didn't tell me why," Tom persisted.

"I don't know!"

"You mind if I talk to her?"

"If you want!" Though glum in appearance, Tom felt that the boy was pleased. He sensed his time was up in the exchange, but he'd got the permission he sought.

The phone call to Mrs Elaine Wallace was going to be difficult he knew, and he must not overstep the mark. He also knew that unsolicited approaches from the school automatically meant trouble in the minds of parents. Then he remembered that Mrs. Wallace had not attended the recent parents evening, so on the pretext of delivering her son's report as he was passing by on his way home, he arranged to call that day. After he had done an extensive tour of the giant Eden Towers council estate, he finally found Flat 28, Regent House on the fourth floor of a tall tower block, a post war construction, but already showing distinct signs of wear and tear. Breathless after his climb up through the heart of the building, with its myriad of side landings, he knocked on the door of number 28.

Elaine Wallace opened the door and nervously invited him in to the lounge, short on furniture but neat and well kept. She was in her late twenties, with shoulder length dark brown hair with streaks of blond, framing a face bereft of make-up, but nevertheless attractive. At her invitation, he sat down on the sofa and she sat in the armchair on the opposite side of a black and white tiled coffee table. He gave her the report and she thanked him nervously before starting to read it. As she read, he commented on her son's steady progress throughout. When she had finished, she carefully put the report back into its envelope.

"Was there anything else?" she asked uneasily.

"I just wanted a chat," he said

"What about?" Her tone was anxious. "What's he done?"

"Nothing, nothing at all," it was said with as much reassurance as he could muster.

"I just wanted to talk about the Ireland trip, if you've got a minute." She straightened in her seat and drew in a deep breath.

"Is there a reason for Glenn dropping out, he seemed so keen."

"It's personal," she answered in a low whisper.

"Can I help?" he volunteered.

"Nobody can. It's such a mess,"

"What is it?" Tom knew that she was crying inside.

"I can't cope!" They had reached a risky moment. Perhaps he should back off? Yet his instincts prevailed, and he said quietly "Tell me what it is."

"My job…and the rent…I'm on my own…I can't…it's hopeless." she sobbed.

"I can help you, if you'll let me," he said. ..

Warming to his concern and recovering some of her calm, she explained that her personal circumstances and finances were in terminal decline. Her husband had left a year before, and she had a meagre income from her job as a cleaner, with which she tried to do her best for her boy. She had defaulted on the rent and eviction from her flat was on the cards. Avoiding personal details was difficult, but as the conversation progressed she became more communicative. He provided her with the names of contacts that he knew in Social Services, who might be of assistance - specially his good friend Bryan Welland.

"I'm sure he can help," he said reassuringly.

"I don't know what to say," she said wiping away a tear. "I'm so grateful."

The trip to Ireland was not mentioned again and he left, pleased that he might have been of use. "But don't get drawn in further," he told himself. It was best to keep things at a respectable distance, but resolutions are transient things, and days later he found himself knocking on Charles Meade's door.

"I told you. No help from School Fund," was the acerbic reply to his request. "I told you from the start."

"Well I can ask the other parents for a bit extra." He knew that neither option had any appeal for Charles Meade. Either way, it might affect the head's approval rating with, on the one hand, staff, who all fought vigorously for school fund money, and on the other, the money- conscious parents. Tom counted on the fact that his head was a paid up coward. Meade cleared his throat.

"As you describe the boy, I can see this might be a special case." Tom knew that Meade did not really know the boy at all.

"How much do you need?"

"Fifty pounds!" was the quick reply. After a pause Meade asserted "A one off!" his stern head master's face set as if in stone

"Thank you!" Tom was genuinely grateful, and, for a moment, felt guilty that he'd already told Elaine Wallace that her boy was still on the trip. *But only for a moment!*

3

Suddenly, a splash of rain on his face, and then another. He remembered the signs, but before he could react, the spots burgeoned into a torrent. Diagonal slashes of rain that made his face smart, and a wind as if from nowhere. At once the quiet of moments before was transformed into the rasping sound of rain on water. It was a kettledrum of a sound that he knew so well. A sound he'd almost forgotten in recent years. He dashed for the cover of trees on the shoreline, and zipped up his coat. In the welcoming arbour, he sat on a fallen tree trunk and watched the rain.

There was something deeply satisfying in watching this fierce shower, safe in the protection of the trees. He had spent many hours in the rain when fishing. Hadn't everyone! In that perverse way fishermen have of thinking, sitting cocooned beneath an umbrella or under a tree in rain, made the solitude complete. As he sat there a song filtered into his consciousness. It had inculcated into his brain those eight years before, and remained a tantalising filament to the past. He knew the first line. He rehearsed it silently to himself.

"Last night I had the finest dream ..."

But what about the tune? It was there for a split second, and then it, and the words, were gone! That tiny scrap had survived as a marker and, however hard it was to recapture it now, the song seemed to have defined his bond with this place. He sat amongst the trees for half an hour, while the downpour exhausted itself. As it stopped, the sun began to show, and the far mists started to dissolve. Now he could see the rich meadows that skirted the other side of the lake. He remembered it, as if it was yesterday: a morning, such as this one had now become.

*

Good sea conditions had made the overnight ferry crossing from Liverpool incident free. They sat in the capacious lounge on board and played cards. One or two managed a fleeting nap. The ferry terminal at Dun Laoghaire, and the journey through Dublin City, gave Tom and Dave a chance to explain something of the culture and history of a country they had just entered. The large crowds they saw going to evening Mass caused the greatest surprise amongst the boys. The teachers both knew that the crossing and a road trip confined in a tightly packed minibus might well result in tiredness, boredom and perhaps squabbles, so a stop at a roadside café brought respite to the journey, and a revitalising snack recharged flagging energy.

It was a relief to Dave Cotter, who was doing a stint driving, when they finally spotted their goal. Shannonbridge House was a white painted, three storey building, sitting comfortably at the top of a gentle incline, and with a sense of quiet dignity. The last, low vestiges of summer sun lit the sky as they parked alongside the pretty little garden that fronted the house.

The front door opened and a tiny figure waived a welcome. Mary McMahon was a diminutive middle forty year old, with dark curly hair, sparkling eyes and smile to match. The lilting voice, which had so captivated Tom Ellison over the phone, with its rise and fall in pitch, could be heard in the warm greeting she gave to each individual member of the group in turn. Her husband, whom she introduced as Michael, stood at the front door until he was summoned to "Give the boys a hand."

With his help, cases and bags were unloaded and the boys were introduced to their rooms. Tom and Dave exchanged a satisfied nod at the tidy, well cared-for accommodation, and very soon a crackling air of excitement filled the house. Mary McMahon set to making fish fingers, chips and mushy peas for all, despite the fact that a first day meal was not in the agreed plan. The boys set to it ravenously, and the accompanying jam cake received the youngsters' accolade as the perfect topping to the ultimate dream meal. Despite the long journey, the relaxed atmosphere they found at Shannonbridge House augured well for the rest of the trip. There was little resistance as Tom called for bed for his tired, but happy troops. After seeing them all settled, he lay on his own bed and reviewed the day. *Not a bad start!*

It was this rested and energised group that made the early rise on their first day. The ever cheerful Mrs McMahon, who took sham offence at those who did not call her Mary, must have been up at first light, and prepared a giant breakfast of assorted cereals, egg, bacon, sausage and fried bread, all delivered with a smile and a gentle hand on the shoulder of each of her guests. Also, in a large cardboard box by the door of the kitchen, which doubled as a dinning room for visiting groups, was a supply of sandwiches and drinks. Tom said jokingly that it was enough to satisfy a battalion of The Royal Engineers and everybody groaned at the weak joke and Mary said "Get away with ya!"

She could not be described as beautiful, but her round moon face with its sparkling green eyes and perpetual smile, must once have been beautiful. Her stumpy hands embellished all that she said in her gentle Irish brogue. She had no children and this was, for her, a chance to lavish her care on her young visitors. Her husband Michael, who appeared several years older, was a tall angular man. His long face, apparently carved from the very wood he felled and worked with in his job at a timber yard. It reminded Tom of stern, impassive faces from the western films of his teenage years. He smiled as he brought to mind Randolph Scott in "Ride The High Country" Michael had few words and let the lady do the talking. "Like Randolph Scott!" Tom smiled to himself. This pair seemed well suited in their differences.

4

Tactics for the first day had been endlessly gone over, and the huge quantity of bait required to entice large shoals of Irish bream had been picked up the night before from the local tackle shop by Michael. The minibus was loaded to the gunnels for the short journey down to Lake Descarr and began with the sun just above the horizon. The lake lay in a dip below their temporary home and Dave drove the minibus on a slalom course to avoid the danger of sticking in the wetter parts.

Tom reflected on the excitement of the boys at the prospect of what lay ahead. He knew that some, perhaps all, would find that first day hard. Lack of skill was one thing, but even Irish bream needed encouragement. The persuasion of a fusillade of balls of ground bait hurled some forty yards out was the tactic. Then, maybe, the huge shoals of bream might move in to feed, as the breadcrumb mixture dissolved into an inviting carpet of sweet confection. He knew it might take a couple of days of bombardment such as this to create a feeding frenzy, and result in the giant catches they had all read about.

In the event, results on that first day were quite good. All the boys had done well. To Tom's delight, the younger ones had all caught large bream, although many potential bites were missed through inexperience. He knew this would improve in the next days. The four older boys, more experienced, had good catches by any standard, and recorded a total of twenty seven bream between them.

Tom had spent much of the day helping the younger ones. Meanwhile Dave Cotter had patrolled the bank, distributing good humour and refreshment. He realised it was best to avoided giving ill-informed advice, and only offered the odd word of encouragement. The role of coach, which he was used to, had to be

21

conceded to his aged friend! It had been a good start and the group loaded up the bus at the end of the day in good humour.

"Slowly, slowly catchee monkey." was Tom's advice as they settled in the bus and made their way back to Shannonbridge House, with anticipation of the food to come uppermost in their minds. They were not disappointed, as Mary presented them with plate of home-made meat loaf, chips and beans. Large slices of apple pie, submerged in custard, were more than some could cope with, and the older boys hoovered up the leftovers. After this giant feast had had time to settle, Tom and Dave decided to take the boys into Drumlasheen, the nearest small town and, on Mary's advice, visit Gerry's Bar.

Half way up the main street Gerry's Bar, like so many in Ireland, was small and compact; made up of two adjoined rooms with the bar at one end and a seated area at the other. The younger boys drank coke, the older boys an adventurous bitter shandy and, despite their recent meal, they all managed to consume a mountain of crisps. As was their custom, Gerry the landlord and his wife Eileen, gave all children who came into the bar a free packet of crisps. Tom had not been in the bar before, but it mattered not, as all children were treated the same. Tom had seen it before, and liked the custom that going down to the bar was a family event. He had admired the way the parents kept it under control as just another thing for a family to do together.

Then, of course, there was the music! In Tom's experience there always seemed to be someone around with a guitar or a squeezebox. He loved the simplicity of the tunes and the often maudlin sentimentality of the words. In Gerry's Bar, at about half past nine when the bar had filled up, the landlord started up the entertainment on a keyboard permanently set up in a tiny alcove next to the bar. First he sang solo to his own faltering accompaniment, and then invited a growing crowd to join in with their favourite songs. There was one that Tom liked in particular. The song seemed to encapsulate all his good times in Ireland. An outrageous monologue, about a farmer and his two goats, found its way into the proceedings. Tom didn't mind that it was a bit rude. The boys heard worse around the school playground! There was a well-established pattern to the programme, and the order of performance was preordained, only to be broken on this occasion, by a visit from a balladeer from a neighbouring village.

He was afforded top billing and the most fulsome introduction. Then, a pretty little girl about eleven years old, with long black hair down to her waist was accompanied by her father on guitar. She sang Dana's Eurovision hit from 1970 "All Kinds of Happiness". Long forgotten by Tom, but it was still held in obvious affection by the audience, who clapped and shouted for more. It was especially at times like this, when "the craic" was in full flow, that the natural ease with which young and old mixed was most noticeable. Tom thought this was a good example for his boys. He saw the local bar as an important part of the learning experience; and it also meant he got to sample the local brew!

It was late when they got back to their digs and the boys took some persuading to go to bed. Marvelling at the boys' stamina and bemoaning their own frailty, Tom and Dave sat in the lounge and enjoyed a surreptitious tot of whisky with their hosts. Mary had welcomed them from the moment they arrived, and the chat flowed as if they were old friends.

For the main part Michael sat in his arm chair and let the conversation flow with a stoic acceptance that Mary would lead the discussion.

"Another glass? Michael!" Mary prompted. He dutifully opened the cupboard and took out the bottle, saved for moments like this, and poured its content into the glasses of the two teachers and his own.

"Not for me love. I'm going up. I'll leave you men to finish off," Mary said. As she lifted the latch of the door leading upstairs to the bedrooms, she called. "Good night and God Bless!"

Free from the noise of young voices, with glass in hand, the two relaxed.

"I've enjoyed today," Dave mused.

"It went well," Tom affirmed, surprised and pleased at his young friend's enthusiasm. Self-congratulation did not seem inappropriate as they clinked glasses. They sat back and enjoyed the warming glow of the whiskey. Michael seemed to feel no need to fill in the gaps and, on downing his glass, stood up.

"I'm off too. Goodnight!" Without addition, he opened the door and clumped up the stairs.

"One of nature's gentlemen," Dave said sardonically. They were left to further reflect on the day and finalise details of the one to come. When they finally retired, Tom lay on his bed, his arm aching from launching over two hundred ground bait missiles towards the offshore shelf, where the bream would eventually patrol. *Perhaps the next day?* He smiled at the prospect and remembered his mum's favourite Peggy Lee song,

"Yes, it's a good day for singin' a song,

And it's a good day for movin' along;

Yes, it's a good day, how could anything go wrong,

A good day from mornin' till night."

5

It was the following day, holding such promise, that had been blocked out from Tom's mind for so long in the days, months and years that followed.

At first, school was still on holiday, and he returned from Ireland to desultory days alone in his room. Driven by press reports and increasing local gossip, the school governors suspended him after a week of his return. At first his union promised an appeal, but with troubles brewing in its fight with the government over pay, they soon came to the conclusion that if the charges of dereliction of duty came to pass, they would be upheld and might be used to weaken the national bargaining position. They made pathetic efforts to use his previous record in mitigation, but their lack of conviction was brushed aside in the face of blame seeking, and finally all they suggested was that he leave, and accept as good a reduced pension as they could cobble together. His first reaction had been to refuse point blank, but the lack of genuine support from colleagues was a shattering disappointment. No one wanted to become embroiled in the case. There was a collective remoteness. He was an anathema.

On threat of his own suspension, Dave Cotter had made it clear that the decisions that had been taken in those days were taken by Tom. Dave was the novice pupil and he received an official warning. On the other hand, so much more was expected of Tom Ellison. It added to the growing thought that something more than carelessness was involved. Tom had only spoken to Headmaster Meade briefly and soon realised he could expect no help from that direction either. The headmaster made it very clear that there was no way that he could mount a defence in face of local gossip and press coverage, now both local and national. Tom was advised he could appeal, but that seemed a pointless token in a lost cause in light of the condemnation he was facing on all sides.

For three months the matter went backward and forward. Frustration brought him to a point where all resistance was gone. He was left with a bitter resentment for the injustice heaped upon him. All that was left was that reduced pension. A poor reward for his service over the years. As time passed, it had been all he could think of. It would not leave him. He inhabited a tiny world, the boundary of which was the shoreline he now stood upon. Slowly the drink had blurred the edges. Another drink helped to keep the memory away. At first he thought it would help him over the pain of that day, but, as time passed, he had needed it all the more for the disaster that was to follow. His mother, who had been traumatised by the humiliation of her son, soon fell into a deep depression, from which she was never to recover, and she died just before his thirty seventh birthday. The thought that he had brought all this down on his mother was his greatest guilt.

*

It had been two years before he was to break free from his confused sense of blame. Pathetic attempts to leave the drink alone had all failed in very short time. Resolutions made in moments of lucidity or worse, self-pity, were doomed to failure. Free of the numbing effect of the drink, the memories flooded back. Just one to steady the nerve! Who was he kidding? He knew well where that would lead. It always did. It always will be, had told himself over and over again, until he believed it. No point in making the effort. No bugger else cared anyway! Why should he?

Very soon he had lost his few friends. Some, the truer ones, stayed constant for a while, but his drinking and its accompanying wildly fluctuating moods soon saw them off. Others had disappeared from sight within weeks. Dave's desertion had been especially hurtful at first. Reluctantly, Tom came to acknowledge that the young PE teacher had done nothing wrong either and that he had had to look to his own future. Tom was glad to hear that he received only an official warning.

Tom Ellison sank into an isolated world. More and more reclusive, as one rebuff followed another. And yet after eight years it only took a note of eight words on a postcard to lift the curtain from those events. He looked at the touristy picture of a bridge over a river and then turned it over. At first he struggled to make out the words through drink-laden eyelids. Next as he fought for air, it was as if all the breath and the alcohol had been knocked from him by the words on the card.

ASK MARY MCMAHON WHAT HAPPENED TO THE BOY. He drew in gulps of breath. He felt dizzy from the effort. "What the bloody hell!"

The card had come in the early morning post and remained on the mat until he noticed it when he went to the kitchen to fix himself some supper. He picked it up, put it in his pocket and forgot about it until he was taking off his clothes to go to bed. He'd had a drink between, and he blinked at it sticking out from his shirt pocket. He had come to hate the arrival of the post. Often, when he knew what the envelopes contained, he threw them away unopened. It had got him into trouble more than once. Bills had been lost, but he had to pay in the end. He had learned not to care about such things, but now he was more collected than he could remember. What did it mean? Why now? He felt both puzzled and exhilarated as his mind grappled with thoughts long since forgotten.

"Hold on," he said out loud. "It's a joke! Another bloody sick joke!"

His euphoria ebbed. Who? Who knew where he was, let alone cared enough to play a cruel joke? They'd had their fun long ago! He reached out over the arm of his chair and picked up the discarded postcard. The address and its message were printed in a bold, confident hand. Across the corner, without token to neatness, was a stamp of The Republic of Ireland. The post mark stamp had only made contact in its lower half and the letters e...t...r...m. could be picked out with difficulty. "County Leitrim!" he muttered.

He picked up a glass from the little side table and put it to his lips without realising it was empty. He put it down again and sat looking at the picture, then the message in turn. He was looking for reasons, for excuses even, to ignore the note. Pay it no heed. Retreat! But he could not. Memories and questions fought for his mental processes. They would not be separated. He decided to sleep on it. He sat for a few minutes on the edge of the crumpled mass that was his bed. He glanced across at the empty glass and sank slowly backwards on top of the covers to put it from his mind. The card was clasped against his chest. Sleep came slowly that night.

The following morning he awoke with a start. The postcard! Where the hell was it? Not in his hand. Frantically he rummaged amongst the bedclothes. Not there either! It dawned on him that it was a figment of his imagination. Or was he going mad? Then, there on the bedside table sat the empty glass, reminding him. He hadn't imagined it!

"But where's the bloody card?"

He stood up and frantically looked all around him in a confused frenzy, and there it was, sticking out from beneath the corner of his pillow that had fallen to the floor. He picked it up and turned it over to reassure himself of its contents.

"ASK MARY MCMAHON WHAT HAPPENED TO THE BOY" It was true! He hadn't imagined it.

"Now let's see what we've got." He tilted the postcard towards the light. He hadn't opened the curtains yet.

"Dammit!" He cursed as he knelt across the bed and stretched to pull the curtains open. The effort was more than he had bargained for in his debilitated state and he felt light headed for a moment. As he peered again at the message, thoughts of a malicious practical joke again crossed his mind momentarily: but he dismissed it. In a burst of logic he found exhilarating, it was clear to him that all those sick people who had made life hell by their whispering behind his back, which soon became headline stories in the papers, had long since forgotten him. After all, he'd moved back to his mother's house to get away from them, hadn't he?

"Anyway," he mumbled to himself "none of 'em live in Leitrim, that's for sure."

If there was an evil intent in the message, he would need to look beyond the staff and parents of Hillpark School and that coterie of neighbours, acquaintances and friends who fed on every rumour and bit of tittle tattle! He had been consumed by anger that all of his life that had gone before, had been consumed by lies, and relegated to the dustbin with the rest of the stories of weirdoes, perverts and social misfits. And all because he took some boys fishing! All that he had ever done counted for nothing. That his intentions were good, counted for nothing. They needed a scapegoat, and he was it! He had been tried and found guilty by reason of over-enthusiasm! He'd lost his mother, his job, his friends and his self-respect.

Of course he felt responsible! Personally and professionally responsible! He accepted that. No one needed to remind him of his responsibilities, nor could anyone relieve him of the remorse. They could have tried! His sense of accountability was immediate and total, but his sense of fault was another matter. For it to be his fault meant he had to have done something wrong. His mistake might have been taking the trip in the first place, but he could not feel guilty about that. If he did, then his whole life as a teacher was a mistake. He knew from experience, that the less you did as a teacher, the less aggravation you got. He had always accepted that. "Sod's law," he always said. He had accepted the praise too when things went well, so he knew the balance between an irate message from a parent inconvenienced by an activity he had arranged, and the one thanking him for doing it, was in his favour. That was his justification.

But when the crunch came, there seemed to be no mitigation. He was guilty. Not even guilty of bad luck. That might have been something, but the press, his employers, friends and acquaintances had not even given him that. He was culpable; to blame. *Would he ever lose that burden?*

6

In the early hours of the second day of "The Irish Experience", there came a timid knock on the door of Tom's bedroom.

"What?" he grumped, half asleep. He looked at his watch. It was five past four.

"It's Colin," whispered Gavin Green. "He's been sick." In his waking state he went to the room shared by three of the boys, and on examining the young boy it was clear from his appearance that something was wrong. His face was a pallid grey. He complained of stomach pains.

"He's been to the loo three times already," volunteered his brother

"Sick as a dog," it was said with a certain lack of filial sympathy. Dave appeared at the door. "What is it?" he asked.

"Don't know," Tom replied "but I think he should see a doctor." Mary McMahon, by now on the scene, squeezed into the crowded room and felt the boy's forehead.

"He's got a temperature for sure," she said. They gathered on the corridor outside the room.

"I don't think it's serious," Mary said reassuringly "but I'll give Doctor Keane a ring," and she went downstairs while Tom and Dave checked on the other boys. Everyone seemed well and even energised by the event.

It took a while to settle the boys down, but Tom knew there wouldn't be a lot more sleeping that night. On her return Mary said "Doc's away fishing!"

Tom saw the irony.

"But I'm sure they'll have a look at him at the hospital in the town," she added.

"You think they will?"

"Sure it's their job, isn't it!" replied Mary. "I'll go and start breakfast."

By now it was after five o'clock, the boys were all awake and chatting, so it seemed a good idea in order to calm things down a bit.

"Do you mind? It's very early."

"Course not dear, it's only a wee bit early," She was used to early starts on fishing days, as it was what her customers wanted.

"But we'll have to cancel today," he muttered to Dave

"That'll go down well," Dave said when Tom brought it up again at the breakfast table before the boys appeared. "They're going to be really upset."

From personal experience with children injured in school sports, Tom knew that you could never say how long you would have to wait in Accident and Emergency. He had once sat in the waiting room for three hours with a boy with a suspected broken arm. Add to that the half hour journey to and from the hospital, and most of the day was eaten up. Teachers hated the hospital run. In this case, seven disappointed youngsters at a loose end would be a handful, but it was the prudent decision to make.

"Why don't I take him to the hospital and you go on with the kids?" Dave interrupted his thought process.

"Only one bus," Tom replied.

"I'll take 'em in my car," Mary interjected from her place by the cooker.

"Michael's got something on," she added by way of explanation. Tom felt the pressure that was building up inside him. At that moment the first of the boys came into the kitchen, refreshed and eager to tuck into the food and looking forward to the day's fishing. Tom's heart sank. He knew how much expectation the previous day had created. It had been the main subject in the pub last night.

Excitement was palpable as the company gathered. To give himself more time and to reappraise the sick boy's condition, Tom went upstairs. Colin looked pale and drained through lack of sleep, but put on a brave face. As he sat on the bed consoling the boy, Tom weighed up the situation. Could he justify a cancellation of the day to the boys? What would he want in their shoes? The group's disappointment could be managed for sure, but would it do irreparable damage to the rest of the trip. He looked down at the ashen faced boy and thought of the others downstairs. He made a decision. Delivering his promises to the group, but at the same time having the one boy's well-being in mind, could be accommodated if he took the remaining seven and Dave accompanied Mary McMahon to the nearby hospital. It would represent the best to be gained from the situation.

He announced his decision over breakfast and discussed the details with his colleague and Mary. It was a plan and it raised a cheer from the assembly.

"I'll take charge of this shower and you see to Colin," Tom said. "Leave it to me," Dave replied confidently.

"I'll keep an eye on the two of 'em," Mary joked.

Satisfied that the plan was a good compromise, Tom added a caveat to the remaining group. "Step out of line and we come straight back."

After annihilating another huge breakfast, they set about loading up the minibus while Tom finalised the details of the plan with Dave and Mary. The unease Tom had felt earlier was dispelled by their enthusiasm to help.

They started off in perfect conditions. The sun was just tiptoeing above ground when they pulled out of the McMahon's drive, the white painted stones edging the neat flower beds, bright even in the filtered gloom. There was great excitement on the bus at the prospect that lay ahead. All their planning and preparation must surely bear copious fruit today. Colin hadn't slept well and bemoaned Mary's giant breakfast.

"Your dad'll think I've been buying you Guinness," Tom joked.

"He only lets us drink bitter," boasted Gavin from the back of the bus.

"I'll tell him you said that!" Tom responded as he swung the bus round a bend in the narrow lane.

"I'll be alright Tom!" came the muffled reply. Tom liked that. It had been a matter of pride with him that the kids naturally came to call him by his Christian name in these circumstances. He never initiated it, and they needed no word from him to return to the formal "Sir!" when back at school. He had been surprised by it at first. He had expected some unbridled familiarity with which he would have to deal, but there seemed to be an unspoken agreement between them that inside school was one thing, outside it was another.

"It's just too many cokes at the pub last night," chipped in Glenn, who was perched by the door on a sack of ground bait.

The journey down the lane to the lake was like a trip on a miniature scenic railway, as the bus lurched and bumped along a short stretch of road that barely qualified for the name. From the top of a sloping meadow, they had their first sight of the lake below. A straight course down to the water over meadows soaked with recent rain was an option Tom had already rejected, so he stuck to the drier lay of the land, avoiding boggy hollows and followed a snaking pattern down the slope towards the trees that fringed the lake. A battered iron gate barred the way to the clearing in the trees, which was their destination. Tom stopped and asked Gavin, who had been given the job as outrider for the duration, to open it. Tom eased the bus through with only inches to spare on either side. The lad grabbed the top rail, lifted the structure, which was attached only by hinges of string, and heaved it back into position with a curse and an embarrassed look backwards to see if had been overheard. Tom chose to ignore the expletive and was more annoyed to see that a car was already parked in the clearing ahead.

"Dammit!" he muttered as he swung the bus alongside the black mini.

"We've got competition," he announced amidst a chorus of groans.

They knew their plans would need changing, if the intruder had taken up one of yesterday's fishing spots. It was his right of course, but it meant that yesterday's pre-baiting, for one person at least, would have been wasted. The newcomer might have set himself up in such a way, that Tom's plan of being able to see the whole group from one place, could be in jeopardy.

"You unload the bus while I go and have a look," he said. "Careful how you unload that bait," he shouted as he made his way along a narrow path, through waist high ferns and into the wood leading down to the water's edge.

He came out of the shadow of the trees and into the burgeoning brightness of the lakeside, at a point where large stones in the shallow fringes made, with careful balance, a short pier into the water and gave him a clear view in both directions. He scanned both ways for evidence of the owner of the black mini. There was none. "Good," he said to himself and turned to retrace his teetering steps over the stones. As he made his way back through the trees he shouted ahead.

"It's alright. No one's there! Get your stuff!"

He wanted them to set off quickly to avoid intrusion by the owner of the black mini, who may be indulging in a reccy before setting himself up. It mattered a great deal to him that his revised plans worked today, and he did not want an interloper to spoil things. He need not have worried, because before he had penetrated the bank of ferns, he was met by the first of the boys, laden down with rod bag, seat box, net bag and bait bucket. He always marvelled at the ease with which, even the youngest of them, managed to carry so much gear. He waited at the edge of the wood to watch each one of the group set off to their allotted place. Some had found a direct route the day before, but others preferred to follow the path down to the stepping stones and move along the shore from there. It was like a jungle expedition, as they humped the gear through the undergrowth. Soon they were swallowed up by the trees and all was silent.

Back at the bus, he surveyed the scatter of equipment that was his, and he decided to make his own hike to his peg in two journeys. He sat on his tackle box, with a murmur of satisfaction and eased on the new hip-length waders he had bought for the trip. The old ones had succumbed to the strain and stress of constant use over twenty years, and no longer afforded protection against mud, snow and water. He caught a glimpse of himself in the wing mirror. In a childish flash, he found himself waving at his own reflection. Embarrassed by his silliness, he looked about to see if he was observed. He was alone – save for the presence of the black mini. Soon he had secured the bus and completed the double journey to his spot by the stones.

7

When Tom finally set down the last of his tackle, the boys had finished setting up, and the regular splosh of ground bait missiles hitting the water could be heard from all sides.

"Further out, Gavin!" he shouted as the boy's bombs fell short of the underwater shelf where he knew the fish patrolled.

He spent a few minutes encouraging each boy in turn. Then he settled himself on his spot from the day before. His own salvo complete, he looked about making sure that everything was easily to hand. Each bit of equipment was in its place, ready for that moment when action would have to be decisive. He knew well the need for economy of movement. To get additional feed to the area of his baited hook, he had attached a feeder, a small wire mesh tube, into which a cocktail of wetted breadcrumb and maggots was pressed. If cast accurately, to the area he had fed the day before, the mixture would slowly escape and prove a renewed attraction to the patrolling bream.

"Here we go!" he announced loudly. "Catch me if you can!"

Three times he filled the feeder with the inviting concoction and, with a glow of satisfaction, cast the projectile some forty yards out and to within a couple of feet of his target area. Twice he placed the rod on its rest and took up the slack line to await the tell-tale twitch of the rod tip. Each time he waited several minutes for the feeder to slowly empty its inviting mixture. There was no response, but on the third occasion, barely before he had had put the rod down, the brightly painted rod tip flickered. Picking up the rod in one movement, he took it backwards in a diagonal sweep. The soft tipped rod curved in a triumphant arc as it made contact with the hungry fish. He knew at once that it was a good fish. Its weight and swimming power could be felt all the way through the pliant rod and down its extension – his arm! He raised the rod to a more vertical position and started to reel in the fish. He thrilled at the power, as it fought against his will. Twice he felt the struggle was over, but twice the fish found new energy to resist. At last he was able to bring the fish up from the depths, where resistance was greatest, and on to the surface. Confident of its position, he grabbed the handle of the landing net without looking. Gently he slid the landing net under the tiring fish. For a moment he drew in fresh air. Then, with great care, he picked the fish from the net between finger and thumb, released the hook and looked at it with admiration.

It was a bream of about four pounds. Deep in the body and black backed, it was a handsome specimen deserving of his respect and affection. Delicately he slid the fish into his keep net. He was startled by a whoop, followed by a round of applause from the boys who had stopped to watch the struggle. He raised his hand in a regal salute. That was to be the first of many conquests that day.

He kept the fish feeding and by late afternoon, with well over a twenty fish in his net, his arm was beginning to feel the strain. He poured the last of the coffee from the flask Mary had prepared for them that morning, and lit a sly duty free cigar. He looked to left and right at his boys. Satisfied that they had all been catching fish at regular intervals, he had decided to leave them largely to their own devices. He had limited himself to a single visit, sandwich and coffee in hand at midday. He had stood behind each boy in turn and exchanged views and encouraging words. He savoured the cigar and the satisfaction of knowing that plans had worked out. Few things gave him greater pleasure than this. All the elements were there in conjunction. He decided to take a few photographs of the scene. Tom Ellison was a happy man.

He wondered how the hospital trip had gone. He had confidence in Dave's ability to cope. His greatest worry was that the boy had missed a day's fishing, but he felt sure that Colin would be alright after medication. The last two hours of the day were a more leisurely affair than the frantic forenoon. Fish came less frequently but he was satisfied to spend the time in company of a tiny wren. Seemingly without fear, and with an endless appetite, the tiny gem of a bird sat within feet of him and waited until maggot or breadcrumb fell from his fingers. Then with a purr of its wings, it tripped in and out again, with the morsel in its beak. He wondered at the minute perfection of the bird and the uncanny look of intelligence it bore.

It was at times like this that he was glad his life had turned out as it had. He remembered days, it seemed from another life now, when working class ambition had driven him; ambition to "go places" and the need to prove himself. A university place had been his first goal. Tom Ellison had decided that whatever it would take, he would do it to make himself the first member of his family to gain academic success and, with it, the social success that it assured. It was hard for him. He was not an academic high flier, but at grammar school he made up for it by reading voraciously, driven by the desire not to show his lowly roots. Looking back he despised the motivation, but it had given him a breadth of factual knowledge that few of his contemporaries could match. His late teenage years had been lost in this pursuit of self-justification. His place in the world as someone of value, had seemed, at the time, to depend on getting himself out of the class group that saw a job as a Co-op insurance agent as a social triumph.

His father had spent the whole of his working life using his considerable physical strength in a variety of jobs. As a teenager he hod gone down the pit in the family tradition. As a younger man he had delivered coal and then worked at the gasworks where coke was a valued bi-product.

Tom remembered pushing an old pram, brimming over with coke, up Goddard's Brew, a steep local hill at the top of which was the tiny council house his mother and father had lived in for all their married life. He invariably left behind a trail of porous, dark grey nuggets, testimony to the strain that the pram's suspension was under, and his own reluctance to try to park the overloaded workhorse and try to pick them up on such a fierce incline. Thoughts of the brakes failing, and the entire load finishing in the canal at the bottom of the hill had counselled caution. These regular supplies of coke, obtained by avoiding the queue that always formed on Tuesdays and Thursdays, were the only, but valued perk that the Ellisons had in those early post war days.

The Ellison house was always warm and it was always neat and clean too. Tom's mother had never gone out to work since she married Tom Senior. All of her time was spent in ensuring that clothes were clean and food, though simple, was always ready at the set times. She lavished great care on the tiny front room of the terraced house, where pride of place was taken by the folding table, lovingly polished every day, which had been given to them as a wedding present, but hardly ever used. Across the mantlepiece over the open fire, arranged in serried ranks, were the horse brasses and little brass bells that she had collected over the years; her cherished mementoes from Southport or Blackpool. These days out were also recorded in the box of postcards she kept in the sideboard. These were her personal treasures.

A feeling of security, of dependability, of permanency pervaded the fabric and the relationships of the Ellison household. For the young Tom Ellison it was a reassurance that made childhood free and easy. But, as he grew into his teenage years he took an interest in the wider world and it seemed to him that his place in it would not, could not, change. Unbreachable boundaries were in place. Both of his parents assumed their lot with a cheerful, almost religious acceptance. As soon as he was old enough to talk to them about it, he would question them about their ambitions and found an unflinching view that life is preordained, and that they felt that it had dealt them generously on the whole.

"There's a lot worse off than us," his father would say and his mother, always the supportive wife, would smile and nod in dignified agreement.

As Tom reminisced, he conjured up a clear picture of them both. His mother perched on the arm of his father's chair, her hand resting on his shoulder, a gentle but clear affirmation of the love she had for him over forty years. Tom Senior sat there, thickset and as impermeable as the local millstone grit. He was the older of the two, and as a young lad, he was promised an apprenticeship in a factory repairing railway rolling stock. He was conscripted into the Army at eighteen, but he never spoke about his time in Belgium and France. On his return from the war, he found his promised apprenticeship as a wagon builder was lost in post war austerity and he was forced to work down the pit which he did for twenty years before he took a job delivering coke from the Canal Street gasworks.

Only as he grew older did Tom's father's physical presence soften. Shoulders, once square as a garden shed, became rounded and hands that once seemed vice-like had a surprising gentleness as he worked with wood in his back yard shed. It seemed churlish now to think, as he did in his youthfulness, that this wonderful couple lacked ambition. He did not realise at the time that the kind of ambition he espoused was a shallow thing. Eventually he would come to realise that there could be no greater dignity than his parents showed in every aspect of their lives. But youthful arrogance had blinded him to this, and he resolved to move heaven and earth to establish an enhanced status for himself.

It seemed this could only be achieved by first succeeding at school, and then at university. He wasn't sure what would happen after that, but he was always sure that this path bode well.

And that was Tom Ellison's problem. He had never acquired the ruthlessness of the real world. As a young man at university, he played the part of the social radical with theatrical conviction. He adopted an abrasive manner from the first day. It took him some time to realise it was only a sad creation, as an insurance against failure.

If he did not "make it" he could always rail against the injustice of heredity. However, there were too many clever people about him who saw through the pretence. By the end of the first year, and with the help of a few perceptive friends, the edifice he had built crumbled and Tom did a lot of his growing up in the next two years at university, and his latent creativity emerged slowly. When reality dawned, Tom felt ashamed of the wrong he had done to his parents: his father in particular. He knew he must have given much pain by his assertiveness and his single mindedness.

Even now, sitting in such ideal surroundings, and at peace with the world, the sense of guilt he had felt came to him. He had determined to make amends by first returning to his home area after university. A measly £36 a month salary meant that at first, living at home was his best option as he settled in to his new job. The circle had not really been broken and he had learned that there was no shame in that. He had become a teacher and that pleased his parents. They had never flinched in their love for him, and they had not been discouraged by his questioning of their style of life, but had a fierce pride in his achievements. Sadly his father had died suddenly a year later at the age of fifty seven, without Tom fully expunging his guilt for the pain he had caused. He had resolved then not to allow his mother to pass, without constantly re-enforcing his respect and love for her. These were bitter-sweet memories for him.

With a sigh, he looked at his watch and realised that he should soon have to call an end to the day earlier than he had planned, in order to find out what had happened to the sickly boy. He readied himself to record the day's catch by weight and on film. He put a new roll of film in his camera and checked the settings. He never liked to use the first few frames on important shots, so he took a couple of panoramic views to left and right assuring himself that the film was winding on. He waited in vain for the wren to return

"Alright fellas! Time to pack up," he bellowed through cupped hands. He decided to start the weigh in at his end of the group. Armed with net and scales, he made his way over the stones and turned into the trees. Following a well worn path through the dense groupings of slender silver birch, he came upon a barbed wire fence barring his way. He'd taken the wrong path. Looking to left and right he saw a breach in the wire with several posts flattened to the ground. Testimony he thought to the activity of anglers.

"Bloody vandals!" he muttered.

He often despaired for a minority of his fellow anglers. It irritated him that the generality of anglers were often lumped together in the face of such vandalism. He had drilled the need to care for the environment into his boys. He pulled the loose wire and wound it round a wooden post for safety. On the other side of the fence was a typical boggy lakeside pasture. By now he wished he had gone by the direct route along the water's edge. Coming out of the trees he picked his way carefully avoiding flashes of deeper water: down to the lakeside where he was greeted by the widest of grins on the face of young Ben.

"Got a few?" he asked, laying the ground for justifiable pride. "Ten!" There was a tremble in the voice.

"Well done! That's more than me. Let's have a look then." Tom took the cap off his camera lens and readied himself, as the boy took the net from the water.

He needed both hands to lift it, and the fish inside, seeking escape, thrashed wildly. With his arms held wide apart, holding the rings at both ends, Ben's net hung low in the middle with a dazzling silver harvest. Tom took several photographs, before the combined weight of fish and net became too much for the youngster. Between them they set about the task of weighing the catch. Three times a number of fish slid into the weighing net and the scales flickered round towards the 20 pound maximum, and the beaming young angler had registered a combined weight of 37 pounds.

The sequence was repeated six times, as each boy delighted in showing off his catch. They had all done well and Tom was filled with a glow of satisfaction as he swung around the trunk of a tree which overhung the water.

"What've you got Glenn?" he asked, expecting to find the last youngster waiting for him, net at the ready.

But the tackle box sat alone in the shallow water.

8

"Glenn! Where are you?" he shouted. He leaned backwards holding on to the tree trunk with one hand and looked towards the other boys. They were all busy packing their gear away and there was no sign of Glenn.

"Where the hell is the boy?" Tom muttered and then bellowed "Glenn!"

Just the slip slap of the water breaking on the bank came in reply. He stepped into the water, which was only inches deep, and splashed towards the abandoned tackle box. One of the rocks beside it had been used as an improvised table. A cup and plastic sandwich box lay empty. He looked to his left and from this point a long stretch of tall reeds followed the shoreline to the far corner of the lake. They spread far into the water making that part of the lake unfishable from the land. There was no sign of the boy.

"Glenn!" This time even louder and with unmistakeable anger.

No reply. Perhaps the little devil had passed him by, going in amongst the trees! There was no sign of the green and black waterproof coat that made Glenn so instantly recognisable.

"Anyone seen Glenn?" he shouted.

Ben, who was nearest, moved towards him.

"Haven't seen him since you last came round."

"I'll give him a few minutes. Can you go up to the bus and see if he's there for some reason? I'll wait here," Tom said.

"O.K!" Ben made his way towards a gap in the trees.

"And tell him I'll have his guts for garters!" It was heartfelt. By this time the other boys had started to gather. Each in turn could offer no clue as to Glenn's whereabouts. Gavin had chatted with him about an hour earlier, when he had taken a toilet break. Apart from that, no one could remember seeing him for some time. This was not surprising, as Tom suddenly realised that, for some reason, Glenn must have moved his seat box a few yards from his allocated spot, and out of sight of the others.

"He hasn't fallen in, has he?" asked Gavin in thoughtless jest.

They'd talked about water safety before and Tom had joked about falling off their tackle boxes into six inches of water. However, the thought struck home and Tom scanned the water for any tell-tale signs. There were none. Tom remonstrated internally for thinking that there might be.

"Have you all packed up?" he asked. They had, except for Ben.

"Then you make your way back to the bus. If you see Glenn, tell him to get back here quick. Here's the key. Start loading the gear on the bus and leave space for me, O.K.?"

If they followed the same route back to the bus as the way they came, most of the accessible part of that side of the lake would be in view. He watched the boys make their way back to their tackle. Gathering it together, one by one, they disappeared briefly from sight amongst the trees.

"And give me a blast on the horn if you find him!" he shouted to Ian, the last to go.

He moved back along the shore and sat on the boy's tackle box and struck a suitably aggravated pose, expecting any minute for its owner to appear full of apologies. Ten minutes went by. No boy. No horn. In his mystified state, he decided his best option was to move back towards the bus and closer to the other boys. It was now over fifteen minutes since the others had left. He made to pick up the boy's tackle.

"Soddit! Let him fetch it himself," he muttered.

Tom's dominant feeling was one of annoyance that one of his boys could be so stupid; so thoughtless. He made his way back to the bus. Colin was sitting on an upturned bait bucket.

"Where is everybody?"

"We didn't see him, so they decided go up the hill to look. They left me here to tell you."

"I told them to stay here," he snapped as he moved round the bus and scoured the hillside beyond. To his relief he could see the boys. They were heading back, and a quick count of the tiny dots indicated they were five in number. No Glenn!

Soon they were in clear view, climbing the old gate and trudging down the worn track towards the bus.

"No sign?"

"No," said Ben, the first to arrive, breathless from the effort. One by one they slumped down in a semi-circle around Tom.

"I think the silly twerp has gone down the other end of the lake to reccy another spot," said Gavin.

"He wouldn't be that stupid would he?" chipped in Ben to general agreement.

"I'll go down and have another look. Gavin you come with me," Tom said.

"I'm hungry," whispered Colin, but loud enough to hear. "We'll be in plenty of time for tea," Tom answered, ruffling the boy's hair.

Accompanied by Gavin, Tom made his way back to the spot where Glenn's gear had been left. Tom explained he would make his way to the distant reed bed, whilst Gavin gathered up Glenn's gear. He was able to walk along the pebbly shore for quite a way without obstruction. Then, at the start of the reeds, he was forced to move into the trees to make progress along the lakeside. It soon became clear that few, if any, anglers could, or would want to, penetrate the wildness of the lakeside spinney. Gaps in the trees were few, and barely wide enough to squeeze a body through, let alone a mountain of fishing tackle. But it might be just the site of an adventure for a twelve year old boy. Through the gaps in the trees he kept an eye on the reeds, looking for a tell-tale gap that might attract the eye of a fearless explorer. But there was none.

Then, his attention elsewhere, his foot found a hidden tree root and he staggered clumsily into a cluster of saplings. They yielded under his weight and, feeling himself falling, he put his hand out in protection. There was an involuntary cry of pain, as the tip of a broken branch cut into the fleshy part at the base of his thumb. Then a gasp as he landed amongst tree roots. He lay there, sucking air into his expelled lungs. Instinctively he cursed the boy that brought him to this. He looked at his hand and was shocked to see a three inch sliver of twig deeply embedded on the flesh. There was no blood, he marvelled. Holding the injured hand well away from himself, he took the protruding end of the splinter between finger and thumb; turned his head, closed his eyes and pulled. There was no noticeable pain at the moment of extraction, but as he examined the surgery, the pain became excruciating and blood began to trickle down his wrist. He felt in his pocket for a handkerchief and dabbed the wound. It seemed as if the splinter had come out cleanly, so he wound the hanky round his hand. He mopped his brow with the back of his free hand, and felt the sting of sweat penetrating a cut. He dabbed his forehead with the back of his bandaged hand and saw spots of blood. The cut above his left eye didn't feel serious, but he held the handkerchief firmly to his head. He sat amongst the tree roots for a few moments, gathering himself together. He couldn't stop now, but it was one more item on Glenn's bill!

Slowly and more carefully now, he picked his way through the trees. They were becoming less dense and soon he came into bright sunlight as he reached an opening in the spinney, before it continued up the hill and away from the lake. He was now on higher ground above the lake and he could see to the far end. He sighed at the prospect ahead. He started to make his way down from his new elevated position, but before he reached the first of the reeds he found himself confronted by a boggy meadow. Just a few steps into it, and his waders sank almost up to the knees with a squelch. For a moment he could neither move forwards nor backwards. It was as if he had been set in quick drying concrete. Then slowly and with a loud sucking sound, he eased one foot and then the other through the engulfing mud and fell backwards in a heap.

"That's it," he muttered.

There was certainly no way forward, so he picked his way carefully, stride by stride, back to the edge of the spinney, avoiding his own deep footmarks. He sat on a fallen tree, exhausted. From now on he would stay on the higher ground, some distance from the water to avoid the treacherous ground of the meadow that surrounded the lake.

Gaps in the reeds indicated likely fishing spots, but each time he found one, his path was barred by conditions that threatened to take him under. No one in their right mind would venture there, and he saw no tell-tale footprints indicating a recent visitor, but he had to carry on just in case. He could not afford to get too far away from the lake. Even in the outer reaches of the bog, his waders sank in up the welt with every step. He needed to be able to see the lake at all times for the slightest sign. He was now half way round the giant reed bed and feeling the strain. He wished he'd left his waterproof jacket back at the bus. It was covered in mud and streams of perspiration dripped down his arms. He wiped the sweat from his brow with his bandaged hand and, grateful of the rest, surveyed the scene.

At this point the reeds stretched ten metres into the water, but at the far end of the lake, some hundred and fifty metres away, the reed bed must be thirty metres deep. Ancient monster pike could inhabit the area and never have seen man's bait. Nor ever would! Only errant sheep, lost to their owner, would have been stupid enough to try to penetrate it. It was a primeval place.

Tom was convinced his boys were not made of the foolish stuff to test out this kind of danger. Convinced that further struggle in the energy-sapping bog was futile, he decided to make his way back. As he trudged on, the thought that the boy would appear unabashed, overrode any thoughts of impending tragedy. Now as he found the conditions more and more of a test of endurance, he plotted retribution on the boy.

"He can bloody well stay at the house tomorrow!"

The journey back to the bus was made at declining pace, as mud and undergrowth took their toll. He reached Glenn's fishing spot dishevelled and out of breath. He took a few moments to gather himself, both physically and mentally, before he reunited with the boys. He wanted to be composed. If he couldn't be it, he was going to look it! He took a comb from his trouser pocket and drew it through his hair, not realising how incongruous this token to neatness looked in one so bedraggled and mud-splattered. He made his way along the beach and through the trees towards the bus. The boys, hearing his approach, met him at the edge of the clearing.

"Any sign?" he asked.

"No!" came back in unison. Tom Ellison slumped down in the driver's seat. Throughout the search he had found sufficient energy to keep going in the growing panic that gripped him. Now it drained from him in an instant, and his whole body broke out in an involuntary convulsion. He wrapped his arms around himself. "Oh God!"

He sat there, consumed by the ache in his heart and the pain in his arms and legs. A sense of self pity started to take hold of him, but it was cast aside as the thought of the boy punctured his selfishness like an arrow.

"Oh my God!" Only this time the plea was not for his aching body, but for the awfulness of the situation. If only! If only there was a knock on the bus window and Glenn would be standing there covered in mud, explaining that he had wandered off and got lost.

It was a vain hope in the light of his trek. Perhaps the boy had fallen into the water and, in panic, swum to another shore and was lying there exhausted? Or perhaps the scoundrel had played a cruel joke, which had backfired and he was too ashamed to own up. If only that was the explanation. For whatever the reason, the boy was lost, and he knew he needed help in the search. From whom? He looked round for the black mini. It had gone. Concealing his panic as best he could, he suddenly he announced

"I'm going for help. I'll take the bus," and added "don't you move from here again!"

As he moved off, through the rear mirror he could see their confused faces, drained of colour.

9

Those bewildered faces were an image he had contrived to forget since that day, but Tom remembered it these years later, on his return to the spot.

The rain had stopped and the clouds were stretched to reveal blue sky beyond. He had re-run the events of that appalling day over and over as, from his shelter, he watched the weather clear until the lake was bathed in a bright sunlight. Its warmth on his face suddenly brought him back into the present.

Now that he had established a starting point, a point of reference, he could begin his search in earnest. On the journey on the ferry he had considered a plan. The obvious solution was to confront Mary McMahon with the note. It would be no good turning up on the doorstep if she wasn't at Shannonbridge House. He rang Directory Enquiries, giving them the name and address. It was two years ago, he cautioned himself, so he felt an enormous sense of relief when the operator recited "The number you require is Drumlasheen two, six, seven five."

The McMahons were still there! That was a start.

The start of what? What could she know?

Within a week of receiving the note, he was standing on the spot where it all started; but he was no more certain of anything than he had been years before.

"What did Mary McMahon know?"

He had had this conversation with himself many times before. He hadn't had a drink for a week. Well, only one to celebrate the first stage of his plan! To finance the trip he had redeemed an insurance policy early, and he booked a ticket for the crossing for the following weekend. Then he thought about Stage Two and when he found the McMahon's number, he was tempted to celebrate again. No! There was a new clarity, a rejuvenated determination in his thinking, bolstered only by the most tenuous of leads. He recognised the weakness, and better still, the uncertainty of his plans. He resolved to stay off the drink during the search. After that who knew? He was surprised that once he had made the decision, he had not been desperate for a drink for over a week. Each time the thought weedled its way into his head, he took out the crumpled card and read the words "Ask Mary McMahon what happened to the boy," and the urge went away.

It was a mantra that fuelled his new-found determination. His thoughts jumbled as he walked along the stony beach, up the path in the trees and back to his hired car. The black mini came to mind. They had never found out who it belonged to. It was as if it never existed. He sat for a few minutes and re- traced the events of the day of the search.

*

He remembered well entering the bungalow that doubled as the police station on the edge of Drumlasheen. He could smile now at the recollection of the constable answering his ring on the button marked "Press if you want attention."

Why anyone should be standing in a police station and not want attention, he could not imagine! Through a door behind the tiny counter came a young constable pulling his jacket on with one hand, a half-eaten something in the other. He remembered he could see a table in the room beyond with the remains of a meal on it.

"Sorry to disturb your meal," he heard himself saying. It seemed ridiculously English now. He was reporting a missing boy and he was sorry to disturb a meal!

"That's alright sir. I've been way down to Mohill all day with the trottin'."

Tom had remarked on the singular Irish equine sport to the boys, as events were heralded on one poster after another on telegraph poles and fence posts on their journey. But he didn't need a diversion now.

Pointing to a hand written card on the counter, the officer said "I'm Garda Constable Finbar Reeve," and then "What's the problem?" taking a large book from beneath the counter, and a pencil from the top pocket of his, now fully buttoned-up jacket.

He was younger than Tom and considerably taller. Atop a long, fine boned face, a flurry of light coloured hair emphasized his handsome youthfulness. He stood about six feet tall and emanated a sure calmness. Tom explained who he was, and the circumstances. Later he recalled the irritation he had felt at the catalogue of questions he was asked about the boy's age, his address and the name of the school.

Each answer was dutifully recorded in the large book. The policeman looked at the cut forehead and the crudely bandaged hand.

"You're injured sir!"

"Oh I'm alright, nothing serious," Tom said, feeling the cut on his forehead. "Look… the boy's missing for God's sake. We need to do something!"

"All in good time sir. Just checking, you understand!" There was a quiet challenge to Tom's maturity in the remark: a calming reassurance in the cadence of the voice and quickly the tension between the two slipped away.

When all the information had been recorded, the constable picked up the phone, fingered a number and, with a hand over the mouthpiece, confided "Regional H.Q." The one sided conversation that followed gave Tom a growing confidence that here was a man to be relied on. He knew what he was doing, this young man with the bright eyes and the open face.

"How long will they be?" he asked.

"Likely they'll be there before we get there. I'll drive the bus shall I?" Garda Reeve said, pointing outside. The constable had taken charge and Tom felt immediate gratitude. For the last hour or so he had been flying on automatic pilot. Perhaps someone with a more detached view of the situation would see it more clearly and resolve, what had become, a growing horror.

On the short journey, Tom sat in the front passenger seat thinking of all the things he might have done. Perhaps he should have contacted the police earlier, but then how foolish he was going to look if the boy had turned up while he was away. He felt ashamed at the thought. "But what would happen if..?" He sought a diversion from the thought of the worst of all possible endings to the day's events, and told himself he'd done his best. Somehow that didn't count. He gained no solace from the thought.

They completed the journey to the lake and pulled up beside two green Gardai cars, their lights flashing wildly in the fading light, as the sun began to sink. The constable nodded a respectful greeting to a large man bearing sergeant's stripes.

"Now then Fin, what's about?" said the big man.

Garda Reeve recounted the details that Tom had given to him, without embellishment.

The sergeant asked Tom to show him where the boy was last seen, and they made their way down to the water in Indian file. The boys were left in the charge of a woman constable. On the foreshore Tom went through the events of the day and explained his own search. By now there were two policemen on the beach and the sergeant sent them off in different directions. He had a small radio handset, with which he began communication with someone on the far side of the lake. The plan was to cover as much ground as possible quickly. Tom pointed out the problem of the reed beds to the sergeant.

"Thanks for your advice sir!"

It was said with a marked lack of gratitude and Tom realised his relationship with the sergeant had reached a low point. It was Finbar Reeve's suggestion that he took Tom back to the minibus that fractured the tension. This reawakened in Tom his sense of responsibility to the other boys, which he had almost forgotten in his panic. He arrived back at the bus, got the boys to gather their gear together and load it up. Sharing out the remaining coffee and sandwiches, he tried to reassure them. He was touched that they seemed more concerned to reassure him. There was an understanding of his situation beyond their years, and he felt a sense of pride in his young men. His concern for them was heightened and he looked for signs of stress, which he knew they must be feeling. It seemed that Dave had done a good job in keeping them calm. They sat in the bus chatting away the time. Only a determined joviality indicated any strain.

"What's that?"

Colin was looking out of the backdoor window, and pointed into the encroaching gloom. Over the top of the trees was a moving, flashing light, followed seconds later by the steady slap slap of an approaching helicopter. Circumstances forgotten, they all scrambled out of the bus to see the landing in the field just up the hill from where they were. Tom watched their excitement, grateful for the distraction. The sergeant appeared from the woods and, with one hand anchoring his peaked hat against the downdraught, lent up the slope towards the helicopter. He approached the machine and held an opened door while he had an animated conversation with someone inside.

By now the slicing blades had stopped, and in the still night the trees appeared and disappeared in the intermittent gaze of the helicopter's flashing navigation lights. Stooping instinctively, the sergeant moved away from the machine and waved. The engine started up and the sagging blades spun and lifted as the noise built up. Even in this pandemonium, the moment when the machine's weight lifted from the ground just a foot or two or two, excited all but the most blasé. For a minute Tom marvelled at the sight, as the helicopter rose, stepped back and then, tail up, swept sideways towards the trees and disappeared into the encroaching night.

"Any news,?" Tom asked as the sergeant approached.

"Not yet sir! To be sure they've only arrived just now. Give 'em a chance!"

"But it's getting dark!"

"I know that sir!" The stricture was delivered without subtlety and hit its mark.

"I'm sorry sergeant."

"I know how you must feel sir."

Tom doubted that he did, but thanked him for it.

"Could you tell me how you got the cuts sir?"

Tom explained his injuries. It was the second time he'd been asked, but this time he understood the thought behind the question. He strove to avoid any hesitancy that could be misconstrued. At that moment he knew he was suspect. *But of what?*

Before the thought had time to expand, Finbar Reeve put his hand gently on Tom's shoulder and led him to one side.

"Don't you think your boys should go on and get something to eat?" He had kept a professional eye on the English school teacher from the time he had entered the Police Station. He watched his every gesture and grimace for tell-tale signs of wrongdoings, but after an hour he had become as convinced as he could be that his man was genuine. There was a deep concern in his reactions which Finbar sensed was true. He had an instinct for these things, but he knew he must not mislay his objectivity.

Garda Finbar Reeve had spent five years in his little bungalow as the guardian of the law to the community of Drumlasheen and was well liked and respected for the undemonstrative way he went about his business. He knew when to be firm and when to use discretion in the way he dealt with local problems. He could not pretend that the area around Drumlasheen represented a major test of law enforcement. The odd enterprising young thief or a fiery dispute after too many Blacks at the three pubs in what was little more than a village, were about as serious a problem as Finbar Reeve had to deal with.

Here was something different! He sensed that this current episode had darker implications. A local lad going missing for a few hours was one thing, but this boy's disappearance seemed filled with ill omens. Over the years he had come to understand what fishing in Ireland meant to English visitors. He had never truly understood the reason for the passion. A fat trout or two for the table was one thing, but catching fish all day, only to return them to the water, defeated him. Experience showed him that coming to Drumlasheen to fish meant that the boy would have a singleness of purpose and would be difficult to divert. What might have distracted the boy? What diversion could have taken him away from fishing? It was difficult to avoid the thought that some accident had overtaken the lad. He knew that the local lakes had a benign appearance. It was strange that the boy could have gone off unnoticed, but he had come to realise that anglers had a singleness of purpose once they started fishing. He was told the boy could swim. Falling in the shallow margins of the lake should not have been a problem, especially with others nearby.

What explanation could there be?

10

As he watched the English teacher mustering his charges with what appeared a quiet calm, Finbar Reeve knew that the same fear he was experiencing must be magnified within him. Reeve felt a growing compassion for the man and reassured him that he would bring any news to him personally. He pushed the driver's door of the minibus shut. The window was down and he placed a reassuring hand on the Englishman's arm.

"Don't worry! You look after the boys!"

It was said in a whisper that acknowledged the futility of the remark. But it had to be said. They both understood. He shepherded the bus through the gate and watched its lights disappear over the hill in the gloom He took a deep breath, as if to re-tune into the search, and made his way back through the trees. The sergeant was talking into his handset.

"I know it is! But my instincts tell me if we don't find this laddie soon, we won't find him alive. So keep looking until you hear from me. Over!" There was a muffled acknowledgement and a crackle. Then silence.

"What's your feeling on this one Fin? Do you think our English friend's been up to no good?" Although he had considered the thought himself, it was now said so full of knowing that it shocked him.

"I don't think so Donal." was all he could say.

"There's not too many alternatives d'ya know Fin. My money's on him, it is. And you saw his face and hand," It seemed logical that if there had been any misdeed, the Englishman would be the prime suspect, but Finbar Reeve had more than a feeling that the solution lay elsewhere.

"We may find him yet," he said without conviction.

"Ay! You may be right," the sergeant crunched across the stones and then turned. "But I doubt it! Come on! There's work to be done!"

Fin broke a stout branch off a nearby tree, and followed the sergeant along the shore. They searched in the creeping dark for almost two hours, keeping a short distance between them, so as not to miss anything. The sergeant, at the water's edge, swept the shallows with his powerful torch, whilst Finbar cut a swathe through the light undergrowth that skirted the beach. Several times the helicopter passed overhead.

The sergeant acknowledged a message, and shook his head vigorously at Reeve. Sergeant Donal Quinn had been on several searches like this in a long career, and experience told him that time was already up in finding the boy alive. By now they had reached a part of the lough almost a mile from where the boy was last seen. Larger trees had taken over and in the dark, progress became impossible.

Cupping his hands he announced to all who could hear "That's it 'till first light Fin! Let's get back to the car and sort out some kind of a plan. We'll need more men than this."

They made their way along the shore towards the car. It was a dull cloudy night and there was a chill in the air that Fin had not felt for several weeks. He slid his hands deep into his pockets, and with the stick in the crook of his elbow followed the glow from his sergeant's torch. Once more the sound of the helicopter built up until the bright searchlight appeared above the trees ahead of him. Fin shaded his eyes against the light, momentarily blinded; then it disappeared behind the trees again. As he blinked to re- accustom his eyes to the dark, his foot slid from beneath him and he found himself falling through a bank of ferns and landing in a sitting position at the bottom of a shallow bank. The ferns had acted as a cushion, so he was not hurt, but he felt foolish. He put his right hand out to lever himself up. The grass beneath parted and he felt a solid, smooth shape beneath. He gasped in surprise. Nervous fingers explored the contours of the shape. The smooth shape gave slightly to his squeeze. He sagged back on his haunches, recoiling in his instant reaction.

"The good lord Jesus and Mary!"

He sat there for a moment, afraid to engage his thoughts. Slowly, on his knees, he inched back to where he thought the shape was. He could not see anything in that shallow gully beside the path. Much as a blind man would, he stretched his hands out in front of himself and nervously ran his palms over the ground to left and right. With a shudder, he felt again the smooth surface he had felt before.

He slid his hand beneath the shape and tried to move it. It was heavy: heavy, but yielding.

"You alright Fin?" Sergeant Donal Quinn's words and the torchlight cut the night and Fin sat back in the bracken.

"I'm fine, but shine your torch down here." The light from the torch swept the bracken to his right.

"No! More this way," he insisted.

"There!" he exclaimed as the light caught something dark in the grass. "Hold it there!"

Still on his knees, he moved towards the dark object. Whatever it was, he couldn't see all of it. It was buried deep in the grass. It seemed incredibly smooth to his faltering touch. He eased both hands under the shape and lifted. As he did, he could hear the whisper of something spilling on to the grass. He recoiled in horror, releasing the object to the ground with a dull thump.

"What have we here, d'ya think?" Donal's torch was now centred on the object. The surface glistened in the light. It was black and at one end there was a light coloured gash. As Donal came closer with the torch and, much to the relief of both men, it was clear that it was a plastic bag. By now they were both standing over it. Fin prodded it with the stick. A hole appeared; a light substance, like sand through an egg timer, ran out onto the grass.

"Breadcrumbs!" Donal exclaimed. "Some bugger's left a bag of ground bait behind! Would ya credit that now! You alright?"

"I'm fine!" Finbar said, lacking conviction. He brushed himself down, although he couldn't see what poor shape his uniform was in. He followed the torch back to the car. Donal Quinn slumped down into the front seat.

"Don't know about you," he said "but I'm feckin' crackered! I'm too old for this type o' thing."

"You and me both!" Fin said, leaning against the car and taking in deep gulps of air.

"Do you need me for a while Donal? Only I said I'd let the Englishman know how we'd got on."

"Let him wait a bit. It won't harm. If he's been up to no good, he knows more than we do," he warned. "If he hasn't, then perhaps no news is good news."

The sergeant plucked the radio mike from the dashboard and called the other searchers in turn. Each one reported no sign of the boy. The sergeant conveyed the situation and quickly received the order to stand down until first light. They sat in the car rehearsing the possibilities. Donal Quinn was almost as certain of the Englishman's involvement as Finbar Reeve was not.

"You get a nose for this type of thing in time," Quinn said, and Reeve bristled at the implication. Quinn added "It's your first."

"No!" Reeve responded, hurt by the Sergeant's ill- informed suggestion. He had had to deal with several cases of missing persons, and on one occasion with tragic results. "And I can't believe he..,"

"Trust me," said the sergeant with a tapping of the side of his nose and one eye closed. Finn knew there was nothing he could say to shake the sergeant's judgement. *He might be right*!

*

It was no coincidence that Mary McMahon's house was on his route back to the police house to get a change of clothes. Finbar Reeve had developed a confidence in his own instinct. He judged this to be a moment to follow it. His conscience and sense of fairness was overriding his loyalty to Donal Quinn. He turned into the drive and parked outside the house. Before he could turn off the car lights, the front door opened and the Englishman stood there, still in his fishing clothes. Beside him was his colleague.

"Any news?" Ellison asked.

"No! Nothing yet sir! It's dark just now, so we've been told to stand down. The helicopter's still up though."

"It's not so dark that you can't carry on, surely?"

"It comes from the top," Reeve explained.

"It seems too soon. When will you start again?" he urged.

"As soon as it's light."

"I want to come."

"I think the other boys need you. You'll be more use here," "Dave can look after them. They're good kids," Tom countered. "That's why they need you. Here!"

"I can't stay."

"You must!" Reeve insisted.

Tom Ellison knew, deep-down, that Reeve was right.

By now the constable was at the doorway. He put his hand on the teacher's shoulder and guided him back inside into the hallway with a finger crooked at Dave, inviting him to follow.

"How's the other boy?" he whispered.

"Much better! They gave him some medicine and he's got some colour back," Dave responded.

Reeve expressed the hope that the manpower for the following day would be increased. With added resources, they could search a larger area. The sound of crockery clashing came from the kitchen.

"Any chance of a cup of tea?" the Garda asked mundanely, establishing a moment of normality.

"Mary's been making a brew every half hour," Dave responded, putting his arm around his colleague. "You alright mate?"

He led Tom down the hall and into the large, neat, kitchen. At its centre the large table, covered in a sheet of plastic decorated with images of imaginary birds, was already set for breakfast. Mary McMahon twirled from her duties at the sink, and in a stage whisper asked "What news have you got Fin?"

The conversation that followed was conducted beside the sink, away from the boys, in muted tones.

"Well now Mary, we've none."

"No signs?"

"Not a trace, but it's early days," he knew there was a hollow ring to the remark, but there was nothing else he could say. Even a sliver of evidence would give him more excuse for optimism.

"We couldn't see. It was a waste of time." At once he knew his error.

"Waste?" her tone raised.

"What are you saying Finbar Reeve? This gentleman's lost a boy and you talk of waste. What would your mother say hearing you talk so? She'd turn in her grave so she would. God rest her soul!" It hit the mark.

"Mary, that's not fair," it sounded weak but he was hurt. "Well get out there and find him," then an afterthought, "though you'll have a cup of tea first." The offer didn't help.

"No! I'll be about my business," he said, stung by the response.

He moved to the kitchen door and walked down the hallway to the front door. Silhouetted against the exterior porch light, he straightened his cap and said quietly

"I'll keep you informed. Try to get some rest." Reeve pulled the door to behind him, and Tom Ellison stood for a moment in the darkened passage, not knowing whether to be angry at the lack of action

"He's a good man! And conscientious! You can rely on Fin." McMahon stood at the open kitchen door. Half the passage was lit with bright light from the kitchen beyond. She beckoned him back in. He followed her into the warm glow of the kitchen's open fire. Michael sat silent in his usual chair.

After a warming cup of tea, Tom and Dave checked that all the boys, who had already eaten and gone upstairs, were prepared to go to sleep. Tom had a reassuring word with the recovered Colin. They might not sleep easily, but they were all tired. Back in the kitchen, the conversation between the two teachers stuttered for the next hour. Dave rehearsed in his mind his own concerns. Could he have done more? Surely not! He wasn't there. The thought that these events might have an effect on his career crept into to mind. The lack of anything positive to fasten on to made it impossible to sustain any encouraging line of thought. The boy had disappeared without trace, and as far as they knew, without reason. That was all they had. Neither could make any sense out of it.

*

"How could this happen?" The conversation was a blur, but Charles Meade's unanswered question remained with Tom Ellison long after he had put the phone down. He knew he had to do it. He put off the deed as long as he could, but the headmaster had to know. *But what had he to tell? How could he tell it?*

When he did, his anguish deepened.

"How could this happen? Meade repeated.

There was a panic in the headmaster's voice that left Tom feeling even more alone; more exposed than before.

He sensed, there and then, a distance being set between them.

How could that be? Solidarity at least for God's sake! They were colleagues. Professionalism required it. Humanity required it.

But at once he had a bad feeling.

Deliberately, and as calmly as he could, Tom explained what was happening and asked Meade to deal with matters at that end.

"What do I tell his parents?"

"Just the mother," Tom corrected. "For the rest, I'd leave it until the morning."

He was shocked that the head teacher had not yet got a grasp of his responsibility in the situation "Yes. Perhaps that would be best. I'll try to contact someone at the Office. God knows what they'll say!" He meant the Local Authority. "They have to know."

"Right!" Tom said, too tired to discuss.

"Well I'll leave it to you," said Meade. "You'll ring in the morning. If you don't hear from me first. O.K.!" followed by an afterthought, "I'll not sleep tonight." Tom bit back a reply and simply said "Goodnight!"

When he put the phone down, he stood by the table in the hall for a few moments, conjuring thoughts of distant treachery. Much as he did later when the deep shadows from the fire only served to emphasize the blankness of his unseeing gaze. He did not respond to Mary McMahon's sympathetic hand on his arm. Dave was standing by the window looking out aimlessly.

"I'll go and check upstairs before I turn in."

"Thanks Dave! I'll be up soon."

"Goodnight Mary," said the young teacher at the kitchen door.

"Goodnight my love," she replied, with warmth in her voice.

Mary finished drying off some plates and put them on the table. She leant over, her face close to his.

"How about a wee tot?" she whispered.

"No thanks Mary," he said. "I'd better go and check on the boys." He slid the chair under the table and made for the door. As he opened it, he turned and muttered a trembling "Thanks!"

"Goodnight and God Bless!" She nodded.

Tom Ellison closed the door behind him and, in the darkness of the hallway, wiped away a tear and slowly climbed the stairs.

At the same time Finbar Reeve sat at home gathering his thoughts. What else could be done? There was no evidence. No clues. Nothing to fasten on to. Could he be wrong about the Englishman? *How could he let the boy disappear?*

He seemed a careful type.

Could Donal be right? The teacher did have those cuts.

Had he been up to no good?

What motive could he have?

Finbar knew what conclusion Donal had come to, but he could not believe the teacher was perverted in some way. There was nothing about him, or his young colleague to suggest that. In fact his every response spoke of a deep concern for his missing boy and his other charges. There was still a chance that the boy would be found. The thought needed to be kept alive, but they had to assume that he had not just wandered off and got lost. If he had, surely all the activity around the lake would have found him, or he would have found his own way back. Fin concluded that, at best, he was lying injured somewhere. At worst, he had either been taken by the water or some malevolent hand had struck him down. Either way, a tragedy had struck Drumlasheen.

He felt sickened at the prospect.

"God help us all!"

11

Tom Ellison nodded off fitfully through the crawling night. Each time he woke, it was with the expectation that daylight had come, and the search was to be resumed. But each time a still blackness filled the bedroom window that he had left with curtains open. One o'clock, two o'clock, three o'clock went by. It was as if life had been put into slow motion. It gave all the more time for bewilderment to enter his confused brain. Each befuddled notion became immediately enmeshed with another and there was no chain of thought. No logic. No sense. He was a man derailed. Images flashed in and out of his thoughts. They had no sequence. Everything was confusion. It was like a vast painting by Hieronymus Bosch, but without a frame. No edge; just a convulsing mass spreading to the corners of his mind. He got out of bed and moved towards the window and he could see the moon glinting off the lake below. The knock on the door shattered the silent world of his dementia.

"Mister Ellison!" He was too afraid to answer.

"Mister Ellison! It's Mary! I heard you moving about, so I've put the kettle on. Mr Ellison?" she whispered.

"Yes, Mary." he answered. "I'll come down. Thank you."

He blessed the intrusion. In the gloom, he saw his reflection in the mirror above the sink. "God you look a mess!" he muttered to himself and, on aching legs, tottered towards the sink and poured some cold water. Wearily he cupped his hands and splashed the ice cold water over his face to shock himself into life. Some of it went down the front of his open shirt and found its way down his chest and across his stomach. It took his breath away and he was wrenched back into the world of reality. Drying himself in the gloom, he peered at his watch. Five o'clock!

In those moments he determined to be at the lake, whatever the police said. That was his place, his heart told him. He reasoned that Dave could look after the boys. Mary would help, he was sure. After a cup of tea, all he could manage, he felt more alert. When Dave, bleary eyed, came downstairs, they decided to let the boys sleep as long as possible.

"They'll be alright," Dave said reassuringly. "Let's hope there's good news." There was a brief discussion, but neither could give voice to more than wishful thoughts of hope. It went without saying that Tom was deeply concerned for the well-being of the other boys, but at the moment he was convinced that his place was with the search.

Mary, who had been busily preparing for the boys' breakfast at the stove, turned and with a tremble in her voice, said "We'll take care of them don't you worry."

"Will you deal with Meade if he rings?" Tom asked Dave.

"Sure!" he replied.

Stepping out into the early morning drizzle, Ellison got into the minibus, assured that the boys would be alright, for the time being at least. The short journey down to the lake seemed longer than before, and he tried to cultivate an inner calm. He wanted to be effective. The sight of three police cars and a large van in the parking area disturbed the brittle composure that Tom had created for himself. There was no sign of activity about the group of vehicles. Tom sat in the bus for a few minutes, mustering his thoughts and his resolve.

It didn't look as if the search had been stepped up. A large policeman, wearing a long black cape to combat the worst of weathers, stepped down from the back of the van and moved towards him. He decided to take the initiative.

"My name's Ellison. Any news?" he asked.

"Not yet sir! They went out about a quarter of an hour ago."

"Couldn't they start earlier?"

"Well now!" The Chief decided to take charge. Things slow down do ya know." Tom felt angry that time was wasted on oiling the wheels of the establishment. He bit back his criticism.

"What can I do?"

"They said if you turned up you were to stay here."

"You're joking!"

"No! They're well away by now. Spread all over the place. They've worked out a pattern. They know what they're doing."

It was meant to reassure, but Ellison felt that nothing he'd seen so far indicated a well tried and tested approach. In his midnight ramblings he had come to think that there had been a chaotic randomness about it all the night before. At that moment two cars appeared over the brow of the hill and bounced their way down to the car park.

"Volunteers?" offered the Garda, moving towards where the cars had stopped.

He peered into the front of the first one and proceeded to give directions, which Tom could not hear from his position. The doors of the cars opened and five men gathered around him. By now he was using his arm more as a scythe, indicating a wide sweep in the search. This demonstration finished, the group gathered into a tighter knot suggesting the sharing of some special, confidential information. Heads turned in Tom's direction. For him, no words needed to be spoken to establish the sense of recrimination he sensed in those looks. There was no compassion for him in that dour collection.

The group parted like a wave into two groups, with individuals moving to their allocated starting points. Thinking to add himself to the search party, Tom made to head for the stony beach.

"Let me help!" It was not an offer, but a plea. It was made to anyone who would listen. The men moved as one, and disappeared amongst the trees and were gone.

His way was now blocked by the stout policeman, feet wide apart, arms crossed. Holding his hand in front of his face, as if directing traffic, he announced "You can't go down here sir!" Frustration and anger collided.

"Look!" Ellison responded angrily. "You can take your instructions and stick 'em up your arse. I'm going!" There was a fury and determination in the words that shook the Garda. He responded "Them's my orders!"

"You just watch me!" snapped Ellison, his stride lengthening as his determination grew. The policeman hunched his shoulders in resignation, as the teacher marched past and down the path, disappearing into the trees beyond. It was more than his job was worth to leave the parked cars! Tom made his way through the trees, feeling a bristle of self- satisfaction that he had so easily quenched the constable's resolve.

12

Tom recalled the isolation he had felt back in 1985, as he turned into the drive of Mary McMahon's house He was surprised at the ease with which he had retraced the route down to the lake, and then to the house above. He had rehearsed the moment many times since he received the postcard. But this wasn't the audition. This was opening night!

The track up to Shannonbridge House was more arduous than he remembered, and he slowed down over the rutted drive to protect the suspension of his hire car. As he pulled up outside the front door, he was shocked to see the once pristine white frontage, now a grey and stained imitation of itself. The front door, its brass knocker once lovingly polished, showed the consequence of years of lack of attention. The small manicured square of lawn and carefully planned flower borders, of distant memory, showed equal signs of neglect. There was an all pervading sense of degeneration about what had once been Mary McMahon's pride and joy. Tom Ellison felt completely disorientated as he moved towards the front door. It was as if the image of Shannonbridge House that he had carried around for so long, had faded like a crumpled photograph: all ochre, no colour. Briefly it had been his home! If Mary McMahon stilled lived here, it shook the confidence that any of his memories were true.

For a moment he stood by the door, unsure of what he would discover if he knocked. Perhaps she'd moved? But he'd checked the telephone number. He chided himself for his lack of confidence. Anyway he was here now.

Four strong raps on the door, and he stood back. There was a faint sound from the other side. The latch clicked and a tiny gap opened. A nose appeared.

"Is Mary McMahon in?" He peered intently at the nose. No reply. "I'm looking for Mary McMahon. Is she in? "

The door snapped shut. He stepped back, shocked at the response. What the hell to do now? He hadn't come all this way just to be snubbed. The nose couldn't be Mary, could it? He looked around at the shambles around him and he wasn't sure. He moved back to the door, bent low and pushed at the flap of the letter box. It was stiff but, with an effort, he managed to pry it open sufficiently to see just a pair of tartan slippers disappear towards the kitchen, as he remembered. He shouted into the letterbox.

"Hello! Is Mary McMahon there? Hello!"

He waited a few moments for an answer. Nothing! He walked backwards to the gate to get a better view, and then decided to look around the back. He passed through a disintegrating gate to the rear garden. At least it had been a garden – once! Now it was more like a jungle. The long grass was above the top of his shoes, and rose bushes ran amok in every corner. The delicate pink of the flowers were in stark contrast to the rest of the enveloping weeds. He remembered the kitchen had once overlooked a well cared for lawn, where he and the boys had played football. Now the kitchen window was almost blocked by the rampant bushes. He moved some branches aside and peered in. A net curtain barred his view. He tapped on the window.

"Hello!"

He pressed his nose against the window to try to detect some semblance of movement. There was none. He pushed aside the grass that overhung the path and made for the back door. His knock was harder and went on longer than he intended, but he was desperate and increasingly annoyed. No response. Anyone inside must have heard. He knew someone was there. This wasn't how it was supposed to be! He turned sharply and picking his way through the undergrowth, made his way back to the front of the house. Standing well back, he scrutinised every window for a tell-tale sign. There was no sign of movement.

"I'll be back!" he said out loud. It was a ridiculous threat, but he felt the better for it.

He got back into the car and for a time he sat there, not knowing just what to do next. His plans had been simple. Face Mary McMahon with the note, and take it on from there. It was his only clue. "Hell it wasn't even a clue!" But it was all he had. He couldn't see his next step forward but, if it didn't lie at Shannonbridge House, it had to be in Drumlasheen village. Somebody there could explain to him, surely!

It was midday in light drizzle as he drove down the wide main street of Drumlasheen with its low, whitewashed buildings on either side. Time seemed to have passed the village by, and left it trapped in the 1900's. There were few ostentatious concessions to the 1980's. For want of a better idea he stopped outside Gerry's Bar. It was the one he had been in before, and he entered, concerned at the recent dent in his plan. He needed somewhere to marshal his thoughts. He parted the multi coloured plastic strips that served as a curtain across the doorway, and passed into the long room that was the bar. Two men sat on stools along the bar. Almost out of sight at a solitary table in the far corner, beneath a dart board, another sat hunched over an empty glass. Behind the bar, a fresh faced man, in a mustard-coloured waistcoat, was polishing glasses.

"Good mornin' to you," he said with a ready smile that revealed a dazzling set of teeth. The dark hair, meticulously scalloped in waves and slightly greased, helped to create a dapper, but slightly comic appearance. This wasn't the Gerry he remembered.

"What'll you have?"

"A pint of Guinness," he said automatically. He perched himself on a stool next to the two men.

"Good morning," he said

"Mornin'!" Their response was ready and encouraging. He watched the man behind the bar pour a glass of thick black stout. An ever increasing pale head formed as the glass filled. The man stopped pouring.

"Y'here on holidays?"

"Well not really. No!" He had forgotten how easy it was to fall into the speech pattern. "I've come to see someone I knew years ago."

"Oh ay!" The barman started to pour again. As the brown foam crept over the lip of the glass, he made a deft slicing action with what looked like a child's wooden ruler, and took the head off the swirling pint. He presented it to Tom.

"That'll be one ten."

"Do you take English?" he asked. In the turmoil of events following the postcard, Tom had forgotten to buy in a supply of Irish currency. He'd paid for the ferry and hire car in pounds, so this was his first money transaction.

"Sure!" He handed over a five pound note and the barman gave him change. He put it in his pocket without checking, not even sure of the exchange rate.

"And who might your friend be?"

"Not a friend, really. Someone I stayed with two years ago. Mary McMahon, Shannonbridge House. You know her, I expect?" he prompted. From experience Tom knew it was difficult to be unknown in villages like Drumlasheen. At the mention of the name, the swiftest of glances flashed between the barman and the two silent drinkers.

"To be sure! Owd Mary. From years ago y'say?"

"Two years ago."

"'Tis a shame an all."

"A shame," echoed one of the drinkers.

"A cryin' shame," said another. All three shook their heads in mournful union.

"Is something the matter?" Tom wanted to retain an appearance of innocence. That way he might get the information he needed.

"Well now, y'know her husband Michael died?"

"Oh yes!" he lied.

"Terrible business, so t'was. Terrible!" The others nodded as one.

"I never really heard the details," Tom said, his mind racing to keep up the pretence.

The barman picked up a towel and started polishing a glass.

"Y'know he worked down the timber yard." Tom nodded, though in truth he knew very little about Michael McMahon.

"Twenty ton of logs they reckon. Terrible!" he continued.

"Terrible!" chimed all three.

"They sent for Mary. She got there just before he passed away. But he was in a terrible mess they say. Poor Mary's never been the same since."

"How?" Both his mind and his mouth had lost the race and Tom was floundering.

"Went downhill fast!" The taller of the two drinkers pirouetted on his stool and faced Tom. He was a man in his fifties and bore the signs of an outdoor life. Skin like tanned leather, hair that showed no knowledge of a comb and a dark blue suit that must have been his Sunday best many years ago. Now it bore the stains of working with animals and fitted just here and there.

"Let everything go," he reported. The second man leant over his friend. He was clearly in the middle of a day's work, for the hand that rested on the shoulder was black. The boiler suit he wore beneath a tatty jacket was also engrained with grease and the cloth cap completed a well-oiled ensemble. But he had a cheerful cherubic face, testimony Tom thought, to many a mid-day visit to Reynolds' Bar; or one of the others in Drumlasheen.

"I've been up to the house." Tom wanted to show he was leading the conversation as much for himself as his audience. "I couldn't believe it!"

"She's lost it," said the oily one, drawing circles on his temple with his finger.

"Mad as a hatter," confirmed the suit "Shut herself away, so she did." The barman had finished polishing glasses and came round from behind the bar to where Tom had eased himself onto a stool.

"The village tried to help, but she's lost the thread. Father O'Mahony's the only one she'll allow in the house. Word is the place is filthy. Can you imagine it? Mary always bein' so neat and house proud an' all."

The barman heralded a young man who had come into the bar and moved back behind the bar to pour out "the usual". The young man greeted the suit and the oily one and they responded in cheery unison. He offered them information on a horse that could not lose and they laughed it off dismissively. The interruption had taken the impetus out of his conversation, so Tom decided to leave. It wasn't until he was sitting in the car, rain dripping down his face, that he realised that he had been in a bar and come out with his full pint still on the bar..

"Bloody hell!" he muttered to himself in a mixture of surprise and pride. Not much to write home about – but progress.

By now it was raining hard. The moment was interrupted by a knock on the car window. A face peered in at him, blurred by the increasing rain. He wound the window down. It was a round unshaven face, the whiteness of several days' stubble indicating a man of mature years; but there was an impish ness about the eyes that gave it a contradictory youthfulness.

"You've been to the house then," he said.

"I'm sorry..,"

"Mary McMahon's house."

"How..?"

"In there!" The face pointed a thumb over his shoulder. Now Tom realised that this was the man, sitting in the corner of the bar.

"Oh yes!"

"Will ya be stayin' on?" he asked.

"I'm not sure. Why?" He was tempted to object to the man's inquisitiveness, but he was fast learning the technique.

"She's not the same woman you knew."

"What do you know about me?"

"What you said in there. Besides..,"

"Yes?" he asked instantly, but he had been too quick. *Technical fault!*

"No matter!" The man stood up and momentarily his face was no longer framed in the car window. Tom leaned over.

"Have we met before?" The face reappeared. "Maybe we have. Maybe we havn't. It's hard to say."

"But you know Mary?"

"I do."

"I want to talk to her?"

"From what I've heard recently, you'll likely get more sense from my dog, so ya will."

"But I'd like to try. How can I get in touch with her? She won't answer the door,"

"Try Father O'Mahony. Church at top o' the town." The rain was suddenly harder and the man pulled up the collar of his coat.

"Can I give you a lift?" Tom offered.

"Thank you, no. I've business to attend to." As the man started to walk away, bending into the rain, Tom shouted "We have met before havn't we?" The man turned, rain dripping down his nose.

"I helped to search for the boy. We never spoke."

"None of them did," Tom mused, as he watched the man disappear through the rain spattered windscreen.

"Thank you!" he shouted into the rain.

13

Tom Ellison arrived on the stony beach on that second day and watched pairs of men, one of them at the water's edge, the other at the tree line, trudging along with their heads down and prodding the ground with sticks. He walked into the shallow water to get a better view of the other end of the curving beach, and he saw figures on the far bank move about in the early murkiness of what promised to be another grey day. The activity before him looked controlled. He wasn't part of it, but he knew he would have a role to play, if things turned out badly. He watched the systematic hunt for clues as the rain got harder, the circulation to his hands and feet blunted to a painful level. He stamped his feet and shook his hands vigorously. Despite the fact that he was wearing waders, a water proof coat and gloves, the cold insinuated itself to his whole body. The increasing rain scuttered across the surface of the lake, drowning the diminishing sounds of the search party, as they moved along the bank and out of sight. He knew that these men, called upon to help search for the boy, had made up their minds about him.

For half an hour he wandered aimlessly up and down the beach and into the trees following the searchers. What was he looking for? He was getting increasingly frustrated and sitting on the tree by the boy's fishing spot, he knew he had done all he could, but inaction was not an option. He weighed up the situation. The search must be concentrated on the reedy area, out of sight from where he was. He knew only too well how difficult the search would be in amongst the trees and along the boggy pasture. The memory of his own search persuaded him against a token individual foray into the dense coppice. He was neither fit enough for the task, nor did he have the local knowledge to make his search effective. In fact he was useless.

"Bloody useless!" He was relegated to the position of observer. The sergeant had been right to tell his man to keep him away! He sat on the fallen tree for a while and then walked through the copse back to the car park.

Sheepishly he greeted the policeman on guard, who saluted respectfully. Ellison nodded in response and, climbing into the back of the minibus, said "Any news?"

"No Sir!" The response was icy and no more than he deserved.

"None at all?" he persisted.

"There's no sign over the far side. The frogmen are moving down towards the far end."

Tom Ellison's body stiffened at the word. The frogmen! He really knew that any effective search needed frogmen, but the reality of their involvement shook him to the core. What had been a nightmare, and perhaps unreal, was now inescapable. All his warnings about the danger of water might have been for nothing.

The next two hours passed very slowly. The policeman remained tight lipped and volunteered information only when pressed. Tom knew he had overshot the mark before, but there was more to it than that. Was he being paranoid? Had this man judged him too? What could he say or do to change his opinion? He turned the question over and over in his mind, as he sat there, alternately scanning the sky and the ground beneath his feet. He thought of confronting it head on.

"You don't think I had anything to do with him going missing?" he rehearsed to himself, but it was too pleading, too defensive and was never asked. Any persistent interest he showed in the organisation of the search could be misconstrued as nervous guilt. Perhaps a jovial, optimistic approach would unfreeze the atmosphere, but then he would be thought uncaring and unfeeling! Maybe, if he explained what he had already done in his search for the boy, he could establish that he cared? Would this be seen as laying the ground for an alibi? He decided that there was nothing he could do to dislodge the opinion that the constable and others seemed to hold. Whatever it was! Twice the helicopter hovered over head and his pulse raced. He couldn't make out what was said over the radio. Each time the answer to his unasked question was a shake of the head and "No! Nothing!"

Garda Constable Finbar Reeve, looking exhausted, trudged towards him from the area beyond the stony beach, drawing in deep breaths and brushing his arms free of debris.

"I'm to take you to make a statement," he puffed. "Just a formality."

All of Ellison's frustrations had, by now, taken their toll and he presented no objection to the Garda's message. He was not in control of events and had to take his designated place in police procedure. They made their way back to the car park in silence. The journey took about twenty minutes until they arrived at the wrought iron gates to the area HQ. An officer waved them through.

Inside the Victorian building Tom Ellison was conducted to a ground floor room, painted grey, and furnished sparsely with just a Formica-topped table and three chairs. Ellison sat down, Finbar Reeve stood to attention by the door.

Date August 28th. 1985 Time: 10.15 a.m.

"My name is Thomas James Ellison and my permanent address is 7, Stanley Close, Millerton in Lancashire. I am a teacher at Hillpark School and have come to Drumlasheen with a group of eight children and my colleague David Cotter for a week of fishing. We arrived on August 27th 1985...,"

Tom Ellison read through his statement. It was a distillation of the hour long grilling he endured at the hands of Inspector Eric Blane. The detective had stumped into the tiny interview room with a bundle of papers under him arm from another case in which he was already deeply involved, With man power over stretched in the search, his brief was to question Ellison about the missing boy. It was clear he was not well pleased at the diversion.

On entering, Blane removed a dark brown trilby, which was turned down front and back, and looked like an upturned basin. He was a short, stocky man in his early forties. Two slabs of dark hair were separated by a centre parting. A tiny moustache tight beneath a squat nose and a prominent lower lip gave him a belligerent look. A colourful floral patterned handkerchief popping out of the top pocket of his three piece suit and a brightly coloured tie, were a bizarre nod to the times. Tom smiled through his apprehension.

Blane eased into the chair opposite, and then very deliberately placed the sheaf of papers on to the table, and beside it his trilby. He sat back in the chair, his fingers entwined, and looked at Ellison as if getting him into focus. It seemed to Tom that the moment passed in slow motion, and he moved uncomfortable in his chair. After a long silence, the detective introduced himself in a matter-of-fact sort of way, and acknowledge the constable, standing beneath the single window that gave the room its meagre light. After establishing Tom's identity, and the details of the others on the trip, Blane leaned forward slowly and in a conspiratorial whisper said "Now Mr Ellison, what do you think has happened to the boy Eh?" It was the "Eh?" at the end of the question that set the mood for the interrogation that followed.

"I don't know!" It was said with as much fortitude as Tom could marshal.

"Surely you must have some idea?"

Tom mustered all the resolve he could find in fighting off any suggestion that he had some hidden knowledge of the episode. The boy had disappeared and that's all he knew. Sequences and times were endlessly scrutinised. Tom rigorously defended his management of the trip. Questions came fast and loose, in a voice that sounded like a rusty gate.

"A pub. Was it a suitable place to take the boys?"

"Was there sufficient supervision of the boys?"

"Were they well prepared to be by water?"

"Could they all swim?"

"Were they all in sight at all times?"

All were designed to seek out any vulnerability in Tom's testimony.

"Let's talk about you shall we Mr Ellison?"

"Here we go!" Tom thought. He couldn't help adjusting his sitting position in the chair once more. His heart was thumping. He must keep calm. He knew that he needed to choose his words very carefully. Inexorably the questions homed in on his relationship with the boy.

"How long had you known him?"

"What was he like? Did you get on?"

"What do you know about the boy's background?"

"Did you have other dealings with him outside school?" Tom responded truthfully to all of Blane's questions and had almost recovered his equilibrium, but after a lengthy pause, full of feigned contemplation, Blane said

"Remind me about the boy dropping out of the trip."

"His mother had problems," Tom answered.

"His mother?" A sharp glance up from his note book.

"Her husband had left her." A longer stare.

"Do you know why?" Blane lent forward, sensing an opening.

"No! But she said she was struggling on her own."

"And..," followed by a well-practiced, knowing pause "you said you could help her?" Pause.

"I put her in touch with someone."

"Nothing else?" There could be no ambiguity in the question.

As if triggered by a remote switch, Tom smashed his fist into the detective's pile of papers, all the tension of the day bursting out.

"You sanctimonious bastard!" They were now nose to nose. The constable moved forward instinctively.

"It's alright!" Blane sat back in his chair, his open palm signalling to Reeve that he was in control of the situation. There was a hint of a self-satisfied look on his face. He'd got enough. If he, or anyone else, had to speak to the teacher further, he knew where they should start. He had done what was asked of him.

"That'll be all for now Mr Ellison," he said flatly. "Garda Reeve will take you through making a statement."

Before gathering his papers together, Blane put a hand on either side of his parting and, with a smoothing sweep, slicked his hair into place. The final gesture of delicately replacing his trilby on his head brought the interview to a close.

"... *signed Thomas James Ellison*"

As he looked at the completed statement Tom wondered what use it might be to the investigation. Had the detective drawn positive conclusions from the process, enough to pass on to the investigation?

Was it form filling for form filling's sake, or was it all just lining up the blame?

14

Tom Ellison parked his rented car in front of the huge basilica- like church dominating the top end of Drumlasheen's main street. The Church of Mary The Blessed Virgin seemed out of scale with the rest of the town, with its huge dome and its elaborate decoration, in stark contrast to the self-effacing simplicity of the buildings sitting at its feet. It made an unambiguous statement about the church's position in the town. Here was the centre of Drumlasheen's little universe. Tom Ellison looked up nervously as he walked towards it. He was on foreign ground. He had no sense of how he should conduct himself in the heavy, alien, atmosphere that surrounded the building and its status. It boomed out its eminence. He stopped half way down the path, feigning a tourist's look at the church's green dome. In fact he was considering ignominious retreat.

He had felt ill at ease around all things religious since his youth. The three years in his church choir from age eight, for his mother's sake, had done nothing but to confirm in him a deep and lasting distrust of the church. It was its rituals that concerned him most. They seemed, to him, designed to both mesmerise and demean the congregation. In recent years, as drink and depression had gripped him, religion had totally failed to represent any hope of salvation, despite the efforts of a well-meaning local cleric. Had he been judged by the almighty too, he had wanted to know? He found no absolution from the blame heaped upon him. He took it to be another reproach. Friend Booze gave no answers, but he asked no questions either! Self-doubt, anger and distrust, mixed in equal portions, made up the feeling that now caused Tom to break into a sweat. Momentarily he turned his anger inwards to his own weakness. He recognised that the paranoia that had overtaken his life was grappling for the ascendancy again.

"No way," he muttered to himself, slapping the side of his leg fiercely. "I'm free of that!"

Almost as quickly as it came, the self-doubt and uncertainties were dispelled and he was in control again. He opened the gate to the manse, which lay to the side of the church. The large black door, its icy smooth surface a credit to the loving attention of generations of willing parishioners, stood before him. He pulled a knob set to one side, and the response was the muffled tinkle of a bell inside. Seconds later the door opened, and was held back by a goblin of a man. Short would not sufficiently describe the man that greeted Tom.

"Gooday!" the round face split into a ready smile.

"Father O'Mahony," Tom asked.

"The same!" In acknowledgement a pink hand was laid across his chest, in sharp contrast to his black cassock.

"I wonder if you can help me? My name's Tom Ellison and I've come over to see Mary McMahon."

"Ooooh..," It was an involuntary response. A sharp intake of breath released almost as a sigh.

"I've been up to the house. I can't get an answer. Someone in the village said you might help me."

"Come in!" said the priest with a sweeping action.

The door was held open and Tom entered a hallway, whose outer sparkle matched the door, but it was a polish that disguised the ravages of time. A pink and grey tiled floor, tired from years of wear, led to rooms left and right, and a door at the end that Tom assumed was the kitchen. A staircase curling to the right and out of sight, once covered with the finest carpet money could buy, was reduced to hints of its former glory between strips of a modern substitute, tacked on to the lip of worn treads. The banister was further testament to endless polishing, as was the wooden panelling. The colour and texture of black treacle, it skirted the hallway up to waist height. Above it, red flocked wallpaper reached up to the high ceiling. At the foot of the stairs stood a plaster sculpture of the Virgin Mary, blue and red colour faded, but with its gilt newly painted. The priest nodded acknowledgement to it and crossed himself.

"Come through," he said, pushing aside a sausage shaped draft excluder with his foot. Tom entered a room which, although gloomy, had a pleasing, well used feel to it and an invigorating smell of polish. A large flat-topped desk beneath a bay window was covered in books, files and paperwork, and dominated the room. On the walls, in addition to a picture of Christ in a richly decorated frame, were dozens of more modestly framed pictures of birds of all sorts, winging their way in every direction. In one corner, next to a heavily carved cupboard, were two fishing rods in bags and a wicker creel with a canvas strap. A kindred spirit, Tom guessed.

On the mantelpiece above, a black cast-iron fireplace, an old leather football held pride of place. The informality was in stark contrast to the polished austerity of the hall.

"Will ya have a drink?"

"No. Thank you!"

As the priest moved to the cupboard and opened it, Tom took a closer look at his host. As he stood, to reveal a comprehensive collection of bottles, his head was only inches higher than the nearby mantelshelf. What hair he had was almost a creamy colour, indicating a tendency to gingery ness.

"What'd ya like?" the priest said, ignoring Tom's reply and with an expansive gesture of his tiny hands and added "A fruit juice perhaps. Orange, or something. Thank you." Tom replied.

"Nothing stronger?"

"Thank you. No," he bit his lip. A cut glass schooner, much too fine for orange juice, was filled from a carton.

"You don't mind if I join you?"

Tom nodded in assent.

The whisky was already out on top of the cupboard. A flat sided glass was filled half way to the top. Tom was invited to sit in one of the arm chairs on either side of the fireplace. He sank down amongst springs, which had long since given up the ghost. Father O'Mahony sat in its twin. He seemed even smaller, engulfed by the embrace of the chair.

"Well now. What can I do for you?" He took a substantial swig of his drink.

Tom stumbled his way through his story – or at least as much of it as he felt able to reveal to a stranger. The priest did not make matters easy by maintaining a silence, forcing Tom to drive through the tale at breakneck speed. Arriving at that day's visit to Mary McMahon's house, Tom was drained. He felt awkward in the moments that followed, but it gave him some time to regain his composure. Having sipped away at his drink, as Tom recounted the story, the priest's glass was now empty. He hauled himself from the depths of his chair.

"You want another?" he asked holding out the carton.

"No. Thank you," Tom insisted, indicating a half full glass.

Without regard for niceties, the priest poured a generous shot from the decanter into his own glass.

"Mr Ellison, I don't know what I can do to help. Mary's not herself just now."

"I know. I'm sorry." It seemed the thing to say.

"Been like it for several years. Even if she was prepared to talk to you, I don't think it would help. Her thoughts are all jumbled. It's taken me nearly four years to find a way of communicating with her on any meaningful level,"

"What exactly is the matter?"

"The Lord above knows," he said looking upwards.

"Her husband died?" Tom said. It was a shameless prompt.

"So he did. . Yes!"

"I didn't hear how." Another lie.

"A terrible thing so 'twas, an accident at work y'know. He was horribly crushed when some timber fell on him."

"And Mary's been ill ever since?" Ellison's hesitation was deliberate. He needed someone to tell him what the matter was with Mary McMahon.

"So to speak. Sure it's a mystery an' all."

"Can't the doctors help?"

"She's refuses to have anything to do with them. After the funeral she shut herself away," he shook his head mournfully.

"There's a little mobile shop. She leaves a note by the front door." Tom looked at the recumbent goblin and asked him "Do you think you could try to get her to see me? It's very important." Was he rushing things he wondered?

"Mr Ellison. I don't understand. Why is it so vital that you see her?" Up to now, Tom had not mentioned the postcard and his mission. He looked at the open face opposite, knowing he only had an instant to make a decision.

"You see I had this message," he began. There was no turning back now.

In more measured fashion, he told of the card, his hopes and that day's disappointment. As the conversation moved back and forth in the story, Tom knew he was revealing more and more of himself and his vulnerability than he would have liked. It seemed to matter less and less, as he had become comfortable with the tiny priest. There was no hint of judgement in the questions and comments.

Tom was telling his story for the first time without defensiveness, at least for the first time in years.

Father O'Mahony had listened as the story unfolded with an occasional nod and a sip of his drink.

"Had you no help from your colleagues?" the Father asked.

"No help! They were worse than that! In the first days back, they sympathised. It was what they were supposed to do. Soon they distanced themselves from me in a hundred subtle ways. After two weeks, the governors held their own version of the Inquisition and eventually, after weeks, I was dumped."

Tom regretted his choice of historical reference instantly.

He had not intended to upset the tiny priest; who nodded and smiled, acknowledging that he understood.

Tom continued "They called it "leave of absence". For my own good they said, to give me time. What it did was to give them time to make their own position as watertight as possible."

"Had you no one to speak up for you?"

"I was represented by a solicitor from my union. He did a good enough job, but by then the suspicions and the rumours were stacked against me."

"The rumours?" The priest asked.

"The English Press. It stated as soon as I got home and they got hold of the story."

"How?"

"Well the boy had disappeared without trace. I soon discovered that when you have a ready scapegoat, you start looking for all those things from the past that might give substance to the suspicion. Every parent, child and teacher has their memory of you, and unless you are a saint, your tiny foibles can easily be aggregated into a creature you would not recognise. If I had disciplined a child, I was a tyrant. If I had made allowances for a misdemeanour, I was weak. If I showed interest in the putting on a play, I was a pervert. All the lost causes that I had championed in the past made me a string of beads short of being a hippy. The papers fired the rumours and, before long, the figment of people's imagination was reported as fact. I was photographed coming out of an off licence. I was a drunk. I had even taken the boys to a pub, they discovered. Was I plying them with booze to get my evil way?"

The priest shifted uneasily in his chair.

"One paper flew over a spiritualist to look for a body."

"I remember that, I do," the priest said with distaste.

Tom was aware that he was being given full rein to tell his story, and it gave him solace that he had been able to unburden himself in that way, after so long.

"Tell me Father. Do you believe me when I tell you I did not do the boy harm?"

"I do!" the priest answered at once. The answer was breathtaking in its directness. Tom did not know what to say next.

"I always did!" the priest added. It was a comment more stunning than the last.

"You see, the tragedy of the boy was felt very deeply here. You'd not know that, I daresay. We prayed for him - and you for months after." There was a sudden dawning of memory.

Tom said "I remember you now Father. You came to the house that night."

"I did!"

"Why didn't you say so before?"

"I think you needed to tell the story. Besides you had no use of me that night." Tom suddenly remembered that the priest had arrived soon after he got back to the house on that blackest of days.

"I was very rude to you," Tom admitted.

"Ah t'was nothing! You were tired and upset. I understood."

"I'm sorry," Tom confessed. Very few words had passed between him and the priest that night. The bitterness over Meade's reaction had still been with him.

"Will you speak to Mary, father?" he asked earnestly.

"Of course, I'll try. I'm going in the morning for my usual visit. I'll do it then, but I'm not hopeful, mind."

"Thank you," Tom responded with genuine gratitude. "I've taken far too much of your time," he said as he stood to leave. "And I need to find somewhere to stay," he explained.

At once the priest ran through a number of places offering board in the village. In particular he recommended accommodation with a Mrs Elizabeth Murtagh.

"She a widow woman and keeps a spotless place. I can ring her if you like?"

"Thank you. Yes!"

"I'll do it now."

"If it's no trouble."

"No trouble at all!" Father O'Mahony levered himself from his chair and made for the door.

"It won't take a minute."

Tom looked around the room as the muffled conversation over the hallway phone began. Now that his eyes were accustomed to the light, he could see the delicate skill of the bird paintings clearly. He moved closer to one group of wading birds for a closer look. It was obvious, even to his untrained eye that they were all by the same hand. There was great attention to detail in the feathering and around eye, beak and foot. But the overriding impression was one of movement; living creatures, no doubt about it. These were no copied imitations. He squinted to see the tiny signature in the bottom right corner of each one. It was the same signature he was sure, but too small and quickly done to decipher.

"Ah! Pay them no heed!" the priest said, standing by the door.

"They're very good," Tom responded.

"I'm no expert mind. They fill a space on the wall, so they do."

"They're yours!" His admiration was genuine and matched the artist's modesty.

"It's all arranged. Mrs Mutagh's got no one staying at the moment, so you'll get the full treatment."

"Sounds intimidating," Tom joked.

"Lord save us! Men'd travel miles to be the sole beneficiary of Mrs Murtagh's cooking."

Tom thanked the priest, who in turn gave him detailed instructions on how to get to Mrs Murtagh's house. There was a noise on the corridor outside, and the door opened. Standing there was a man in his middle forties, tall and full suited in black, with an upright bearing.

"Sorry!" he said apologetically. "I didn't know you had someone..,"

"This is my nephew Patrick," said the priest

"I can come back later," the visitor said, turning to the door.

"I'd better go," Tom responded quickly and added "If you do talk to ..," he hesitated. "I'd really like to see her."

"I'll try," Father O'Mahony said with a resigned shake of the head. The nephew moved to one side, as Tom was shepherded out of the room and to the front door of the manse. Tom thanked the priest for his time.

15

They had spent seven hours searching for the boy. Finbar Reeve had been without sleep for almost twenty four hours, and was feeling the mental strain: that and the physical pain of aching legs forced to plough through water and the energy-sapping bog. Morning was passing into afternoon and there had not been a scrap of evidence about the boy. All the land in the immediate area of the lake had been searched and, as the shadows lengthened in late afternoon, it was decided to regroup the search party. The frogmen, whose number had been swelled by members of a local sub aqua club, would continue their search. The helicopter scuttled overhead.

The new plan was to spread out beyond the boundary of the lake, which had been the outer edge of their search so far. Cars could be used to spread the search wider if required. Finbar Reeve was glad to see the car park area again, promising a short rest and perhaps a cup of tea, but in the concentration of the search, he had forgotten the English teacher. He was a pathetic figure, standing by his minibus, ignored by the gathering searchers. As Finbar approached, he raised his hand to greet the policeman.

"Anything?" Tom asked, rubbing his hand across his face, brushing his eye, fearing a tear.

"No. Sorry. The divers are carrying on. We're spreading out."

"Have you any ideas…?"

"Just now we're following procedures. It's laid down. 'Tis the best we can do." It was said with a hint of scepticism.

Reeve made his way towards a patrol car which had just arrived and was immediately surrounded by police and a bunch of volunteers. Tom Ellison followed and stood at the back of the crowd, as a tall moustached man eased himself out of the car. Tom could see from his uniform and the braid on his cap that this was top brass.

"I'm Chief Superintendent Quinlan. Thank you for comin'. I'll be taking charge of the search. Give me five minutes to bone up. Sergeant!" He beckoned, and the sergeant and a thickset man in a waxed jacket followed him to a spot well away from the searchers.

Tom watched anxiously at the animated conversation between the two uniformed men. The waxed jacket stood close by listening. At one point, he thought they looked in his direction and he turned away instinctively. After several minutes they came back and the Superintendent outlined the next stage to his searchers. He allocated an officer and pairs of volunteers to cover areas, indicated on a large map held by the sergeant. The wax jacket looked on, but made no contribution. A female Garda, with the help of an old lady volunteer, started distributing cups of tea and thick sandwiches from the back of a battered Land Rover. One group went straight to their vehicles without refreshment and moved off. The others collected a cup of tea, drank it quickly, and left. Plastic cup steaming in his hand, the Superintendent approached.

"Mr Ellison. Have you contacted the boy's parents?"

"I rang my headmaster last night. He was going to contact his mother," Tom replied.

"I think she might like to be here," the Commander said gravely.

"Why? Have you..," Tom moved closer, anxiously.

"I think it would be best, whatever the outcome." It was nothing short of an instruction.

"Of course," Tom agreed. This was no time to be unhelpful.

"Right! Well now, you go ahead and arrange it. I'll go down and have a look round."

Ramrod straight, he strode out, the waxed jacket at his side and the sergeant, clearly exhausted, trailing behind. They soon disappeared out of sight through the trees. For a moment Tom reflected on developments. What new information could he give to Meade? Nothing he might say would avoid the assumption that the boy was dead.

"Christ!" The thought became all the more shocking as Tom realised that he too believed it to be so. The boy was dead!

It took all his inner strength to muster himself for the task ahead. He knew it must be done. There could be no excuses. He decided to make the call from a public box. He hated the thought of doing it with the other boys around. "Thank God for Dave!" He knew there was a telephone box by a small cluster of cottages on a sharp bend on the road in to Drumlasheen. He was grateful for the isolation. The call was a tense affair, with long silences at the other end: but not silences of shock. Tom could sense that Meade was working out his position, considering his options, already looking to cover his back. Altruism was pushed to one side, replaced by self interest.

"He's already started to pull up the ladder," Tom thought. "The bastard!" He repeated the next necessary steps, to be sure that the Head teacher had taken them in.

"And can you let me know what arrangements you make. I'll be at the house," he insisted.

"The house?"

"Mrs McMahon's. I left you the number."

"Oh yes!"

The extended bleep tone sounded the exhaustion of his money. There seemed little point in further conversation. He was just able to blurt out "Give me a ring," when the line went dead. For a minute he stood in the telephone box with the phone still in his hand. Meade had not asked how he was, shown any sign of solidarity or offered moral support! Bitterness boiled in his mouth. His thoughts turned to all the extra work he had done for the school, for which he had expected no reward. But here? Now? Surely they owed him support?

"Who are THEY?" he muttered to himself. "It's just bloody Meade. No-one else! He's bloody useless!" He was zoning in his anger to assuage his own sense of uselessness. It would not be played out fully for a long time.

Having arrived back at Shannonbridge House, he took the other boys into the dining room and, gathering all his strength, told them of the day's developments. They had spent the day under Dave's watchful eye playing board games and cards. The pent up frustration was not difficult to see. In a whispered conversation with Dave, they decided to take the boys to the small woody coppice that Tom had noticed in a dip on the other side of the house, away from the lake. He thought the fresh air would do them good and they could try to mend relations, which had obviously come under stress in his absence. He had been pleased and grateful for the mature way that Dave had dealt with the events. He had stepped up when needed. They all sat on a fallen tree near a ramshackle shed, and in a flood of questions and opinions, let free their confusion and unspoken fears. At first he tried to reassure them about the boy, but he knew he lacked conviction. It fooled no one, not even the youngest of the group. The heads of the two youngest dropped to cover their distress, and the older boys gripped them for comfort. He was in awe of their maturity. It was a pathetic sight and more than he could bear.

If he was to cope and help his boys through, he needed a plan.

"We'd better get back. There might be news," he said

He strode out ahead of the boys hoping inspiration would come before he reached the house. It did not. A diversion was needed, and he could not find it. He stood at the front door and when the boys arrived he wrapped his arms around each in turn.

"It'll be alright."

In that moment Tom Ellison's own feelings burst within, and at the fading of the second day, he stood with his boys and finally wept.

16

After his interview with Father O'Mahony, Tom drove down the main street of Drumlasheen and at the bottom turned into Weir Lane. He parked his car outside Number 3 and, standing at the top of a set of steps up to the front door, was the diminutive figure of Mrs Elizabeth Murtagh. She could not have been more than five feet tall. He thought that with the priest they would make a matching pair of book ends. Her grey hair was severely swept back, culminating in a giant bun in stark contrast to her delicate, pointed face. Thin in the extreme, at once he had the impression of a clockwork mouse, wound up in the morning, never to stop until it was time to go to bed.

"Oh Lord you look so tired. Come in," she gestured.

"Father told me you hadn't been too well. You'll have a cup of tea?"

"No thank you. I just had a drink with the father."

"I'm sure you did," she responded with a gentle sense of irony.

"But I would like a bath, if that's alright?"

"To be sure! I'll show you to your room and where everything is." Before he could move, the old lady had picked up his case, entered the house and made to haul it upstairs.

"Let me," he offered. It was a futile gesture. The tiny bent figure disappeared up the stairs and he followed. By the time he reached the top of the stairs, Mrs Murtagh was standing by an open door half way down the corridor,

"Here's your room. Right next to the bathroom."

"Let me take that!" he picked up the case and she proffered the key.

"Supper at seven alright?" Mrs Murtagh said.

"Yes! Thank you."

"Make yourself to home."

Alone in the room, he slumped on to the bed. He was, indeed, very tired now. It had been a long day and had taxed his physical strength. Though the outcome had at first been disappointing, he felt reassured by the understanding Father O'Mahony, and his promise of help. So, all in all, Tom Ellison felt in good mental shape at least. He laid soaking in the bath for half an hour, easing his aching limbs and re-running the events of the day.

After a splendid meal of ham, cut straight from a boiled hock, mashed potatoes and beans, he realised it represented his first food of the day. It was followed by a slice of fruit cake, topped with marzipan and icing, reminding him of youthful Christmases. Afterwards he sat with Mrs. Murtagh in the sitting room, with its roomy arm chairs. They chatted their way through an episode of "The High Chaperal" and watched the television news. When it seemed alright to do so, he excused himself. As he reached the bottom of the stairs, he remembered he had left his wet coat in the car. He would need it next day.

"Best hang it up somewhere inside," he thought. He searched around in his trouser pockets for the keys as he went out through the front door and down the steps.

It was dark now, and the lane was unlit. The car was parked right in front of him, as he opened the front gate. He fumbled for the right key, turned it in the lock and it clicked in reply. As he made to open the door, something white fell to the ground at his feet. It was a piece of paper. It must have been jammed in the gap between the bottom of the door and the door sill. He bent to pick it up. In the darkness, he turned towards the light from the house to see what was on it. He could not. He opened the car door, slid inside and turned on the interior light. Even now the paper appeared blank. He turned it over and held it hard up against the light and tilted it towards himself. His eyes took a second to focus. The message printed on it was simple, but clear. "DONT GIVE UP". His heart leapt in his chest, as he read it again. His brain was consumed in a maelstrom of confused thoughts. What was he to make of this bewildering message? Still bemused, he fumbled again with the car keys and needed several attempts before his finger found the door lock. When he reached the top of the steps to the house, he turned around and peered into the depths of the darkness beyond the car. Was his mysterious postman still out there? Upstairs in his room, he placed it on the table at the side of his bed and lay there looking at it, unknotting his confusion. His coat was still in the car.

Tom Ellison woke up next morning in his new surroundings, feeling elated at the turn of events. Although there was no clue to the authorship of the note, of one thing he was sure, it was the same simple hand as the one that had set him on his quest. A distinctive curl at the centre of the letter "O" gave the hand away. His ally, if ally it be, was in the area and knew of his activities. Could it be someone he had met since his arrival? He ran through the day's events. Almost everyone he had met was a candidate: The Suit, The Oily One, The Man in the Rain – even Father O'Mahony. All possibilities! Or perhaps his mysterious correspondent was keeping watch on him from a distance? Either way, Tom was encouraged.

There was a revived spring in his step as he walked up the main street of Drumlasheen later that morning. He needed to know how the people of the town had learned about, and responded to the disappearance of Glenn Wallace in 1985. Father O'Mahony said the events had had a significant affect. If nothing else, he might be able to get a clue about how the people felt towards him, all those years ago: how was he perceived in the town? The previous day he had noticed that a library was part of the Town Hall, a grey stone building full of its own importance on its separate site in the middle of the main street. He walked up the steps and in through the large oak doors to a cold, unwelcoming hallway with a wide staircase spiralling its way up through the building. His steps echoed as he walked along the tiled corridor to a small apologetic window, tucked round a corner out of open view, with a notice Sellotaped to one corner. DO YOU NEED HELP? PLEASE RING. He pushed the button.

The frosted window slid open and a headless body filled the space. A dazzlingly white blouse was filled to bursting by the biggest breasts he had ever seen. The breasts moved down and disappeared out of sight like a submerging submarine, to be replaced by a beaming face, topped by the most amazing red hair. It belonged to a woman in her forties, never a beauty queen, but, even now, capable of taking his breath away.

"Can I help you?" She leant forward and looked at him through sparkling green eyes. For a moment he felt like a schoolboy, tongue-tied by pubescent desire.

"Yes. Thank you. I was wondering if your library had back numbers of your local newspaper?" The eyes sparkled even more and the rich red lips parted in a smile.

"Why yes, we do!" There followed an awkward silence as he struggled not to stare.

"Do you want to see them?" she asked and he nodded mutely, his mind on one thing, his eyes elsewhere.

"Do you know where the door is?" she asked politely.

"No!" he answered, but he wasn't sure he remembered the question.

"Down the passage, turn right and through the double doors. You'll see a sign," she said and he watched the breasts re-surfaced, and the window slide shut.

He followed the directions, and found himself in a long room. Wood panelled up to a waist – high dado rail, and with the walls above painted cream - or was it a subtle shade of white? The room was divided by tall bookshelves with signs indicating various categories. At the far end there was a counter and behind it a door leading off. He wandered through the bookshelves until he came to a single large cupboard labelled LEITRIM OBSERVER. He opened it and inside he saw serried ranks of large green leather bound books, with numbers in gold lettering down the spine. He slid out the one marked 1986 and placed it on top of a table nearby. He fingered his way through the early months of the year, and smiled at the mundane news that had excited the folk of Drumlasheen He swept pages aside until he came to an edition of the paper which had come out two days after Glenn Wallace's disappearance. Across the top of the front page was the headline BOY MISSING. He shivered at the stark reality of the headline. Its simplicity hit him in the pit of his stomach. He sat down in a chair and took in a lung stretching breath. Being so soon after the event, information was sparse, but the banner headline on the front page of the next edition announced "MISSING SCHOOLBOY" and beneath it, in smaller print. "YOUNG FISHERMAN FEARED DROWNED" Here we go!

He read the story as if he was being told it for the first time. Perhaps, if he could strip away his own recollection of events, he might find a new slant on things. He was mentioned by name in the story and quoted as saying he could not understand what had happened to the boy. Had he spoken to a reporter? He could have done, but he did not remember it. Besides, very soon he had discovered that all the press invented quotes like that. There was much worse invention to follow than that. He remembered the story in The Daily Mail days later. "DON'T BLAME ME! SOBS LOST BOY'S TEACHER".

He had always remembered that particular headline. It leaves no room for explanation. What he had said was that he did not know what else he could have done for the boy's safety. The local paper repeated the Mail's "quote" and did a survey on public reaction to it. Soon the reaction became the story. Education chiefs were asked if he failed in his duty. County Guide Lines were quoted endlessly. Backs were being covered. It was the responsibility of the School Governors they said. New umbrellas were up there too! Relatives and neighbours of the boy were hounded into reactions by press eager for any scrap of gossip. Staff at the school had been instructed to refuse to comment, and that was presumed to be a lack of support. The Head held a press conference, but would not be drawn on the possibility of disciplinary action. They could read into that what they might! And they did! Why had he spent his day fishing out of sight of the boy? Why had he taken the boys on a drinking binge? Were tales of poor decisions true? All the questions he'd been asked by the police. He had felt the culture of blame growing and consuming him.

Within two weeks the Governors' Meeting had quizzed him and put him on indefinite suspension. They would not sack him. Yet! That would ensure a continued interest, so they could let some time pass and then ease him out; that was their ploy.

All this, and hours of questioning by the English police, left him vulnerable to press interpretation. Or misinterpretation! He was an anathema to many of those he had once called friends. At first one or two had voiced their support. In private, of course! As the heat was turned up, they began to distance themselves from him. Within two months he was completely isolated.

All this seemed ironic as he read the last sentence of the piece. "Headmaster Charles Meade, said that Mr Ellison is held in high regard at the school and our hearts go out to him too."

"Bastard!" he muttered and looked round nervously in case he had been heard.

He turned to the next week's copy of The Leitrim Observer. "NO SIGN OF MISSING BOY," The story beneath the headline told of the two week long search, and was accompanied by a photograph of the police frogmen. The caption beneath read: "POLICE CHIEFS SUPERVISE SEARCH (STOREY),"

There was nothing of note in the article, except that he sensed sympathy for his position, in stark contrast to the home press. He looked again at the photograph. The print quality was poor and it was difficult to see any detail. The Commander was pointing something out to two frogmen. Behind them, in shadow, were what seemed to be two uniformed policemen and, at the edge of the photograph, a figure dressed in a long black coat and wearing a trilby hat. He could not make anything of these dark background figures.

"Do you have a magnifying glass I can borrow?" he asked the back of the figure behind the counter, who was busy sorting books. To his surprise and delight, it was the same red hair and sparkling blouse that had excited him some minutes before. He looked at her and then back to the doors he had come through.

"Oh! I do reception sometimes," she said in explanation, and they both smiled.

"I'm sure I've got one somewhere."

She rummaged in a drawer beneath the counter and handed him a huge and ancient magnifying glass reminiscent of Sherlock Holmes. He mumbled his gratitude, as he restored his composure, and returned to the table. He scoured the enlarged view for details, but the picture would not take that kind of scrutiny and he was left with large expanses of black and grey dots. All he could discern was that from the stripes on his arm, one of the policemen was a sergeant. He did not know why, but he felt a sense of disappointment that he could not decipher the photograph. He read the caption again. "POLICE CHIEFS SUPERVISE THE SEARCH (STOREY)".

What of "(STOREY)?

He looked through another three months of The Leitrim Observer and, save for a small piece that mentioned his dismissal, found nothing else. He carried the huge bound ledger to the counter.

"Thanks very much. You've been very helpful,."

"Not at all," she smiled in return.

"Oh! I wonder if you can tell me what this is?" he said, opening the volume bookmarked by his finger, and pointing to the picture.

"A printer's error?"

"Oh no! That's Patrick Storey the photographer. They used to print the photographer's name next to the picture. They don't do it now. They've got their own photographer."

"And Mr Storey?"

"Old Mr Storey is dead these last two years, but his son still runs the chemist shop down the street. Next to the bank."

Suddenly another thought struck him. What about Michael McMahon's death? He was guessing that she would know of his death, and perhaps she could provide him with a date to start this part of his search.

"Did you know a Michael McMahon?" he started nervously.

"I did," she replied "And Mary too!"

"I'm looking for some information about his death."

"Tragic it was," she whispered, crossing herself.

"Did it get in the papers?"

"Of course! T'was a big story."

"Can you find it for me, please?"

"I'm sure I can. Just a moment," she moved towards the cupboard and returning with another one of the huge volumes, she eased it on to the table and drew back a handful of pages. Here we are. May 24th 1986," she muttered as she swept back the pages. "The tragic death of well-known Drumlasheen man. Last Friday Michael McMahon (61) was killed in a tragic accident at his place of work. It appears that Mr McMahon was working alone amongst some recently felled trees, which toppled, and he was crushed. It was sometime afterwards that a passer-by noticed the accident and phoned the police. Services made the site safe and Mr McMahon was taken to St Brigid's Hospital where he died later. Mr McMahon's wife Mary was at his side. A spokesman for the Aidan Timber Company expressed their regret at Mr McMahon's death and added that safety measures had been in place."

Ellison tensed as she read it. He understood that this would have been traumatic for Mary. Had it caused her to become deranged? By now the blouse was leaning further over the counter and he smelled a gentle drift of perfume. Momentarily he was transfixed as an arm reached over and turned to the next edition of the newspaper. A long, vermillion tipped finger pointed to a place on the obituary page.

"There we are," she said as a smile of satisfaction lit her face. The smile on Ellison's face owed more to her lingering presence than the page that lay in front of him.

"I'll leave you to it," she said

"Thank you. That's very…kind," he mumbled. It was the standard newspaper announcement of a death. Inside a two inch square bordered by a thick black line, was recorded details of Michael's tragic accidental death and his life. He read it again. Born in County Wicklow. A former shipyard worker.

"That's a surprise," he said to himself. At the end it expressed the gratitude of his wife Mary for wishes of condolence.

Ellison took stock. In the last hour he had gathered shards of information that might help his search. He was starting to get a clearer picture of a sequence of events that might have some bearing on his quest. Could it be that the timber yard incident was part of it? Perhaps he was seeing ghosts where there were none. How might it relate to the story of the missing boy? At least he had a bit more background. Much as he might have liked to, he could not think of a plausible reason to remain in the library longer without embarrassment, so he thanked the librarian profusely for her help.

"And you name is?" he asked.

"Rhiannan!" she replied.

"Thank you Rhiannan. I'm Tom."

"I know," she said mysteriously. For a moment she looked at him full in the face and then glanced down at the book she was holding. Was he reading the signs? It hadn't been that long! Go on Tom! Panic struck, and all he could say was "Thanks again."

"T'is nothing. Come again." She smiled.

He left the library and made his way back to the entrance hall. With no reason to do so, he rang the bell and waited. The window slid open and a spotty young man peered out.

"Yes?" he said, devoid of interest.

"I spoke to a lady just now. Rhiannan." He had no idea what he would say next.

"Yes!" the youth repeated, his mouth narrowed and a grimace formed as if he had experienced a bad smell. Then the green eyes appeared beyond his shoulder, he moved aside and at once the window was ablaze with the red hair.

"Oh yes!" Tom said with relief." I just wanted to thank you."

"That's fine," she said hesitantly. He knew how pathetic he must seem.

"Come again," she added. Could there be more than just a return visit to the library he thought? By this time he was in no position to rationalise. His mind was hazed.

"Thank you," he repeated pathetically.

The green eyes sparkled, and he was mumbling his farewell as the window slid shut. Even in this moment of near panic, he knew he would return.

In contrast to the gloom of the inside of the Town Hall, the bright light of a blossoming day met him, as he pulled open the heavy door. He had no idea what he might achieve, but he decided to visit Storey's Chemist. By now the main street of Drumlasheen had come to life. Every available space was filled with some vehicle or other. Only in Ireland, Tom thought, would some of these machines be allowed on the road. Of course there were new shining cars, but nowhere else, in Tom's experience, would you see so many rust buckets in one place. The fact that some of these geriatric motors were capable of forward motion was testimony to the attention of countless back yard, part-time mechanics. It was as if the bodywork repair section of the manual had gone missing." Bodging was a national pastime.

He waited for a gap in the traffic, crossed the road and made his way to Storey's Chemist. A bell jingled above his head as he entered the shop, and in response, a voice from a room at the end of a long single counter.

"I'll be with you just now!" The man who appeared from the back of the shop was small and thickset. Older than Tom, he sported a luxurious dark moustache, in stark contrast to his total baldness. Tom thought he had never seen anyone with so little hair on his head and yet such a splendid growth beneath his nose. It gave him a comical look. This was emphasised by tiny, pale eyes which almost disappeared, creating the impression of a hairy egg. As the man spoke, his moustache quivered, but there was no sign of a mouth.

"Can I help you now?"

"I'm looking for Mr Storey."

"That's me!"

"I was over at the library and they said you might be able to help me."

"If I can! He nodded. Tom explained that he was hoping to get hold of copies of photographs his father had taken for the paper some seven years before. To his amazement and delight, the chemist said he had kept all his father's photographs in the back of the shop.

"Can I see them?" he asked nervously.

"Of course! Come on through. Help yourself."

Tom was beckoned through the door at the end of the counter. To the right was a room that was the pharmacy with a window overlooking the shop, and to the left a room which was still impregnated with the smell of chemicals, but which clearly had not played its role as a darkroom for some time. Developing dishes and an enlarger shared a bench with boxes of hand lotion and baby food.

"How long ago did you say?" the chemist asked.

"Seven years."

"Now let me see..," he bent down on one knee and his head disappeared into the empty space beneath the bench. Reappearing with a cardboard box tied with string, he pushed aside a carton of beauty products and dumped it on the bench.

"All this lot's from the seventies. Most of it never got published." He undid the string and delved inside. One by one he brought out eight yellow boxes: the type that once held new photographic paper.

"There's no system you understand. Just put together at the end of the year. You'll have to go through the lot for that year if you're to find what you want," she said.

"Is there somewhere I can look at them?"

"You're staying at Mrs Murtagh's?"

"That's right!"

"Who else knows?" he wondered.

"Father O Mahony was in just now," the chemist said in explanation. "Why don't you take them away and have a proper look at your leisure? You can bring them back tomorrow."

"That's very kind of you."

"Sure, they're old news now. Nobody else is interested in them. They've not been opened since my Da died. Take 'em and welcome," he said with an expansive waive of his hand. Tom could hardly believe his luck. He thanked the chemist, perhaps too effusively he thought, as the shop bell tinkled behind him. His presence in Drumlasheen had been noted, and by more than the writer of the notes!

With the help of Father Goblin, he was sure that he had become something of a celebrity!

17

The problem of sorting through the photographs was made easier by hand written dates in the top corner of the back of each one. Sitting on his bed in his digs, he undid the string and separated them into two piles. One pile, the larger, contained pictures which were not relevant, or taken before the date of Glenn's disappearance. They were the usual collection of weddings, portraits of local worthies, sports groups, church events and fund raising events. Rather good all the same, he thought and they brought a smile to Tom's face, which froze as he turned over one picture. A policeman was standing by a car pointing towards the unknown. Tom turned the picture over and read the caption. First, in capitals, "MISSING ENGLISH SCHOOLBOY" and below in a scrawling hand "Police continue their search."

He separated out a number of photographs taken during the search, including the one he had seen in the paper; seven in all. He spread them on the floor and felt sadness mixing with his excitement, as he scanned the images. There he was, looking like a lost soul. Stern faces all around him; men leaning on sticks and listening to instructions. A policeman was prodding into a bank of fern; the helicopter low over the trees; and a tracker dog deep in ferns. He'd not remembered that. There was a stunning view of the lake from the high pastures above the wood. He picked up the print of the one he had seen in the newspaper for a closer look. Detail was much clearer. Certainly the two figures in the background were uniformed policemen. One he recognised at once. Constable Finbar Reeve. He smiled remembering the kind policeman. The Commander was obviously aware of the camera and his gesture had a comic quality about it. More akin to a leading player in a silent movie than a man involved in a real life drama.

"Yonder, lies the pass through to Tombstone!" Tom mocked.

Then his eyes strayed to the edge of the picture. He was surprised to see that the hazy figure cut off in the newspaper copy, now stood well in from the edge of this print. He had been partially cropped out from this original. It was easy to see why. His face was turned away from the camera, with a spread hand dramatically in focus thrust directly towards it. Tom imagined the photographer's irritation when he printed the image and found this intrusion. Tom turned one of the other photographs over and used its clean white edge to make a new edge to the composition. Cut out the whole of this unwanted figure and the Commander was sliced too. Just cut out the raised hand and the picture worked. Sort of worked anyway! No Photographer of the Year award for this one. Yet as Tom looked again at the whole print, the raised hand was the only clear thing about the picture. He looked closely at the figure. The back of the head, the ear and the side of the face were blurred into indistinguishable shades of grey and black. He sighed. What was he to make of this? He truly had no right to make anything of it at all, but this and the other photographs were all he had. That and notes from someone who, for all he knew, was unhinged.

He poured over the photographs for two hours. He scoured each one for a fact, a detail either new or out of place; something to re-enforce a growing feeling that he was on to something. He had nothing more than a collection of random events that only he thought should lead somewhere. In exasperation he threw the bundle of photographs on to the floor and sank back on the bed. One thing that the photographs had done was sharpen up some of his own recollections. He lay there and re-ran the events of that harrowing day once more. As he recalled the sequence, suddenly he stopped at the point where the search was taken out of the hands of the sergeant and Garda Sergeant Reeve, and transferred to the Commander and his associates.

"That's the chap!" he cried out loud and slid off the bed and on to the photographs. Frantically he shuffled through the pile.

"Gotcha!" He picked up a photograph and leaned up against the side of the bed, a look of triumph on his face. He recognised the figure at the edge of the photograph! The man who had been so camera shy was the tall man in the long black coat and who was at the Commander's side that night. Everyone else at the head of the search had been recognisably police, but this man, clearly important, bore no identifying insignia or police garb. He should have seen it before. Who the hell was he? He looked more closely at the image and released a sigh of frustration at the haziness of the facial detail. Unrecognisable.

The front door bell rang distantly. He focused again on the photograph, armed with his new piece of information. There was a knock on the door. He scrambled to his feet and opened the door to Mrs Murtagh.

"It's Father O'Mahony. He's in the front room." He thanked her and slipped on his shoes. Father O'Mahony was standing with his back to the door as Tom entered.

"Good morning Father!" The priest turned to face him. The puckish twinkle was dimmed.

"I've bad news Mr Ellison. He moved to a chair next to the window and sat down. "Mary McMahon's passed away. I found her in the kitchen this morning." He steepled his hands and looked up in silent prayer.

All the new found enthusiasm of a few seconds before left Tom Ellison. He felt weak and groped his way to a chair by the table. He sat down and, for a moment, could not speak.

"How?"

"I don't know."

"But she wasn't ill, was she?"

"Physically she wasn't good. But then, she would not have said anything."

"Even to you?"

"As I said before Mr Ellison, you have to understand that my relationship with Mary was a very basic one. I always knew that it was the collar she responded to – not the person. Despite her confused state, she still had a strong sense of her God. She could not express it, other than in a simple obedience to the ways of the church. So really, I knew her no better than anyone else."

"But she confided in you."

"Not really. Our conversations tended to the mundane. How she was caring for herself. Sometimes she talked of her childhood, but never of more recent times." Tom knew sanctity of Confession would not be breached.

"In the kitchen you say? You found her," he wanted detail. "Yes. She was on the floor by the sink. Poor soul!" Ellison hesitated for a moment but the question would not be denied.

"Were there any signs of..?"

"No!" The answer bit out before the question was complete. "No. I'm sure there wasn't. Mr Ellison I know how desperate you are to make some sense of recent goings on, but I'm sure that Mary would not be able to help with the things you are looking for. She was hardly able to organise her daily life and she could barely remember yesterday."

"I just wanted the chance to see her. I would know," Tom responded sadly.

"Believe me, Mary would not understand your questions – let alone know the answers. Trust me," it was said with genuine feeling.

Although such was the sincerity of the plea, Ellison could not let go of the one thought that had rekindled his life. There was something unresolved at Drumlasheen and even if she did not know the answer, in some way Mary McMahon was part of it.

"Thank you Father! You have been very helpful," he didn't know what else to say.

"Not at all! I must away back to the house. Arrangements to make. But I thought I'd let you know first." He thanked the priest again, and was ushered to the front door.

"Is something wrong?" It was Mrs Murtagh at the kitchen door.

"It's Mary McMahon. She's dead!"

"Lord save her! Poor demented soul!" She crossed herself and kissed the crucifix that was her constant companion. Tom made to go upstairs to his room.

"Will you be leaving now Mr Ellison?" she asked.

For a second it seemed the logical thing to do, now that his main contact was no more. And money was tight.

"No. I think I'll stay a few more days if that's alright." He did not wait for an answer and he made his way upstairs to his room.

"Just a few more days," he thought.

18

Finbar Reeve looked at the body lying face down on the kitchen floor. Now that the scene had been photographed, he knelt down and gently turned it over. He shook his head. The woman he had known as a young boy was gone from this face. This face was old and tormented. In place of the plump roundness that he had lusted for in his youth, was skin which had been drawn tightly across bones and now, in death, resembled crepe paper. He slid fingers over the staring eyes that once sparkled. As he did, he noticed a cut to the right side of the forehead; semi-circular or crescent shaped and about two inches across. It was deep, but there was no great show of blood. He sat back on his haunches and brushed his hands up and over his forehead, where youthful blond hair was giving way at the temples to signs of white.

"Where have the years gone Mary?" he whispered.

Reeve surveyed the scene. The large kitchen, once the pride and joy of a vibrant woman, bore the unmistakable marks of neglect. Available surfaces were littered with items once removed from cupboards, forgotten, and never put back. The large table with just one accompanying chair sat in the centre of the kitchen. From the middle he picked up a jar, unscrewed the top and looked inside. It contained the last vestiges of strawberry jam. A plate and cup and saucer lay unwashed in the sink, the last drains of milky tea, now grey, flooding the saucer. Next to it on the draining board was a teapot in a knitted cosy. Instinctively he slid his fingers under the cosy. The pot was cold. He eased the cosy off and lifted the lid. Inside the rich brown liquid filled the pot almost to the brim. How long had it been there, he wondered. Today? Yesterday? He looked down again at the body of Mary McMahon and muttered to himself, "Could have been days!"

He cast an eye over the scene. He'd been a detective for almost a year now, but his experience gave him no clear picture of the circumstance of this tragedy. In this clutter, what could seem out of place to give him a clue? Had she collapsed and hit her head on the table or the chair? He could not see tell-tale evidence of blood on either. Perhaps she had been attacked by an intruder? There was no obvious evidence of a break in. Or, he wondered if it could be the work of someone she knew? Whilst considering these options, he left the kitchen and opened the door to the sitting room; off to the left of the hallway. The curtains were drawn shut. In the gloom he could pick out the chairs, table and sideboard. There was a lingering smell of mustiness which suggested a room no longer used.

He decided to familiarise himself with the rest of the house, and he moved upstairs. He opened the door to the first of the bedrooms. The same musty smell hung in the air of the room which had two sets of bunk beds. Next was a room with two single beds. At the end of the corridor he opened another door. This room was not quite like the others. He got the impression that this room, at least, was given special treatment. Things were in their expected place and surfaces were polished and free from clutter. A collection of ornaments lined the mantelpiece over the tiled fireplace. A Madonna stood in pride of place in the centre of the top of a dressing table. A large picture of the risen Christ filled the wall above the head board of a double bed. A small television sat atop a chest of drawers. This room had an appearance of normalcy. A neat room. This was the Mary McMahon he remembered. The rest he did not understand. He had not seen Mary for years. It was hard to believe the transformation reflected in the condition of most of the house

Promotion had meant that Finbar Reeve had worked from headquarters for the last year and left the Drumlasheen police house for rooms nearer his office. He had taken the promotion because it was expected of him, rather than because he wanted it. "Rationalisation of Resources" dictated that the little police house be closed and sold off. He'd loved the independence of life in the tiny house, despite being on call at all times of day. Someone must have thought well of him, and he was offered a place in the detective division. It was either that or a huge patch covered by car. He didn't fancy that. He had been content as the local policeman and enjoyed the place he occupied in the life of the area. For a long time he struggled with the formality of H.Q. life. He missed the daily contact with street people and dealing with their problems, however mundane. But in time, the challenge of being a good detective took over, and Finbar Reeve had become a good detective.

It was not a day to day crime in County Leitrim, but it presented a problems which was not likely to solved by spectacular initiatives. Much of it involved tedious legwork and even more tedious paperwork. But he had evolved a system and it seemed to work. His greatest strength was his ability to work with others and to get others to work with and for him. Finbar Reeve was popular amongst the lower ranks and highly regarded by the top brass. His promotion to Detective Sergeant had been anticipated by all.

He opened the top drawers in a chest that stood at the foot of the double bed. The first one was full of woollen sweaters and blouses. In turn, the two other drawers also contained a selection of ladies clothing. He bent to open the bottom drawer. This was full of men's clothes. As he had done with the other drawers, he slid his hand under the clothes to see if there was anything beneath. His fingers found a hard edge and he slid it to the front of the drawer. It was a red mock-leather photo album with a gilt edge. He opened it, and on the first page was a rather stiffly-posed wedding group, which could not hide the handsomeness of the couple. Mary and Michael Mc Mahon had been a fine looking pair. Even in black and white, the vibrant wavy hair, turning to red in reality, was striking and Mary's full figure, crisply defined in the white wedding dress, was testimony to a desirable woman. Michael stood stiffly to attention, but handsome in his new suit, tall and well built; a lock forward Fin remembered. As strong as a young bullock when close to the try line. Off the field he was a dour, quiet man.

Reeve quickly fingered through the pages of their life together, put the book under his arm and left the room. At the end of the corridor, he opened the door that lay under the eaves of the house and stooped as he mounted the stairs to a long loft room that, he deduced, had once been used as a bedroom for visiting anglers, but now was the resting place of the detritus of several disorganised years. Garda Danny MacAlinden stood at the bottom of the stairs.

"The Doc's here sir," he shouted.

"Right! Tell him I'm on my way."

"Sir!"

In the kitchen, Doctor Andrew Kerr the Medical Examiner, on one knee by the body, rose creakily.

"How long has she been dead Doc?"

"Oh I should say about fourteen fifteen hours; sometime last evening. Don't you go quoting me mind. I'll know more later on." Reeve calculated this meant between seven and eight the previous night

"Cause?" Reeve asked tentatively.

"A stroke I thought – at first."

"And now?"

"Can't say – for sure."

"A guess."

"Not even for you Fin."

"You noticed the cut then?"

"Not trying to teach me my job now are you?" Kerr feigned mock offence.

"Would I dare! Natural causes?" he persevered.

"Later!" The rubber gloves snapped as he removed them.

"Have you finished here?"

"Just about," answered Reeve. "Unless there's something I should be looking for." The detective knew that would do the trick.

"Let's say you shouldn't take anything for granted." The doctor put his gloves into an old leather bag and clicked it shut. Picking up his hat from the kitchen table he moved to leave. "What do you mean?" Reeve asked.

"Later Fin, you'll know soon enough."

"Doc! I need to know whether I'm dealing with a natural death or not. For god's sake tell me what you suspect? Just me and you," he said confidentially. Kerr cast a glance through the open door. The constable was standing guard at the end of the front door.

"Alright! But it'll cost you."

"Cheap at half the price," retorted the detective, knowing from experience that the price was a bottle of whisky.

"And a nice salmon from that cousin of yours."

"It's a deal!" Reeve threw his hands up in mock submission.

"What have you got?"

"Well, all I'll say is that I don't think dear Mary died alone."

"The cut?" Reeve enquired, his theory already forming.

"Almost perfectly round. Not much like the kind of shape caused by hitting the head in a fall. Besides, there's no blood here. If that wound bled somewhere, it wasn't here."

"She's been moved."

"I'd say so!" said the doctor.

"Excuse me sir!" It was the young constable. "It's Father O'Mahony." Before he could answer, the priest was at the door and stepped into the kitchen. He peered round the table at the body, crossed himself and muttered an inaudible prayer.

"Good day Fin. Good day doctor."

"Good afternoon Father," Finbar replied with a respectful nod. He was about to warn the priest, but it was too late. He was kneeling over the body of Mary McMahon and made to lay his hand on her forehead.

"If you don't mind Father." Reeve raised his hand

"Of course!" said the priest as he struggled to his feet. Finbar slid a helping hand under his elbow.

"She's not been a well woman, bless her. But she was faithful and took the sacraments every week." Father O'Mahony looked over his shoulder at the body and added "Pity she missed them today." He realised his faux pas and raised his hand to his mouth.

"What time did you find her?"

"Just after ten o'clock. Every Tuesday and Thursday, same time." He nodded.

"Did you see her on Tuesday?"

"Yes!"

"Did anyone else visit her do you know? "

"No! No.! She'd not seen a soul for months. I tried to get people in to visit, but she would have none of it. Shut herself away completely. The Englishman tried to see her though."

"The Englishman?" Reeve responded quickly.

"Yes. The one who was involved in that business of the missing boy: all those years ago. Ellison. Tom Ellison."

"He's here? Now?" Reeve was wide-eyed in surprise.

"Yes. He called in yesterday, but she wouldn't answer. Not for anyone!"

"What did he want? Ellison."

"I think you should ask him." The priest was reluctant to go further.

"I will," Reeve said resolutely. Taking the priest by the elbow Reeve said "Now then Father, if you'll forgive me, we've got to get on. I'll call round to ask you a few more questions and let you know when matters are sorted here."

"Of course! I'd like to come back before she's moved."

"Sure," Reeve nodded, and as the priest turned to leave asked, "Oh Father. Where is this fella? The Englishman. D'ya know?"

"He's staying at Mrs Murtagh's. Weir Lane. I spoke to him just now."

"He knows then? About Mary ?"

"Yes. I told him she'd passed away." Finbar Reeve knew that, even now, the priest thought that he had come across an accidental death. He wasn't going to disabuse him of that thought. Not yet.

"Thank you father." He escorted him to the door and said to the constable "You stay here and let no-one in, d'ya hear?" and added "There's someone I've got to see."

Garda Reeve was starting to put together his few clues.

19

Finbar Reeve moved stealthily down the garden path at the side of the house, so as not to create a disturbance. As he passed the kitchen window, the surprised face of Mrs Murtagh peered out at him. He put his finger to his lips and beckoned with it for her to come outside. As she came through the kitchen door, he shepherded her away from the house.

"What on earth are you about Finbar?" she exclaimed.

"Sorry Mrs Murtagh. I'll explain later. You've an Englishman staying with you?"

"Yes!"

"Is he in?"

"He went down the town a while ago," she said. "On foot?"

"I believe so. You'll see his car out front. The red one." Reeve had spotted it in the lane outside the front door.

"Can I wait for him?" he asked.

"Sure. But why? What's it about?"

"I'll explain later. Can you show me his room?"

"It's to do with Mary McMahon isn't it?"

"Does the whole world know?" he wondered and replied.

"Later Mrs Murtagh."

Once alone in the bedroom, he systematically opened the wardrobe and then the drawers. Empty save a black leather- bound bible. A striped shirt hung over the back of a chair and a shaving kit sat on the glass shelf above the sink.

"He must be travelling light. Anyway what am I looking for?" he asked himself. He sat on the bed. His eye caught the yellow boxes on the bedside table and he took two pencils from his top pocket. He levered the lid off and tipped its contents on to the bed. He prodded the photographs apart to look at each one in turn. He wondered where the teacher had got such a collection of local pictures. He came across the pictures from the time of the boy's disappearance and saw himself looking wearied and strained as he prodded through long grass. However his distress was nothing compared to the look of total despair on the face of the English teacher.

"Surely, this guy had not harmed the boy!"

He remembered that intuition from the day the teacher came into the little police house, looking ashen faced, covered in mud, a dribbled of dried blood down his face. His first thought had been that there had been a road accident. It was not unusual for visitors to find the local roads a test of their driving skills. A combination of narrowness, uneven, ill-repaired surfaces was sufficient to test the best driver. He recalled he had consciously donned his official mode. It slowed the pace and took heat out of situations. Mostly! In this case it took a few moments for him to size up the bedraggled sight before him and register the fragmented story he was being told. He quickly realised that these events were outside the daily norm of his job. He wanted to be in control at his end, before he contacted his superiors, so he drew the English teacher through the details of the day, making careful note of relevant facts. He must have his pocket book in order, he knew. The next judgement he had had to make was the seriousness of the situation, and the level of his response. He looked at the pallid, agonised face and sensed that he had a serious incident on his hands, whatever the outcome.

His conversation with Regional H.Q. was, of necessity, brief and guarded with the teacher so close by. Thankfully on the other end, his sergeant realised the situation and led the conversation, teasing out sufficient information.

"Right! Garda Reeve. We'll meet you at the lake."

"You know the way sir." He bit his tongue at his stupidity. There followed a silence in which he saw his future in the force fading. After a pause, he said "Right then sir! I'll be on my way." Turning to the teacher, he said "Come on sir. We'll take your bus," adding "I'll drive." He took his trench coat from a hook behind the door and with a cursory look about the little office, he led the teacher outside. As he put the key into the ignition, he heard a deep lung clearing sigh from the man in the seat next to him

Words were not necessary on the journey to the lake. He reckoned he knew what the man was thinking. Continued interrogation was inappropriate. That might come later. No words of his would remove the awful pall which engulfed the teacher. As they rolled down the undulating meadow to the lake, he sensed his passenger leaning forward to take in the scene.

He had taken the journey at a steady pace to ensure that assistance would be in place on their arrival. The reassuring bulk of Garda Sergeant Sam Irons blocked their way. Finbar was pleased that the initial search was to be in the hands of the no-nonsense sergeant who had been such a strength in his own early days as a young constable. Sam Irons saw everything as black and white and did not suffer fools gladly, but you always knew where you stood with Sam Irons. Reeve remembered that the next two hours went quickly amid a growing sense of concern. Progress seemed slow. The options were restricted by the nature of the terrain. Not a place for careless wandering; but the situation was contained. He could not resist the thought that, even in these early hours, the growing police presence would reveal the truth of a tragic accident. He had looked across the lake. The waters would soon give up the answer, he thought. But perhaps not that night.

*

Now, as he prodded through the pile of photographs, thinking back over the intervening years, Finbar Reeve remembered his feelings of failure when, after two weeks, the hunt for the boy was suspended. It had been one of the biggest organised searches the County had ever seen. He recalled his own feelings as the search ground slowly to a halt. The lake was searched by divers and the surrounding countryside scoured for evidence. The extraordinary thing was that there was not a scrap of evidence to lead down one avenue of enquiry or another. The physical search was all they had. Glenn Wallace had just disappeared! The rest of the group of boys had been flown home and only the teacher and the boy's mother stayed on. Tom Ellison was their only viable suspect, if the boy had come to harm at the hands of anyone. It was clear from the beginning, to Reeve at least, that the man was not guilty of a crime. His sympathy grew as the two weeks passed.

There was a mounting media interest and the teacher bore the burden of suspicion on the one hand, and the charge of irresponsibility, on the other. He had seen quotes from parents who had valued his commitment to their children. This soon changed as they were challenged, by English press and television, to doubt both his motives and his competence. The growing suspicion and cynicism were all pervading, whenever Ellison appeared in public. Poor sod!

That was then and this is now. Why should there be another unexplained death as soon as the man had returned to Drumlasheen? Had he been so wrong?

At that moment the bedroom door opened and Tom Ellison entered, unsuspecting, and whose surprise was signalled by an involuntary gasp.

Finbar Reeve stood up.

"Hello Mr Ellison."

"Hello Constable…"

"Detective Constable," he corrected. "Reeve," he added

"I'm sorry!" The elevation in rank took on an extra significance Tom thought. He held his hand out instinctively. The policeman responded and shook it firmly.

"I heard you were in the town and I thought I'd ask you a few questions."

"About what?"

"Mary McMahon."

"I went to the house. She won't talk to me."

"No sir. She won't. She's dead!"

"How?" Tom Ellison visibly sagged.

"We're not sure yet."

"When?"

"Some time last night."

It was more than the policeman had planned to reveal. The Englishman sat down on the bedside chair, his chin cupped in his hands. Realisation hit home.

"You're here to ask me a few questions because you think

I had something to do with her death."

"I'll be asking questions of a lot of people. You did say you went to see her."

"But she wouldn't open the door."

"When was this, precisely?"

"About two O'clock yesterday."

"And you saw her?"

"Yes. At least I think it was her. She opened the door a bit and shut it at once.

"I called through the letter box. I gave up in the end."

"And what did you do after that?"

"I came back here."

"And the rest of the evening?"

"I had a meal with Mrs Murtagh and we watched television

'till about ten o'clock."

"And today?"

"After breakfast I went down to the library. I've just come back."

Tom Ellison's plan to revisit the library was far from his thoughts as he sat with the policeman and explained his presence in Drumlasheen. The conversation flitted between the present and the past. The news of Mary's death was a double blow. Fond memories of her kindness stirred feelings of sadness. Her place at the centre of his quest meant her death was a blow to his search for a solution. Sadness and frustration mingled. He showed the postcard to Garda Reeve, who asked if he could keep it for a while. Tom agreed readily, assuming some kind of forensic testing. They talked of the photographs and remembered the events they had captured. Lost confidence was being restored, as they went over all the facts of days past as well as recent developments. Finbar Reeve regretted his moments of doubt.

"Do you see a link between Mary's death and my missing boy?" Tom Ellison asked.

"I can't say. We'll need to examine the evidence," Reeve replied.

"But you're not ruling it out?" Ellison said urgently.

"No! We've made it a possible crime scene," he confided. Realising his error at once, he added quickly "That's confidential!"

His official status restored, he continued "You do realise that any link between this death and the boy's disappearance will bring the press down on our ears again, especially if you stay here. It's my job…but do you want it?" He knew more about the teacher's recent life than perhaps Tom Ellison suspected.

"If it provides a solution yes!" was the firm reply. On his side of the equation, Finbar Reeve was building on his resolve to search out the facts about these events, separated in time. Were the two linked in some way? He was reassured that the teacher was prepared to face whatever might come. They were on the same side. For his part, Tom Ellison felt a pulse of excitement – of euphoria even, as Reeve left.

He was not alone! The meeting they arranged for that evening at Reynold's Bar confirmed it!

20

Finbar Reeve nodded in response to the young constable's salute. He had been away from Shannonbridge House for two hours: longer than he intended. He had stopped off at the library to check the Englishman's story. Procedure demanded it.

Now he re-examined the scene; unchanged, except for a white sheet over the body. He lifted a corner and looked again at the face of Mary McMahon. He peered at the gash above her right eye and looked about again for an edge or corner that could account for a wound, and which could have been inflicted in a fall. The body was lying away from the kitchen table, towards the sink. It was too far away from both for her to have struck her head and fallen in this way. The chance of the gash being caused in a fall where she lay, seemed non existent. He moved towards the door leading to the hallway for a different view of the scene. He turned away from the body, and kneeling to get a different angle, peered down the hallway. In the thin layer of dust, and in the slanting light from the from the kitchen, he could just make out a dust free line about two feet wide on the wooden floor, leading down to the front door. There was no sign of a mat by the door as might be expected, but the echo of something like a mat was clear down the hallway. He could see the trace of how it had been pulled down the hallway towards the kitchen. Supposing a mat had been used to drag the body away from the front door; where was the mat?

He stepped carefully around, what he was now sure, was a murder scene. He looked closely at the floor. A few inches from the skirting board by the door he saw the minute, but unmistakable, splatter of blood; just a few spots. If the scene of the death was not the kitchen, he was convinced that this was not the work of an opportunist. If Mary McMahon died by her own front door, she must have opened it to someone she knew. Remembering Mary's reclusive nature in recent years, he wondered to how many people she would have been prepared to open the door. From the little he understood, it would be a very short list. Finbar Reeve knew that Mary's father died when she was very young, and Father O'Mahony had told him that her mother died in the late sixties. He needed to check if she had other relatives.

His attention turned to the front room. He had left the door off the hallway ajar, and he pushed it open with his foot and stepped into the gloom. He turned the lights on with a prod from the end of his usual pencil and moved to draw the curtains back. Everything was in its place, and he sensed the room was as it might have been for a long time. The curtains, carpets and chairs all spoke of times long past: perhaps pre- war. A small shrine consisting of a plaster Madonna kneeling in front of a picture of the Risen Christ, stood in the centre of an ancient sideboard. On one side next to it, at a respectful distance, in a silver frame, was a photograph of a handsome man he recognised as the young Michael McMahon. Memories of hard fought matches on quagmire pitches came to mind. A young Mary McMahon shone from the silver frame on the other side of the shrine. Resisting the temptation, he didn't touch anything. He decided to let SOCCO do their work and photograph the house before he looked more closely.

He moved back through the kitchen, turned the key in the door that led out to the garden. He strolled round the back of the house, checking windows, confirming in his mind that entrance had not been forced. Then he sat on a rusted wrought iron seat at the edge of what had once been a lawn, and took stock. He assumed he had on his hands an unnatural death of a woman who avoided contact with the outside world and with little to attract the attention of the opportunist criminal. He was starting to rule out gain as a motive. There was no sign of the house being tossed. Everything seemed to be in its place. Uppermost in his mind was the strange business of the Englishman and his link with Mary McMahon. He wondered what the common denominator was. Coincidence? He thought not.

A two man Scene of Crime team arrived and Reeve explained what he wanted of them, and formulated his next move. He knew the nearest neighbour were about a mile away. He called the young constable over.

"You got a map?"

"Yessir! In the car."

"Well get it then!" There was just a touch of authority. He watched the young officer run to the car and back again clutching a map. Reeve took the map and spread it out on the bench and pinpointed two nearby houses.

"Who lives here?" He indicated the nearest building. "Joe Minchin and his family," the constable replied. "'Course! I know Joe!" Reeve brought to mind a likeable local farmer he had known for years.

"And here?" he said pointing to another building on the map.

"That's Gilbert Busey's place. Keeps a few pigs and chickens."

"Been there long?" Reeve asked.

"'Bout three years, I guess."

"I'll go out there." Reeve said. "Meanwhile you keep this place tight." "Yessir!" A ready smile shone at the responsibility.

An hour later, Finbar Reeve was back at the scene and was prepared for closer scrutiny of the house. Sitting outside in his car, he had considered his next step. Forensic had confirmed his suspicions. Mary McMahon had opened her front door to someone. What happened to her next was not clear. There was no obvious sign of an object that might have created the gash on her forehead. He concluded that either the object had always been there and then removed, or her assailant had brought it with him. If the former, what was missing?

He had gained nothing from a visit to the two nearest cottages. They'd had no contact with Mary Mc Mahon for over two years. He was no further on. He passed through the hallway and into the kitchen, where the MD had confirmed he that had finished with the body. As Reeve knew of no immediate close relatives to contact, he told the constable to let Area know the situation and for them to arrange for the body to be taken care of.

"Let the Father know too." He stood by the kitchen door and looked down the hallway to the front door. Next to it, in a dark corner, was a tiny window alcove with a telephone in it. "Have you checked that phone for prints?" he called.

"Just done it," came back the reply.

"Anything?"

" Looks like the priest used it last when he rang in."

"Don't forget the door!"

"Done it!" The young officer turned around, a flash of resentment in his voice. He knew his job, and Finbar Reeve knew he had made a mistake.

"I'm going upstairs," he said flatly. A more careful examination of the upstairs rooms revealed nothing of significance, save the all pervading feeling of sadness. The young officer was standing by the door to the parlour.

"You finished now?" Reeve asked.

"I've got a handprint on the front door and the one print on the phone," Pointing down the hallway, he added "The rest is all clear."

"At least Mary's done some polishing, or perhaps someone's done it for her." In spite of the lack of evidence, or perhaps because of it, Finbar Reeve felt a growing certainty that this was no accidental death.

Stepping round the body, he looked through the kitchen window to the garden beyond, and gave a passing glance at the kitchen door for signs of damage. As he expected, he saw none. He surveyed the overgrown patch of lawn and the chicken run in the corner, attached to a wooden shed. Around three sides of the rectangular garden were the last vestiges of flower beds, which would have been a matter of some pride in times past. Now consumed by weeds, they were stark confirmation of the neglect that hung over the place. He stepped out and crossed to the shed, the long grass making it hard work. Next to it, the chicken run played host to a handful of speckled bantams, over-lorded by a handsome specimen with a voluminous, shiny black tail. They, at least, seemed well cared for.

He pressed the latch of the shed door and pulled on the handle. At first it yielded a little, but the rampant grass blocked further movement. Stepping back he trampled down the offending grass and lifted and pulled on the handle once more. It needed all his strength to pull it open. He felt pretty sure the shed had not been visited for some time.

Once inside, he quickly became accustomed to the light from the one large window. On the far wall, above a bench, was a bank of drawers, the sort used for storing nails, screws, hinges and assorted small ironmongery. Against the right wall was a splendid ancient wood turning lathe, with a thin scattering of wood shavings beneath, the bi-product of its very last use. Gleaming defiantly against the other wall, and caught in the light from the window, was a more modern, compact lathe for metalwork, its crisp neat lines in contrast to its chunkier partner.

"That must have cost a few bob Michael!" Reeve muttered to himself.

Above each lathe, on the wall behind, were racks of tools, their outline in black paint for ease of identification. Pieces of timber and metal rod lay across the bench and in a rack in the ceiling. Reeve made a glove of his handkerchief and slid opened one of the drawers. It revealed tiny jewel-like pieces of the most precise metal turning. Miniature screwdriver, machine parts, brackets and a pair of small pulleys shone brightly. A second and a third drawer bore further testimony to a man with great skills. He had no idea that Michael McMahon was such a craftsman. But then, there was not much he did know about him. He wasn't a Drumlasheen man born and bred. Reeve did know that much.

"Sir!" It was the second SOCO officer Don Latham from the kitchen door, camera in hand.

"You finished in there?" Reeve shouted through the open door.

"Yessir pretty well."

"Then come in here. Get some general shots and look for anything that's missing or out of place."

"Yessir!"

Reeve left the young Garda to get on with recording the shed, and returned to the house. The tape delineating the crime scene had now been extended all the way round the house. He knew that he needed the body to be removed before he could scrutinise the kitchen minutely. Entering the sitting room again, the mid afternoon sun had swung round and light streamed in through the window. Shielding his eyes, he could see a heavy built constable stiffly guarding the front of the house.

"Well done George!" He mimed through the glass, with a thumbs-up sign.

The first drawer in the sideboard would not yield to the pencil, so he threaded his handkerchief through the handle, gathered both ends and pulled on it like a rope. The drawer opened a little and then stuck. He pulled harder, and suddenly the drawer came shooting out and he caught it before it could fall to the floor. He cursed his clumsiness. Rolled up at the front of the drawer was a bundle of place mats made from woven grass, next to a small wooden box containing several pieces of costume jewellery and a necklace of blue stones; too blue to be of any real value. He moved a random collection of pencils and pens, and spotted a collection of keys, which he slipped into his pocket. He would try those later. At the back of the drawer was a faux leather box, containing a glistening set of fish knives, which clearly had never been used. He repeated the procedure with the matching drawer of the sideboard; this time easing it open with greater care. He slid the drawer from its place and put it carefully on the top of the sideboard and, tipping it on its side, a wad of papers fell out. The papers seemed to be in a rational order. The more recent bills lay at the top. As he turned them over with his pencil, he started to come across letters, sometimes addressed to Mary and Michael individually, and sometimes to both. A thin cardboard folder lay at the bottom of the drawer. It was held together by a large elastic band and contained birth certificates, insurance papers and house details. Michael's birth certificate showed that he was born in Belfast.

"Now I never knew that," he said, making a note in his pocket book.

Reeve realised he might need this archive if he was to progress the case. He combed through the papers in turn, making regular notes in his pocket book. When he had read the last of them, he carefully eased them back into the folder and drew the elastic band across. He sat in one of the chairs with the folder on his lap and flicked through his notes. "Not much to go on," he muttered under his breath. He knew that they would have to go through this standard routine throughout the house, but he was already getting a feeling that his best chance would come from the autopsy report.

The manner of Mary McMahon's death might hopefully lead him forward.

21

It was early evening when Finbar Reeve parked his car outside the wrought iron gates leading to the church. The large oaken door to the church was open. He assumed the priest would be inside, and entered the porch past a huge notice board covered in announcements reflecting the church's place in the life of Drumlasheen. Inside the church, the cavernous space amplified his footsteps on the stone floor, announcing his presence.

"Is that you Finbar?" came a disembodied voice from behind the altar.

"Yes father."

"Just a moment."

Finbar on bent knee, bowed his head and crossed himself before making his way down the central aisle towards the voice. The diminutive figure of Father O'Mahony appeared from behind the altar, brush and pan in hand and flora pinafore tied at the waist

"Just tidying up," he said with a hint of embarrassment. "Come through won't you?" he added. Conducting with the brush, he led the way into the vestry and through the door that linked the church to the manse. "Come through! Come through!" he urged as he entered his study.

Finbar Reeve had never been inside the manse before and felt overpowered by the dark and heavy atmosphere that prevailed in the passage. He followed the priest into what he felt, in contrast, had once been a splendid room. The priest, brush still in hand, indicated a spacious arm chair engulfed by an antimacassar depicting men on camels and palm trees. Finbar eased himself over tired springs and sank back.

"Drink?" asked the priest, standing by the sister chair.

"No thank you Father." Disappointed, the priest resisted his own inclination and sat down. Moving forward in his chair to set the mood for asking questions, the detective withdrew his pocket book to signal that the formal part of proceedings had begun.

"I want you to tell me, in order, exactly what happened this morning."

The priest needed no persuasion to give a minute by minute commentary of his actions, starting with the aftermath of the broken night he'd spent with a searing headache. Finbar didn't ask what had been the cause! He then described his usual breakfast of prunes and toast, taken at precisely eight thirty. A walk down to the shops for a paper and fresh milk took another half hour. On his return he spent some time sticking some recently taken photographs of birds into his scrap book. Shortly before ten he left in his car to visit Mary McMahon.

Thus far, he had not interrupted the priest's flow. When he came to his arrival at Shanonbridge House, Reeve interjected, asking "What was your first impression?"

"Impression?"

"Did everything seem normal?"

"Normal? Yes!"

"Nothing unusual?"

"Only that Mary didn't answer when I knocked."

"Was that unusual?"

"It had happened before a few times. That's why I persuaded her to let me have a separate key cut."

"Did she mind?"

"Not really."

"So you let yourself in?"

"The door was always stiff and I had to push it hard."

"That sounds right. Did you touch anything else?"

"I don't think so."

"The telephone?"

"Yes. When I rang the station."

"Then what did you see?" Realising he was now moving into forensic detail, Father OMahony slowly retraced his actions and reaction to the scene.

"The kitchen door was part closed and when I opened it, there she was on the floor. I knelt down beside her and felt for a pulse. There was none. I gave her God's blessing and sat, for a moment, thinking about her life; especially recent times. She was a troubled soul, but a good Christian woman. I wondered who there was for me to contact. Then I realised this was a sudden death and I should let the authorities know. As far as I know she has no relatives. None she spoke about. Poor woman!"

"Then what did you do?" Reeve pressed.

"I phoned the police."

During this exposition, Finbar Reeve had made a few desultory notes; more as a formality, than being points of significance.

"Tell me what you know about Mary," he urged.

"I had come to know her when I was appointed to the church. She had always been a strong church woman. She came to church regularly, sometimes with her husband, and helped at church events. She did a lot of sewing for the church. A pillar of the church you'd say. Then there was poor Michael's tragic death." He crossed himself and took a moment to gather his thoughts.

"She stopped coming to mass. My parishioners became concerned at her absence, and that she wasn't being seen in the town. I tried many times to call on her, but she wouldn't even open the door."

"When was that?" Reeve interjected.

"Three years ago," the priest replied.

"What changed?"

"One day I came and she was out at the back feeding the chickens. She couldn't avoid me. Well, we talked, and I remember I had almost to force her to offer me a cup of tea. I took her confession and from that day on I've come on Tuesdays and Thursdays. Whenever I can, you understand." Reeve nodded. "You know I can't reveal details of her confession," he added quickly.

"Of course," Finbar responded. "What else did you talk about?" He hoped it gave the priest some release from his confessional obligations.

"It was hard to remove her from the deep melancholy that had overtaken her. It consumed her you might say. I could never get from her why she saw her life in such negative terms. Sure, the trauma of Michael's death was part of the answer. I came to the conclusion that I just had to support her as best I could, and pray for God's help." He raised his hands in resignation.

"So you've no idea what made her so depressed? Broken friendships? Money? Health?"

Reeve's promptings were answered with a saddened shake of the head.

"Not that I could discover. No! She didn't take care of herself, but she always seemed in reasonable physical health. That is why this is all such a shock. But it's all relative you understand. She was far from well otherwise." Father O'Mahony tapped his temple.

Finbar Reeve had long since reached the conclusion that Father O'Mahony believed he had come across a tragic accident.

"Would you say she had any enemies?" He realised the implication that the priest might take from his question, but it could not be avoided. There was a long silence and the colour drained from Father O'Mahony's face.

"No! No!" he stuttered. "You can't believe that someone..?" "Did she? Reeve insisted.

"No! Not as far as I know." Reeve thought he might have revealed too much of his thinking.

"Do you know anything about her family?" he continued. "I know she was born in Drumlasheen, as was her father and mother. They're both dead. They were well respected in the town. She told me about an older brother who died from cancer. As far as I know she had no other brothers or sisters. She never mentioned any other relatives."

"And Michael?" Reeve asked.

"From what I gathered he was born in the north and came here as a youth. I never heard her speak about any of his family."

"Did Mary say much about him?"

"She rarely spoke about him directly."

"Isn't that strange if, as you say, his death had meant so much to her?"

"I tried, but she would turn the conversation away whenever it was mentioned."

"What else did you talk about?"

"We talked about death. She needed reassurance about the hereafter."

"Did she say why?"

"That's for the confessional!" Father OMahony was adamant.

Reeve sensed that useful questioning had come to an end and decided to conclude the interview.

"I'm sorry to have to ask you Father, but where were you last night?" The priest paled at the implication of the question. "I took the evening Mass and then I was visiting at the hospital." Reeve bowed his head in embarrassment, and levered himself up from the depth of the chair, thanking the priest for his time. They shook hands warmly at the study door. Reeve made to leave, but with his hand still firmly gripped, the priest leaned forward slightly and cleared his throat.

"You don't think it was a natural death?"

"Early days Father," Reeve answered. "I'll send someone round to take your fingerprints, if that's alright. Just a formality, for comparison." The priest nodded in assent.

Minutes later, driving down the main street of Drumlasheen, Finbar Reeve took stock. He was now pretty sure that Mary McMahon had met an untimely death at the hands of an intruder. But what could be the motive. Burglary? There appeared to be nothing missing. Revenge? Revenge for what?

It all seemed so improbable that the ordinary little woman, cut off from the world outside, could be involved in a matter so deep that she should lose her life. As he drove on, the one thing that drew it all back into the realm of reality was the arrival of the English teacher. However implausible the facts might be, the death of Mary McMahon and the disappearance of the schoolboy appeared to be connected in some bizarre way. Reeve was confident that Tom Ellison could not have been the intruder. Only if the timings were wrong, could he have been in Mary's house at the time of her death. He had to accept the scientific expertise of the doctor, and the unimpeachable word of Mrs Murtagh.

He arrived at Shannonbridge House just in time to see the body being removed in a black van. At the front door to greet him stood Inspector Eric Blane, his immediate boss for the last year. Blane, who was a good boss, albeit sharp of tongue and short on patience, greeted him brusquely.

"Get in here Fin and fill me in!" They entered the house together.

"What have we got?" Blane demanded. It was that gruff uncompromising approach that Reeve had become accustomed to in their association. Blane's hard-nosed demeanour was a device which enabled him to cut through any meanderings presented in evidence. Reeve did not always agree with his unyielding approach, but he usually got things done. Their relationship was founded in respect. As they stood by the door, Reeve gave an account of what he knew of Mary McMahon. Her early life, family connections; her seclusion linked to her mental state in recent years, and his own understanding of the possible events of the day.

"Murder! You sure?" Blane asked.

"It's my guess," Reeve replied.

"Guess?" The question carried all the weight of disapproval that Blane could muster.

"According to the Doc, a cut on her forehead looks like a blow from something round," Reeve asserted, ignoring the ill-disguised rebuke.

"I saw that. What else?" By now they were in the kitchen. Blane bent over the sink and peered out of the window. Reeve reported the coincidence of the death of Mary McMahon at the same time as the English teacher's reappearance in Drumlashen.

"I remember.. Funny business. I fancied him for that." Blane reflected.

"Not our finest hour." As the words passed his lips Finbar Reeve was already regretting his foolishness.

"It might not have been yours. I was on that Carrick fraud case." was the sharp reply. "Have you spoken to him?" Reeve explained that he had sought out the Englishman and was satisfied that he had an alibi for the projected time of Mary's death.

"Doesn't mean he wasn't involved." It was the response Reeve might have expected, but he did not want to go into those instincts that told him that the man was not involved.

"I'll keep an eye on him," he said in mollification.

"Make sure he doesn't leave town." Reeve smiled as he imagined it said with an America twang.

"Sure will sir!" he mocked. It passed Blane by.

They toured the house and garden and agreed on how to take the case forward.

Bringing together the forensic evidence and a more detailed search of the house and its surroundings, were the main priorities.

22

Tom Ellison had decided to take a walk down the narrow lane and spent the remnants of the afternoon on the banks of the river that flowed around the lower part of Drumlasheen. He stopped at a stone bridge and watched a heron searching for fish in the reedy margins of a weir. Deadly still for minutes on end, the bird struck with amazing speed and juggled a small roach in its beak, before the fish disappeared down its gullet. Twice more the long legged fisherman struck, but each time he missed his quarry.

"We've all done that," he said through a smile. He lent over the parapet for a while, watching fish in the clear water, idling against the flow. As he surveyed the peaceful setting, the thought came suddenly to him that he was standing on the bridge pictured in the postcard.

"Bugger me!" he said out loud.

He perched on the parapet and reflected on his journey from the picture on the photograph to the real thing. It focused all he had felt about the last few days: from doubt to certainty – and back. Surely now there were clear links between the postcard; Mary and Michael's deaths; and crucially, his own presence in the town. There were too many coincidences.

Someone knew the story. It might only be his anonymous correspondent, but his feeling was that others knew the boy's fate. How many? He guessed it would be a small handful; maybe two or three. If he was right, had Mary lost her life because of something she knew? He was as certain as he could be that she had no part in the disappearance of Glenn Wallace. What might she have found out, he wondered? He had long struggled with the thought that someone might, in a tiny window of opportunity and out in open countryside, have randomly picked out that particular boy. But it made no sense.

He returned to his accommodation buoyed with a sense of well-being from his riverside walk. He let himself in and went up to his bedroom. Minutes later a gentle tap on the door was followed by "Mr Ellison. It's only me!" Elizabeth Murtagh entered the room with a metal tray, supporting a shining silver teapot, matching sugar bowl, milk jug, cup and saucer, accompanied by a plate of biscuits.

"I thought you'd be better for a nice cup tea," she burbled, "and I found this in a little scrapbook I keep. It's about Mary McMahon's Michael. Did ya know he was a champion rugby player as a young man? Just like my Sam. They played together. That's him!" she pointed. "My Sam!"

She handed the newspaper clipping to Ellison. It showed a recognisable young Michael McMahon, surrounded by mud splattered players, celebrating a momentous result. He thought he remembered it in the library.

"Thank you Mrs Murtagh," he said, his interest mildly aroused. "And thanks for the tea," he added. He picked up the teapot and, in one unbroken movement, put it down again, as awakening dawned. Nervously he refocused on the cutting. He took in a sharp intake of breath as he looked again at the suited man sharing the trophy.

"My God!" There was not a moment's doubt. Instantly he knew! After all these years he remembered the tall figure in the long black coat that haunted his memories of the search for the boy.

"Who's this?" he exclaimed, clearing his throat and pointing at the tall figure.

"I don't know," she replied. "I saved it as a picture of my Sam."

There was no accompanying text. He gathered his racing thoughts.

"Can I keep this for a while? I'll look after it, of course," he added reassuringly. She nodded her approval."

"You drink that tea while it's hot now," an instruction as she closed the door behind her.

He stared at the picture. Another trigger to his memories! He was again taken by a feeling of elation mixed with a sense of disbelief, that so many details had come his way in such a short time. Ideas flew wildly like too many birds in a cage. Hold on! Think it through! All he had was a collection of unconnected titbits. No hard evidence. Not even a theory that made any sense. Could he legitimately link them all together into one cogent whole? He had to yield to the fact that he could not. Not yet! Despite this doubt, he was left with a hellish good feeling about his return to Drumlasheen, and of his own growing sense of well being. He felt better in mind, body and spirit than he had for so long.

As if to force a balance in his psyche, he reminded himself of those dark soul sapping times of the search and of the devastating events that followed. Down this dark tunnel lay the day when he had to face the boy's mother. She arrived in a coach with other parents that were to return the rest of the children to their homes. Elaine Wallace, her face an ashen copy of what Tom remembered, exited the minibus holding desperately on to the handrail. As she adjusted her eyes to her surroundings, Tom stepped forward holding out a hand of support. She stiffened, and without acknowledging his presence, walked past him on teetering legs. In the days that followed, when the search continued, they came face to face a number of times and he shrank beneath the withering look she gave him. Nothing was said. It was a silence full to the brim.

The boys were questioned with a relative present. This was done with an understanding and sympathy that touched the mothers and fathers. The same could not be said for their reaction to the two teachers. Distrust pervaded the group, which found its prime outlet in Tom Ellison. Directing their distrust on one person seemed to help them cope with the distress. But it was more primeval than that. Whatever the outcome, the disaster was not theirs, but it so easily could have been! Their relief mechanism was to apportion blame; and it required the two teachers, the senior in particular, to become their focus.

The following day, after discussion between the relatives and the police, it was decided that Dave Cotter should return home with the boys and their families, and that Tom and Elaine Wallace remain behind. Tom pondered on their thinking. The mother's presence would be vital in the face of news; good or bad. He realised that in his case, keeping him close would mean they could keep an eye on him. Still a suspect!

As one week turned into two, he became marginalised in the day to day events. It became clear he was no longer a part of the search, more a tool of public relations. He might be called to a press conference; a shambolic affair usually. A few questions, and non-committal answers orchestrated by the Gardai, and that was it! He assumed that keeping the case with the two of them alternately out front, was in the hope of stirring any tiny morsel of information. The problem was, how many ways were there of saying "No news!"

In those days, no word passed between Tom and Elaine Wallace, other than through the liaison officer appointed to her by the police. One day, without any pre-warning, they were called together in a tense atmosphere at police HQ and informed that the physical search had yielded no clues and it was to be curtailed. The Gardai's feeling of embarrassment at the failure was manifested in the Inspector who gave the news to the press in a faltering murmur, barely audible. The silent atmosphere was split asunder by Elaine Wallace, standing at the door, her scream echoed in the featureless room

"FIND MY BOY!"

It wrenched his heart then, and Tom Ellison remembered it painfully now. He poured himself some tea, and drowned intermittent biscuits, until the plate was empty. With the physical effect of his riverside walk, his mental energy sapped by the twin forces of past memories and the excitement of potential progress, he sank back on the bed and fell asleep.

*

He was awakened by the sound of the bedroom door being opened. The elfin face of Mrs Murtagh peered in.

"Tea will be ready in half an hour," she announced as she gathered the tea tray. "I'll take these now."

"Thank you," he said, dry scrubbing his face into life. He washed in cold water and changed into his other shirt. As he sat waiting for the call to dinner, he considered that perhaps he had just lifted the corner of a curtain that had shrouded his life.

Having consumed a huge plateful of beef stew and dumplings followed by a sublime rhubarb tart, he gathered himself together for his assignation at Reynolds Bar. He checked his wallet for cash, borrowed a brush to clean his shoes and stepped out on to the lane outside his lodging and turned the corner on to the main street of Drumlasheen, now almost deserted except for a fish and chip van just setting up.

He hadn't realised how steep was the rise from the lane at the bottom of the main street to the bar at the other end. He was starting to feel his prolonged lack of exercise and puffed out his cheeks and lent against the slope. It was quarter past six and he made for a bench beneath the memorial clock to rest, and to take in his surroundings. The low two storey buildings on either side of the narrow street were individually undistinguished, but their frontages painted in a uniform white colour wash made for a clean, if uninspiring, whole. The grey Town Hall stood alone on its patch of land: pride of place in the middle of the street.

When he entered Reynold's Bar he thought he'd walked into a still from a Hitchcock film. The same small group of men, carefully posed, as if frozen in aspic, sat at the bar, and might well have been set up by the master film maker.

At any minute he expected someone would call out "Action!" and he, (Jimmie Stewart) was walking into a place he shouldn't be in. The call did not come and the figures slowly turned in unison, with a scrutinising look at the interloper, and then back to concentrate on their pints of beer.

This twilight time, peopled by old men, would soon be transformed into a noisy, pulsating bedlam, as families came out for the Saturday night ceilidh.

"Guinness!" said the man behind the bar.

Tom thought of his credibility in this setting and answered brightly. "Thanks. You remembered."

"Part o' the job," was the reply and then "Something wrong with the last one?"

"Sorry?" Tom said, uncertain of the meaning of the question.

"You left without finishing it," it was said with mock offence.

"I'd forgotten. There was someone I had arranged to meet," he replied weakly.

At that moment Garda Finbar Reeve dressed casually in sports jacket and jeans, parted the curtain and entered the bar. "Saved by the bell!" Tom turned quickly to greet him.

"What'll you have?" he offered as they shook hands.

"The usual, Bryan," Reeve said, acknowledging the barman, who repeated the routine of the ruler, and presented him with his pint. Ellison paid for the drinks and beckoned towards a table in the corner. The men at the bar nodded in turn as the Garda passed by.

"How are things going?" Tom said in a stage whisper. He tried not to look furtive.

"Much as they were," Reeve replied.

"No clues?"

"You know I can't tell you that." Ellison was disappointed. He had come with the high expectation of news that the cases were coming together. This non-committal reply meant that he was not yet fully in the loop.

"What about you? Have you come up with any information?" Reeve asked.

"Matter of fact I have," Tom replied with a glint of childish delight. Out of his inside pocket he withdrew the photograph of the cup celebrations and moved closer to Reeve. "Here. Look. That's Michael!" Reeve looked closely and nodded acknowledgement.

"And THAT is the man I saw at the start of the search," Tom Ellison said triumphantly, with an implied "and what do you think of that?" After a silence Reeve said "What do you think is the relevance of that?"

"Don't you see? The man who didn't take any part in the search, is the same man as the one presenting the trophy to Michael; who died in a tragic accident. His wife had a breakdown; and died today; when I turned up." He had articulated the items as if adding up a sum. It was a distillation of the whole story as Tom Ellison saw it.

"Hold on," replied the Garda. "In summary, this man, who might have been at the search, also presents rugby trophies, and is therefore guilty of some unspecified crime. It's hard to make a link," Ellison was shocked. This was the first rebuttal he had felt from the Garda detective since his return to Drumlasheen. The enthusiasm for the meeting that he had built up during the day, had just taken a dive.

"Let me ask around about the picture," Reeve said.

"You do know something!" Tom replied, his fire re-ignited.

"Just let me make some enquiries," was the bland reply. Ellison had not expected the stony faced response. He handed the photograph to Reeve, who put it in the pocket of his coat and then downed the last of his beer.

"Another?" He said as he stood up. Ellison realised that he had forgotten the pint at his elbow. Resolutions made earlier were forgotten, as he downed most of the pint in one draught. Almost breathless, he said "Sure!"

Finbar Reeve made his way to the bar and exchanged greetings with the trio leaning there. When he returned, the conversation reverted to their individual memories of the times seven years before. First one, and then the other, looked back at the various phases of that first encounter.

"You checked me out?" Ellison said.

"Of course!" Reeve replied confidently.

"And now?"

"It's standard practice," Reeve answered, a mischievous glint in his eye.

As they talked, it was a relief for Tom Ellison to find that Reeve knew something of his more recent life, and that there was no need for him to be evasive about it.

It seemed that Reeve trusted him. On Finbar Reeve's part, it showed that he was committed to professional procedures where necessary, but that he still wanted to help in Ellison's quest for answers. They mulled over the search and the arrival of the boys' families. Reeve spoke of his sadness at the plight of the boy's mother, and of his despair when the search was scaled down. Ellison asked about Reeve's career and expressed his envy for its stability.

Reeve showed that he understood the pain Ellison had experienced, and did not press that corner of the Englishman's life. Ellison was grateful for that. Over an hour passed with the discussion going back and forth. Ellison cleverly tried to weed out nuggets of information, and Reeve stoically resisted the zest for information. Perhaps because there was none! They finally agreed to let matters develop naturally.

Conversation turned to rugby and films, and a wide range of inconsequentials that made the reunion complete. Tom was no further on than he had been on the river bank, and he felt slightly disappointed. However, so much of his new found confidence stemmed from this man's acceptance of his search for justice for the boy; and himself.

By now the pub was filling up. A group, carrying guitars, fiddles and drums were warmly welcomed and directed to the tiny alcove at the other end of the bar. The noise level increased as their followers and casual drinkers began to fill the tiny space in Reynolds Bar. When it seemed impossible to squeeze any more into the space, the few tables were passed over the bar and through to a room beyond, to accommodate the growing crowd. Now the place was full, the first strains of the pairing of guitar, fiddle and the ancient bodhran drum filled the space that was left.

It was a joyous rustic noise, and each cascading fiddle solo, designed to show virtuosity, was met with an enormous cheer. Ellison peered through the tilting crowd and saw a pair of hands playing a tiny squeezebox. At the end of a long energetic piece, met with rapturous applause, the room went quiet with expectation and Tom heard the sound of a gentle guitar riff and a twinkling penny whistle solo replaced the bucolic uproar. A voice, the owner of which Ellison could not see, floated like a whisper across the silenced room. The voice was sweet and vulnerable, as it rendered the ballad Tom Ellison had long forgotten.

"Last night I had the finest dream that no one can gainsay." He drew in a sharp gasp of surprise. This song was a memory of Drumlasheen encapsulated in simple words about a yearning for home. He joined in excitedly with the resounding applause that greeted its end.

The rest of the evening flew by, as a succession of performers came to the fore. A little girl was lifted onto the bar and executed a dazzling step dance, ramrod straight and her head still, her feet taping at astounding speed. Tom felt exhilarated by the atmosphere, which was now at its height. He was disappointed when Finbar Reeve indicated it was time for him to go.

"I think we should meet tomorrow. I need you to put all this stuff in writing," he said, striving to make himself heard above the noise.

"Of course," Tom agreed readily. They eased their way through the crowd and the overflow that had gathered on the pavement outside the bar. He accepted the Garda's offer of a lift, and was dropped off at the end of Mrs Murtagh's narrow lane to avoid a problem in turning.

"I'll pick you up in the morning at nine," Reeve said. Tom acknowledged him with thumbs up and moved from the light of the main street into the relative gloom of the lane.

There was a partial moon, so Tom could see the line of the frontages of the houses. Then he recognised his car beyond what seemed to be a dustbin. Giving it a wide berth he moved towards the car. As he drew level, he lent to check the car door in case he had forgotten to lock it. A sound split the night air. Phutt! Phutt! Brick dust exploded from the gatepost behind him. Instinct was instant. He was on the ground next to the car before his brain got into gear. As he lay there, he knew, with a weird lucidity what was happening. Some bastard was shooting at him! Where from? In seconds he harnessed clarity of thought and worked out that the safest place to be was behind the low brick wall of Mrs Murtagh's small front garden. With one step backwards and with a modified Fosberry Flop, he leapt the wall and he was lying face down in a border of pansies. He rolled over until he was tight against the wall. He listened for any indication of movement, but the only thing he could hear was his own frantic breathing. Seconds passed and he heard what sounded like someone moving. They're running away! Slowly he raised himself on to his knees, bringing his head just below the top of the wall. "What am I expecting to see?"

He glanced back at the front door estimating the time it would take to open it with his key. A deep breath, and with one stride and a leap up the two steps to the door, with trembling fingers he pressed the key home. The door yielded to his push and he dived into the gap. Once inside he fell to his knees and moved up against the wall, where he thought he would be out of the sight lines of another shot. He pushed the door shut with his foot, at the same time stretching out his hand to push hard on the bolt at the bottom of the door until it slid into place. He sat up exhausted. In the minutes that followed he tried to assess the situation. Was the threat over?

He decided, whatever else, not to arouse Mrs Murtagh. in case the gunman was still around. He would not put her into danger by drawing her into the situation. If she did appear, he would have to deal with it. He looked at his watch. It was ten forty five. He remained there for about twenty minutes, before he decided to crawl on all fours to the sitting room. Feeling his way in the darkened room he found the welcoming arms of one of the chairs. His recent athletics and his cramped position by the door left his legs aching, but soon the adrenalin that had sustained him was shot, and alcohol took over, he fell into a fitful doze.

He woke with a sudden start at the sound of a creaking tread on the stairs. The sitting room door was slightly ajar and with a gasp of relief, the tiny figure of Mrs. Murtagh moved by on her way to the kitchen. Reflecting on his dishevelled appearance, he decided to try to reach his bedroom without detection. He did not want her to be panicked by his bedraggled look. He waited for the sound of rattling crockery, used in the making of her usual late night hot chocolate, and slowly made his way into the hall and put his first faltering step on the stairs. At each slow motion step, he feared a tell-tale squeak, but at last he reached the shelter of the landing. Once in his room he collapsed on to the bed. The first thought that came into his head, was that the situation he was in was no longer cerebral, but wildly visceral.

"They bloodywell tried to kill me!"

23

Sleep would not come that night, so after he had washed and shaved, Tom Ellison changed his shirt to the one he had discarded hours before. He sprayed a generous burst of aftershave over it to disguise its stale smell. He acknowledged Mrs Mutagh's call to breakfast and went downstairs, still unsure whether to tell her about his recent skirmish. He poured a cup of tea from the waiting pot.

"Ah there y'are! Goodmornin!" Mrs Murtagh greeted him as she entered and placed in front of him a sumptuous fried breakfast and toast. He devoured it ravenously as his thoughts raced for a decision. When she came back into the lounge, he asked her to sit down on the chair across the table. He lent forward hesitatingly, and in as calm a voice as he could marshal, retold the events of the night before. She listened impassively and then gently put her hand over his and said "Are you alright my dear?"

He was amazed at the response. The dear old lady had been told of a possible threat to her own life, and yet her first thought was for him. He explained that he had already arranged to meet Finbar Reeve, who now would likely designate the house a crime scene, with all the consequent upheaval.

"That's good!" she said without embellishment.

A few minutes before nine, he unbolted the front door and tentatively stepped out into an early morning sun that temporarily blinded him. Blotting it out with his hand, he surveyed the scene of the night's events. A hawthorn hedge delineated the far side of the lane and beyond it a narrow strip of meadow that skirted the river. A gap in the hedge was guarded by a wooden gate and it was through this gap that the sun was breaking. He gingerly took the two steps down to the garden gate and cast a wary eye on his rented car for signs of damage. Had there been more than two shots? He couldn't be absolutely sure. Reassured that no damage had been done, he turned to the gatepost. Chipped out of the white painted column, revealing the red brick beneath, were the inescapable marks of two bullets. They were both within inches of each other. He moved to the spot where he recalled standing when he heard the sound. The marks were level with his head! Turning round, he guessed the line of fire was in the direction of the gate on the other side of the lane. No grassy knoll here!

His replay was interrupted by the sound of Finbar Reeve's car coming down the lane.

"Morning!" Reeve hailed through the open window. His expectation was that Tom Ellison was standing there ready to meet him.

Ellison raised a weak hand in acknowledgement and Reeve knew that all was not right. Opening the door as far as the tightly parked cars allowed, he eased himself into the gap and sidled his way out.

"You alright?" he asked, and recognised at once that his question was superfluous. The loose set of the jaw was far removed from the face, bright with excitement that he remembered from a few hours before. Standing together on the pavement Tom Ellison was glad that the reassuring figure of Finbar Reeve was at his side.

"Look at this!" He pointed to the gouged holes in the gatepost. Reeve recognised them at once.

"What happened?" he said, knowing how limply foolish the question sounded.

"I got shot at!" was the only reply that Tom felt answered the question succinctly.

"You know what I mean," Reeve replied.

Ellison started to recount without adornment, step by step, his leaving Reeve's car the night before. He described his reactions to the shots. He was sure it was two. The language became more effusive, reflected in a rise in the tenor of his voice almost to soprano pitch until, to Reeve's amazement, he leapt over the low wall and disappeared from sight. Reeve could never have received a more graphic witness report. Without halting the narrative, Ellison completed the aerobic sequence and was standing at the open door. He mimed inserting the key and, searching for breath said

"That's it folks!"

Reeve recognised the trauma this comic re-enactment represented and said "My God!" at the same time absorbing and assessing the information. He took a closer look at the bullet marks.

"No loud bang you say?" He turned and looked across the lane. "Somewhere in that direction I think," he volunteered.

"That's what I thought," said Ellison with mild satisfaction.

"You didn't see anything?"

"I didn't take time to look," was the acerbic reply. Reeve had seen and heard enough, and his brain went into gear, itemising the things he knew that he had to do. Training had taught that the victim's well-being was his first priority. After that he would secure the crime scene.

"Let's go inside," he said, and as he climbed the steps to the front door, added "Does Mrs Murtagh know?"

"Yes she does," was the quick reply, as the door opened wider and the landlady's face appeared in the space. Reeve knew the old lady was made of stern stuff. He acknowledged her presence with a respectful nod and shepherded them inside.

"Can you write all this down while I organise things? Both of you. And don't leave anything out, however trivial." Knowing the uncertainty of radio contact in the area, Reeve asked "Can I use the phone?"

"Of course!" was the reply. "I'll organise pen and paper.

Reeve arranged for a local foot soldier to cordon off the end of the lane, and then ordered a forensic team to come and search and photograph the area.

"It's busy in Drumlasheen," was the ribald comment from the duty sergeant.

"You can say that again!" Reeve replied. He realised that in his years of service he had never had two such major incidents in the space of forty eight hours. Easy for Kojak!

Standing outside the house, he knew the forensic team would take some time to arrive, but after five minutes with no sign of the local man, he began to wonder if resources were stretched – with the two crime scenes in the area. He walked down to the end of the lane, ready to set himself up as his own temporary barrier against intruders on to the scene. A curmudgeonly young officer named Sean Rees appeared ten minutes later, panting as if he'd completed a cross country run.

"Perhaps he had!" Reeve thought in a generous moment and said nothing in rebuke.

Now he concentrated on the area around the house. His first thought was to look at the spot by the gate, where he guessed the shots might have come from. The gate was slightly ajar, enough for him, or an assailant, to pass through. Tight up against the gate, where a marksman could get a solid stance, and parallel to it, were two clear footprints and a confused mash of activity in the recently wet ground. It seemed to confirm his suspicion. He looked around for spent cartridges. From Ellison's description, he imagined a semi-automatic weapon of some kind. He knew better than to disturb the ground further, aware that his own foot prints were already there. He stood on a patch of grass at the side of the gate and made his exit as carefully as possible.

Next he examined the nearside of the car for signs of additional bullet marks. Ellison had been right. The shooter had got off only two shots. By this time, the same forensic team that he had met at Mary McMahon's house arrived. Quickly he briefed them on the incident, and directed them to the area he had already identified as a possible source of forensic interest. Next he needed to find out if anyone from the other two houses in the lane had seen or heard anything.

Reeve knocked gently on the door of the house next to Mrs Murtagh's. The door was opened by Beth Logan, who had gone to school with his mother and had shared the baby sitting duties with her in his own early childhood.

"Why Fin! It's you! I wondered what was going on." She pointed in the direction of the cluster of cars.

"Can I come in?" He remembered the house from his childhood, as he was directed into the sitting room. Many an hour was spent there with the two Logan boys building a crane or a bridge with a Meccano set.

"What's up Fin?" said Ted Logan rising from his chair.

"There's been some bother down the lane," Reeve replied.

He didn't want to frighten the couple, nor did he want to lie to them. "Did you see or hear anything unusual last night?" he asked in as mild a tone as he could avoiding unnecessary gravitas.

"No. I don't think so. What sort of thing?" they replied simultaneously.

"Oh it's nothing to worry about. Some lad with an air rifle I expect."

"We didn't hear anything. Did we Ted?" Beth Logan replied, seeking confirmation from her husband. He nodded in agreement and knocked his pipe out in a glass ashtray perched on the arm of his chair.

"What time?" asked Ted.

"Oh any time from six o'clock onwards, 'til dark." Reeve did not want to lead the couple.

"No! Didn't see anything and my hearing isn't as good as it used to be."

"We were in the kitchen most of the time and we were in bed by half past nine," his wife added.

"That's fine," smiled Reeve "Just checking."

"What's this all about Fin?" Reeve saw no need to unsettle the pair.

"Nothing, I expect," he replied and added "I'd better get on," and he made for the door. "You take care," he wished them as he exited down the steps.

At number one Weir Lane, he knocked on the door and was greeted by Peter Cogan, a man in his eighties, who lived alone, as he had done for forty years. He lent heavily on a stick and he confessed he'd not seen anyone or heard anything.

"Like most days," he added soulfully. Without allowing further question, he closed the door in Reeve's face, who smiled at the grumpy old man's rebuff.

Standing on the steps of Number one Weir Lane, he surveyed the scene. One of the forensic team had made his way, at his instruction, to the area on the far side of the lane that suggested the position of the shooter. Standing next to Ellison's car, the other officer was preparing to take photographs. Reeve shouted across the lane.

"Any sign of any shells?"

"No!" was the reply. "But I've got the shrapnel from the wall bagged."

"Get a cast of those footprints. By the way, some of 'em are mine," he warned. This was met with an exasperated shrug of the shoulders and a sigh, just far enough away from Reeve to avoid him hearing.

Turning to the officer taking photographs of the scene, Reeve said "You got the bullet marks?"

"Yep! But nothing on the car so far," he reported.

"Any idea what did the damage?"

"High velocity, I imagine. From something like one those Czech Parabellum's that are smuggled in by the thousands.

"There's those who love their guns," Reeve reflected, without naming names.

He turned about and stepped up to the front door and knocked. Elizabeth Murtagh opened the door and invited him in.

"He's in the sitting room," she said waiving Reeve through. Standing at the open door to the sitting room, he shepherded her in. "I need to speak to you both."

The three drew up chairs to the table and Finbar Reeve took out his notebook and placed a ballpoint pen on top of it.

"Bit like a staff meeting." Tom Ellison mused.

Finbar Reeve took the initiative. He outlined his understanding of the evening's events, first of all from Ellison's point of view, and then from what little he had gathered from Mrs Murtagh. Opening his notebook and comparing it with their statements, he invited them to add anything that he had missed or left out. The silence that followed indicated that the record was an accurate one. He closed the notebook shut and placed it, and their statements, in his coat pocket.

"Well here's what we're going to do," he said confidently.

"I will carry on with my enquiries. When the boys have finished outside, I will leave a man at the front door. I don't want you to leave the house. Either of you," he stressed.

"Is that really necessary? I've shopping to do," responded Mrs Murtagh.

"That'll wait for now. Not be for long! Just a precaution," said Reeve reassuringly.

Tom Ellison had listened to Garda Reeve and he was sure he had a firm grasp of the situation. He wondered if, like him, Reeve was now convinced that this episode was unquestionably connected to the boy's demise – and more!

"Any clues?" Tom asked hoping to open a dialogue.

"Not so far," was the terse reply, setting up a blockade for further discussion. He rose and made towards the sitting room door. Ellison's understood that he needed to go about his job. At the front door they exchanged silent handshakes. Tom Ellison looked at the ongoing search in front of him.

"Is this what I came for?" he pondered as he re-entered the house. "What have I got myself into?" he mused, closing the door behind him,

"Cup of tea?" Mrs Murtagh asked.

24

County Police headquarters were housed in the shell of a 19th century lodge, acquired to offset death duties of one of the county's long established gentry. It had become an uncomfortable amalgam of tired grandeur and temporary additions. The surrounding garden and the small lake beyond were kept in prime condition by a retired officer, hinting at a future sale, when property prices would be higher. At the front of the house were steps up to the pillared portico, whose heavy oak doors opened to the main reception area with its obligatory Welcome Desk sitting at the foot of the balustraded staircase. On either side of the desk were heavily carved doors with brass name-plaques, announcing senior officers. The staircase led to the second floor, where large rooms had been converted, each divided in open plan style, to accommodate staff of various disciplines. Middle order officers were housed in offices created from what had been, in Victorian times, the library. Traffic shared, what used to be the games room, with the Radio Control team. Records were kept on the upper floor. The basement had been given over to holding cells and a self-help canteen.

In the investigation room, a small team of officers worked from tiny work areas comprised of a desk, phone, filing cabinet and a waste paper basket. In the far corner a separate office had been partitioned off. Jokes and ribald remarks were the common currency in this all male bastion. Few women trod the well worn carpet of the room, without eliciting a muffled comment of salacious innuendo. Only the most confident of female officers braved the predictable reaction without trepidation.

Student Garda Sibohan Farraday was one such. Her youthful good looks made her a prime target for the treatment. However, she was more than capable of a response to deflate the round robin of comments that might transfer from one desk cluster to another, as she passed through.

"Anti-Chauvanist alert!" she announced at the door as she entered. A grudging murmur of welcome was the response. She wended her way to the office at the far end of the room and with a flourish, delivered a thick folder to the desk of Detective Constable Finbar Reeve.

"Pathologist Report sir," she announced.

"Thanks Sibohan," he said, his concentrated gaze unchanged.

"Something I said?" she said in reproach.

Turning to face her, he responded "Oh sorry Sibohan. I was away with the fairies."

"You're forgiven," she whispered in a voice reflecting the strong attraction that she felt for the detective. She had quietly longed for their casual acquaintance to develop into something more. Recognising that his thoughts were elsewhere, she said cheerfully "Must go! People to see! Jobs to do!" And she was gone!

He smiled in response as she moved away. On another occasion his response would have been different. He had lusted for the long legged beauty with black hair cut in the old Mary Quant style. He had held his desire in check because of the age difference. He was thirty two and she was twenty two. A difficult sum to square, he had thought, that was for another time.

Sitting at his desk, Finbar Reeve studied a blackboard on to which he had printed, in yellow chalk, the names of those people, places and events involved in his two cases. Each was circled, and looping lines linked one with another. There was a pleasing symmetry to the picture, as lines of fact and, he had to admit, lines of theory all led to the one name – TOM ELLISON. It seemed undeniable that the English teacher's presence in Drumlashhen and the McMahon case were not a mere coincidence.

He now had a clear basis to re investigate the case that had been a source of personal regret and disappointment. It had left a sense of failure for him and his colleagues and a palpable sadness amongst the local community. The thing that stuck in his craw most was, he had heard later, that the initial search had been called off because of lack of cash. A review of the case had not taken it any further. It pleased him that from that situation, when they were totally bereft of any clues, now there seemed something in the atmosphere that promised developments. He badly wanted to resolve what had happened to Glenn Wallace, and bring anyone responsible to justice. His first job was to ensure it didn't involve anyone else's death. He decided after looking back through the records of the boy's disappearance, he would look at it from the other end and concentrate on more recent events.

At the top of his board he wrote in capitals GLENN WALLACE. He re-played in his mind the incidents of the last two days and then drew a scale at the bottom of the blackboard, dividing it into time segments. At one end, was Ellison's arrival in Drumlasheen. In the middle was the discovery of Mary McMahon's body and next to it was the previous night's attack. Beneath it, he drew another timeline of Ellison's movements, as far as knew them, and added the name or description of anyone to whom the teacher had spoken. By the time he had finished this graphic masterpiece, he needed more space, so he used a board rubber to clear a space down the side of the blackboard. At the top he printed the word MOTIVE and double underlined it. Below it he inscribed

REVENGE

GUILT

SELF PRESERVATION

CONCEALMENT

GAIN

DERANGED

He planned to tackle each heading in turn. He wondered if there was still anyone out there who felt that Ellison had transgressed and that retribution was required. Someone might be acting as judge and jury on the teacher's role. Was it the thought he was guilty of murder, or was it simply a dereliction of his duty towards the boy that motivated someone? Whatever might be driving a vigilante, it was not based on the evidence. Much to everyone's discomfort there was none. Over years, he and the rest of the Gardai hadn't found any, so how had anyone else? It required a detailed knowledge of all the facts to make a judgement, and an unbridled zeal, for it to culminate in Tom Ellison's assassination. Who in Drumlasheen grieved for the boy? His only thought was for the mother and her haunting despair. He drew the sign of the cross and whispered "God bless her! Let's hope we can bring her resolution this time!"

Policing in Leitrim had gone through difficult times recently and the public disdain of the Gardai's failure to find the boy was compounded when the review of the case produced no new facts. It followed the astonishing case of the kidnapping of the wonder horse Shergar. Two years before, the horse which won the Derby in 1981 and had been put to stud, was taken from its stable and never seen again. Theories as to the perpetrators were rife, and the Gardai was ridiculed for its perceived ineffectual investigation. Chief Supt. James "Spud" Murphy became the darling of the media for his bizarre pronouncements and his determination to use psychics and mediums to try to solve the case.

"A clue? That is something we haven't got," he once said.

The quote winged its way round the world, much to the consternation of Reeve and his colleagues. Finbar Reeve remembered that remark now.

His eyes were drawn down to the bottom of his list. Deranged? He wondered if there could just be someone, so unbalanced, that there was no logic at all in the attempt to kill Tom Ellison? Was there a random killer about? It didn't fit. It had to be someone who had a personal reason, justified or not, to kill him. At worst, Mary McMahon might have fallen into that category. Her mental downfall had seemed complete. She was once closely involved in the boy's disappearance, and in a demented fury, perhaps driven by her own guilt, could have decided to settle the score. But Mary could not be a suspect he knew. She was dead. He wondered if there was anyone who might act on her behalf. Her husband was dead and she appeared friendless and cut off from society. He just could not follow that line.

Head in his hands, he pondered this for a while and, with a shake of his head, re-focused on his schematic. Most of the names on his list were dead. Who could have played some part in the initial tragedy and needed to eliminate Tom Ellison, the possible catalyst for a new investigation? He was thinking that the culprit for both crimes was one in the same, and must lie outside his impoverished list. This seemed the most plausible explanation for the shooting, and Reeve drew a large circle round the list and a question mark next to it. Then he considered the category of person who might fit the bill. Criminal or mental? Had the child been the victim of a pervert? Tom Ellison's presence would represent a renewed threat to whoever was responsible. It all seemed to converge on the chapter heads of GUILT, CONCEALMENT and SELF PRESERVATION

His combined experience and intuition reaffirmed that the boy was taken and did not drown. But where was the evidence? Giving himself time to think, he hooked a chair with his foot, moving it closer to the blackboard. With his elbows on the desk top, and his hands supporting his chin, he allowed the thought to take root. It didn't seem possible Tom Ellison had invented the story of the shooting. Could it? As his training had taught him, he weighed up everything he thought he knew about Tom Ellison. The teacher's search for answers seemed paramount in his life just now, so what benefit would be gained by such a deception? It doesn't fit! Reeve sat back shaking his head. His own estimate of Ellison's character and all the other bits of evidence, however small and inconclusive, convinced him that his instincts had been right all along and he chided himself for this momentary aberration.

"We are definitely looking for someone else," he thought

As he ruminated over the chart he had produced, he had no doubt that the cases were linked. Ellison's postcards led positively down that road. Concealment was a strong motivation, but what was being concealed? What, if anything, was Mary's death concealing? Then there was a creeping uncertainty about Michael McMahon's death, which, he had to admit, was pure conjecture on his part. The links were there. Perhaps clearer in Reeve's mind than in the schematic he had produced. He sat deep in his chair and considered his predicament. He had on his hands two possible scenarios that read: three murders and one attempted murder, or an accidental death, two murders and an attempted murder. Whichever the case, Drumlasheen had not seen the like before. He needed to be on his mettle.

At that moment the door to the office opened and Detective Inspector Eric Blane, looking like thunder, stomped into view. Men on either side of his path stiffened in sedentary salute.

"What the hell's going Fin?" he roared, disturbing the quiet of the surrounding work stations.

Before Reeve could reply, his superior continued "First we have the death of a local woman in circumstances we've not yet nailed, and then we have a visitor shot at, by God knows who! It's like bloody Dodge City!"

He was now standing over Reeve, his pose hinting that he was prepared to do unprofessional things to his beleaguered assistant. Reeve, slowly and very deliberately looked up with eyes narrowed and his mouth set firm.

"Afternoon sir," he said quietly. It cut the atmosphere effortlessly and Reeve felt a blush of satisfaction.

"Well then?" Blane's bluster was deflated, and he sank into the chair opposite and Reeve picked up the story.

"As far as Mary McMahon is concerned, the mark on her head was made by contact with the lock fitting on the inside of the front door. We found traces of blood on it, and the mark on her head fits the shape of the knob. We also found small amounts of blood on the skirting board by the door. She must have opened the door and someone smashed against it in order to get in. In her physical state it was probably enough to kill her. There's clear proof that she was dragged into the kitchen. And a rug, that might also have blood on it, has gone missing."

"Is that all?"

"As far as I can see." Blane raised his eyebrows and tutted in exasperation.

"Suspects?" he pressured.

"None!" was the reply

"What about the Englishman?"

"He's got a solid alibi. Old Mrs Murtagh was with him at the time of death."

"And that was?"

"Give or take, about seven Monday night."

"I assume we can discount the priest?" Blane questioned further. Although Reeve was taken aback by the question, protocol insisted it should be asked.

"Yes!" he replied with conviction. "He would have no reason."

"Have you checked his whereabouts at the time?" Blane persisted.

"No!"

"Better do it just to be sure." Blane was establishing his seniority and Reeve recognised it.

"'Course Sir!"

"What have got in the way of forensics?"

Reeve catalogued that fingerprints and blood samples had been taken and the scene comprehensively photographed. The results of tests and photographs should arrive soon. The search for the rug was ongoing.

Taking a piece of paper from a plastic bag and handing it up to his superior, Reeve said "I did find this in a drawer."

Blane looked at it with narrowed eyes. He took a pair of glasses out of his waistcoat pocket and balanced them on the very tip of his nose. What he was straining to read was a newspaper cutting dated August 30th 1985. The headline read: Gardai Review Case of Missing Boy. Blane read on, his lips pursed in concentration.

"And the significance of this?" Blane asked, returning the cutting to Reeve.

"There may be none. Just thought it was interesting it got kept. Then there's these!" Reeve added, enjoying the moment. He handed Blane the messages that Tom Ellison had received. At once the experience detective in Blane accepted that whilst the postcard and the note were not conclusive proof of anything, the connection was inescapable when considering them and the death of Mary McMahon.

"Do we know who sent this?"

"Not so far."

"What about the husband's death? Accident if I remember."

"Nothing to say it wasn't," reported Reeve. "All we have is the Coroner's report. No witnesses, but..,"

"You think it might not be?" Blane pressed.

"What do you think Sir?" The tone suggested it was nearer to a statement than a question and he was seeking confirmation.

Blane took a moment to choose his words.

"I think we should look into it. Fin. I want you to sort this lot out before they send the Special Arseholes down. You know what that'll mean." Memories of joint investigations from the recent past gripped both men.

"I'm wrapping up the Cantrell fraud case today. I'll pick it all up tomorrow," Blane said by way of explanation. He stood up and made his way to the door. "You'll keep me informed. What about the shooting?"

"Nothing so far. I'm waiting for forensics."

Almost as soon as Blane left the office, the phone on Reeve's desk rang. It was Ed Sterne, the younger of the Scene of Crime Officers, reporting on the results of the fingerprint analysis at the scene of the shooting. Mischievously, he confirmed that Reeve's prints were on the gate to the field.

"Cheeky sod!" Reeve muttered. Fortunately there were clear footprints belonging to someone else. Better still, in places they were overlaid by Reeve's prints, indicating that someone stood by the gate earlier than him. The prints were being checked against their meagre records. The bullets found in the house gatepost were nine millimetre. He guessed that they came from a semi-automatic, probably smuggled in from abroad, which meant it probably would be impossible to trace.

"You know the best bit," he added tantalizingly "the prints on the gate are the same as I found on the door in the McMahon house." Finbar struggled to clear his throat.

"Say that again!"

"The prints match," reiterated Sterne.

After a prolonged silence, during which he felt the beginnings of a cold sweat, Reeve thanked his young colleague for a job well done. These cases were imploding in on each other, and making one homogenous whole.

Moving to the door of his office Blane shouted "Get in here!" summoning the attention of the entire office. He wanted to update them on his cases, and ask them all to keep their ears to the ground in their own investigations.

When he had finished, he said "We need a break on this! Go to it!"

They left the room in animated conversation. Bolstered by the anticipation of an impending breakthrough, Finbar Reeve left the office and walked out into the sunshine, and made his way to his car with a spring in his step. He was encouraged to think that if he questioned the two people to whom he had revealed his instinct about Mary McMahon's death, it might complete the circle on this gathering tale.

25

Before he spoke to anyone else, Finbar Reeve decided to cast his eye again over the site of Mary McMahon's tragic death. He wanted to re-assess what had become the scene of a murder. Shannonbridge House lay on his planned route and it was at the heart of his investigation. His ideas were formulating, as he arrived at the house. He took a moment to place the house in the landscape that surrounded it; perched on a knob of land which fell steeply away to the lake below.

Shannonbridge House had everything the McMahons could have wanted for themselves, and its size and location must have been an attractive home-from-home for groups of anglers too. Even in its present run down state, it was part of an attractive vista. He nodded acknowledgement to the young officer guarding the front gate, and asked if everything was in order.

"Sir!" was the wooden reply.

"You got the key?" Reeve asked.

"Here y'are sir," he said, handing over the key. "How're things going sir?"

"As well as could be expected."

"Was it murder?" The young man persisted.

"Well! Let's say we're continuing our investigation," he said mischievously.

Garda Sergeant Reeve walked the overgrown path, looking to left and right for any clues to the happenings of the previous day. At the front door he was able to pick out the signs of fingerprint dusting around and below the doorknocker. He inserted the key and turned it, at the same time gently pushing the door open. As he closed the door behind him, he caught a glimpse of the Yale lock on the inside. He blinked in surprise. Around the tooled edge of the door knob were dark traces.

Blood? It looked as if someone had cleaned the smooth surface of the lock, but the milled edge had been missed. The lock was placed at a height likely to strike a short woman. Reeve made his way to the kitchen. Bereft of the body, he wondered how anyone would know if things were out of place amidst all the clutter. With a little more care than the day before, he looked into drawers and cupboards and under the sink. There was nothing that attracted his interest and, as he was by the kitchen door, he decided to have another look around the back garden and the shed.

He picked his way round the periphery of the overgrown lawn to give himself a different view. Again he was dismayed to see the abandonment of a once loved garden, and he felt for the isolation that Mary McMahon had suffered for so long, at a time when she needed help. How could her decline have been so complete? Looking over the low wooden fence next to the garden shed, he scanned the meadow that dived steeply down to the lake, a sliver of which he could see glinting in the sun beyond the trees.

He pulled hard on the shed door and it yielded more readily than before. He noticed the kettle and mugs high up on the shelf above the bench. Something for forensics to check! He slid out the drawers and rummaged through their contents, in the hope that he might find something new. He contented himself that he had covered everything. As he turned to leave the shed, he noticed a rolled up off cut of linoleum peeping from behind the door. He had not noticed it before.

"You really are slipping!" he chided himself. He pulled it away from the wall, and inside it he found short off cuts of wood saved for kindling. Beneath it was a crushed cardboard box. Trapped within the folds was a white paper sack, flattened and folded in two. Carefully he picked up the bag between finger and thumb, not sure of its previous contents. He laid it on top of the bench and smoothed it out with a piece of wood. He could see no markings on the bag, which he thought strange. Using the stick as a tool, he opened the mouth of the bag. Inside he could see the vestiges of a white crystal substance. Right at the bottom he spotted a screwed up piece of paper. He sniffed the bag instinctively and then scraped the paper out. Holding the corner, he carefully unfolded it.

"Jesus, God and Mary!" he gasped as he focused on the words hand written across one corner. "Ammonium Nitrate!" There was no other information on the paper, but Finbar Reeve knew about this stuff! Its benign use was as a fertiliser in agriculture. But the whole world knew of its devastating use as an oxidising agent in explosives. It had become synonymous with militant movements all over the world.

"Michael McMahon – gardener or bomber?" he pondered. Leitrim's place on the border and its catholic heritage had made its community easy suspects in the growing tension surrounding terror attacks in the North. Reeve's natural pacifism was embedded in his work. Some of the tiny population of Leitrim had contributed to the hatred that permeated the border between North and South. He hated the way the community of Leitrim had been maligned en masse in the eyes of many. The nearby town of Ballinamore had been christened "The Falls Road of the South." He understood that many people supported the aspirations of the Provos, but fewer supported the way they went about trying to achieve them. He too might justify the former, but the latter was an anathema to him. Finbar Reeve was a proud son of Ireland, but he detested the violence perpetrated in its name. His brain turned somersaults, as he carefully folded the sack, and put it under his arm.

"Hell's bells!" he muttered, as he realised that there had been a dramatic shift in his linked cases.

The discovery of the fertiliser bag was a familiar mark of the supporters of The Irish Republican Army. It was inescapable to him that the bizarre sequence of events, now might have the mark of "The Cause" upon it.

The attack on Mary McMahon and the attempt to kill Tom Ellison all bore the signs. How had they missed it before? Of course the name of the IRA was always brought up in cases, because of their predisposition to crime, subterfuge and violence to sustain their agenda. As far as he knew, the Gardai had no clues to take them down that particular route during their search for the boy. Even now, it was hard for him to understand the possible connection with the vanished boy. It didn't fit. but he was being drawn to new conclusions. If true, the boy had not drowned, just as instinct had told him.

To make progress he needed to find out more about the McMahons. His best source was Father O'Mahony. If anyone had any recent information about Mary and her husband, he would have it. Whether Michael had any link with the boy's case, could not be ruled out. Any information about his life, and his tragic death, might have some bearing on the matter. Recognising that he had been less than thorough in his first visit, and in the light of his new discovery, he cast a more careful look at the contents of the garden shed. The lathes might have a greater significance than he thought. He radioed through to HQ and requested a detailed re-examination of the shed for indications of other chemical components. They would know what to look for. Before he left the house, he had another look round and decided to take away the rest of the papers from the drawers in the lounge. Those might give an added perspective on the pair who lived in Shannonbridge

House. He put them in a paper carrier bag he found in the kitchen, and left the house, reminding the young constable that no one was to enter.

"Except SOCO!" he stressed.

His slow journey back to Drumlasheen, along narrow lanes, squeezed between high hedgerows, gave time for thoughts to be filtered, and left him with a better feeling about the chronicle of events that had so troubled him.

26

Tom Ellison parted the dining room curtain and looked out onto Weir Lane; the scene of the previous night's episode. A low sun swept the lane and promised a fine morning to come. At the foot of the steps down from the front door, a policeman stood guard, arms crossed. Two other officers continued to scour the lane and the field beyond. He admired their thoroughness, and considered how stretched were the local police, with a mystery death and a shooting to deal with? Looked at separately, he thought, each would be a major incident for a tiny unit. He knew that the population of Leitrim was less than twenty five thousand and resources must be spread thinly over an essentially rural area.

Beneath the sound of Elvis Presley being "All shook Up", there was the rattle of crockery. As so many things had done since his return to Drumlasheen, it surprised him to remember that the shock news of death of "The King" had been the main headline at the time of the boy's disappearance. *Long live The King!*

Mrs Murtagh entered with a large breakfast tray.

"We might as well enjoy our confinement," she said jauntily, placing breakfast for two on the table. He was amazed at the fortitude with which she had accepted the shooting incident, and the isolation that had been imposed upon her. This grand old lady was showing him the way, and he was grateful. He snapped out of a mood that was part shock from the shooting, and part lack of sleep.

"Hostages together!" he joked.

While he enjoyed a massive fried breakfast, she ate toast and honey.

"I don't usually eat so much," Tom Ellison said apologetically, immediately realising how his appetite had grown without the drink.

She poured them each a second cup of tea and the conversation turned to his first visit to the town and the tragedy that followed. The situation they found themselves in now, and her ready acceptance of his account, made the telling easier. He left out the details of the next six years of his life and she did not pursue the subject.

"Then I had this card telling me to ask Mary McMahon what happened to the boy. What was I to think? I had to come back." She stretched her hand across the table and placed it on his.

"It was all in the papers here. For a long time afterwards there were stories. It was hard to believe that the boy could just disappear. I don't believe you could have done more."

"Thank you," he whispered, putting his cup to his mouth to hide trembling lips. Mrs Murtagh nodded in support. "Did you know what the postcard meant?"

"I only knew that someone thought there was a story to tell and Mary knew about it. I can't believe she had anything to do with it, but she could know who did. Why would she not have said something at the time?"

"Unless..," he pondered "..she didn't know anything about it then. What might she have found out since, and what or who could she be covering for?"

Tom doubted that there could be any other answer than the one that came to mind, but for a moment he dared not mention a name, lest it committed him to too much hope. Elizabeth

Murtagh sensed the moment and she tapped his hand gently.

"Oh my dear!"

It was all becoming too emotional and they both looked relieved when there was a knock on the front door. Mrs Murtagh went to answer and Tom Ellison gathered himself together. He heard her speak to someone, and then she appeared at the lounge door, followed by Finbar Reeve who was invited to take a seat at the table.

"Any news?" Tom Ellison asked expectantly.

"One or two bits and pieces."

"Well..?" Tom Ellison lent on the question, with expectation. Finbar Reeve outlined the evidence of his investigation of the shooting.

"We know the gun was a nine millimetre semi-automatic, virtually untraceable. However, we do have the shells that can be matched later, if we find it. We have fingerprints from the gate opposite and we've made casts of footprints from over there. There's not much else I can tell you."

"What about Mary McMahon?" Ellison asked

"I'd rather not say too much just yet. I've other enquiries to make today."

"Was it murder? Ellison persisted for the time being." Finbar Reeve was torn between the confidentiality of his job, and the desire to help the Englishman rid himself of his demons. He decided there could be nothing lost by revealing the facts, as he knew them.

"Well…we believe her death was not accidental," he said.

"Why was she killed?" Reeve knew that the answer to Ellison's question was vital to him. He had now reached the point of no return. Either he revealed the facts that were driving his newly formed hypothesis, or he stuck to the code of all investigations, not to reveal a hand too soon. His professional instinct prevailed.

"We don't know," he said with as much confidence as he could find within him. It was the truth, and he knew that he needed more facts before he could be more revealing. Expecting that Ellison would push him on the matter, he quickly reverted to his arrangements for the safety of the pair.

"I want you to stay in the house today and I will keep the officer at the front door. We can't be sure that our gunman won't try again, although it may be he just wanted to scare you."

"He certainly did that!" Ellison admitted freely. Reeve took some time reassuring Elizabeth Murtagh that the arrangements were precautionary, and that she had nothing to fear. Her response was quick.

"No matter! Whoever did it was not a very good shot!" It brought laughter to a tense situation and enabled Finbar Reeve to take his leave of them, satisfied that all was well.

Tom Ellison had not played Scrabble since his childhood, but on this day he sat down to play with a feisty old lady; old enough to be his Gran. It was the quiet strength of his grandmother that he saw across the scrabble board now. In such a short time, he had become very attached to Mrs Murtagh, with her sympathetic response to his predicament and her ready acceptance of sharing any danger that it might bring. He had not thought of his Gran for such a long time. He missed her now, with her tales of The Great Depression, told without bitterness, and her habit of slipping him a few bob each time he visited her. He regretted that sometimes his visit was planned specifically with the cash in mind, when he was desperate for some toy or a visit to the pictures.

The game was tough, and Tom's opponent surprised him with her quickness of thought, rapid addition of scores and devious, you could say questionable, strategies. He was at full stretch throughout, and he enjoyed the banter that it caused. He won an epic "Best of Five" match, and he was ashamed to admit that the contest had aroused an intense desire to win. Elizabeth Murtagh went into the kitchen to brew up.

Tom Ellison sat back comfortably in his chair – all tension gone in the moment.

27

Finbar Reeve parked his car on the crowded street in front of the Church of Mary The Blessed Virgin. His Catholic upbringing had instilled in him a healthy respect for the clergy and their place in the community. However it was not a wholly subservient attitude. He gathered his thoughts whilst straightening his tie, in preparation to conduct this vital interview with dispassion and without prejudice or trepidation. He was a good Catholic boy, but he told himself that this would need his best detective skills, uncluttered by religious preconceptions. His curb-side reverie was disturbed by a knock on the window. A round face, framed by a mass of grey hair and criss-crossed by wrinkles, peered in. It was Eva Greagan, the priest's housekeeper, a doer of good deeds and purveyor of service, for which the community held her in high regard. He opened the door and stepped out.

"Morning Mrs Greagan," he said respectfully.

"Mornin' Finbar. You wanting to see the Father?" she asked.

"Yes I am," he replied.

"He's inside," she said pointing to the manse.

"Thank you. How are the boys?" he asked. Mrs Geagan had twin sons, almost his age, who had had failed to escape her all-pervading embrace, and still lived at home to be waited on hand and foot. He always asked her about them, in the hope that one day one of them would have broken the chains that bound them to her, and each to the other. He liked them both as individuals and wished they would break free from her overpowering, maternal grip and their fused identity.

"Oh fine," she reported, as always. "You know they work together at the Water Board now?" He didn't, but he nodded his head.

"Must get on!" he said hurriedly, in an attempt avoid long drawn out tit bits of information.

"Give them my regards," he said, as he headed for the manse.

"Blast!" he muttered quietly, lest she should hear. In his attempt to disengage from the housekeeper, he had forgotten to lock his car. At least he had escaped a protracted conversation! That was something.

He turned about, as if to return to the car, and realised that it was unlikely that anyone would steal a car with a broad yellow line down the side and GUARDA emblazoned across the bonnet.

On reaching the door of the manse, he pulled the knob set into the wall, and heard the bell inside ring. As he waited for a response, he turned about and scanned the main street below. He loved Drumlasheen. It had been his home for all of his life and he could not imagine working anywhere else. He smiled as it went about its business, the street packed solid with cars, a source of much local debate. The door opened and the diminutive figure of Father O'Mahony stood inside.

"Can I have a word Father?" The tone betrayed the policeman's frame of mind.

"Of course! Come in!" the priest had picked up on the formality of the approach and nervously stepped back to beckon his visitor in. He closed the door and led Reeve down the hall and into his study. He offered Reeve a chair, and made his way round his desk and sat down in his high backed swivel chair.

"What can I do for you?" Reeve noticed his demeanor was anxious.

"I wanted to check one or two things relating to Mrs. McMahon's death."

"Oh! I thought it was something about last night's shooting." He seemed nervous, but Reeve marvelled at the speed of the Drumlasheen gossip machine.

"No! It's not that." He moved on quickly. "Can you tell me exactly what happened yesterday?"

"She was just lying there," the priest said anxiously.

"No! I meant from the time you left here. What time was that?" he said getting his purpose back on track. There was a long silence as the priest gathered his thoughts. He cleared his throat.

"Er... I suppose I left here directly after early morning Mass. That would be about ten fifteen. I'd be at Mary's house before half past ten. I telephoned the station that she was dead, and I was there until your man arrived," he moved uncomfortable in his swivel chair and it squeaked.

"What did you do then?" Reeve encouraged. "Why...I... er... came back here," he faltered

"Then I went back to the house later. About one o'clock I suppose. Is there a problem?" The priest put his hand to the side of his face nervously.

"You told me that the English teacher...," he looked deliberately at his notebook.

"Mr Ellison...He came to see you?"

Oh! That was the day before. Reeve was struck by the fluster that seemed to have overtaken the priest.

"Yes of course!" They were now in the area that Reeve really wanted them to be in.

"Did you tell anyone that he had been to see you?"

Nothing could have prepared Reeve for the reaction to his simple question. Colour drained from the priest's face. All semblance of control gone, his hands shook.

"You alright Father?" he asked leaning forward in his chair. With shallow breaths, the priest strove to regain his equilibrium, but here was a man on the brink of collapse. Reeve feared he was on the edge of a heart attack, or an epileptic fit. He stood and made his way around the desk to the priest's side.

"Can I get you anything?" he said, his hands on the cleric's shoulders and looking him hard in the face.

"Give me a minute," he murmured. Slowly Father O'Mahony's breathing became less shallow and the trembling subsided.

"You alright?"

"Yes," he answered unconvincingly.

Still pale and glassy eyed, he seemed to have reclaimed some of his poise. Finbar returned to his seat, unsure of his next move. He was aware that, although the priest was looking at him directly, there were other things going on in his mind. After an awkward pause, the priest drew in a deep breath, stood up shakily and, in a move which surprised Reeve, made his way round the desk and towards the door.

"I can't let this go on any longer," he said opening it. He was in an extreme state of agitation.

"I think you should speak to my nephew." Through the open door he called into the hallway beyond.

"Patrick! Can you come down please?" Reeve strained to hear the muffled conversation that went on in the hallway.

When the priest re-entered the room, he was followed by a man of about forty five with thin, wispy brown hair atop a long mournful face, and dressed in a black three piece suit, which created a sombre presence.

"This is my nephew Patrick Hanlon," announced the priest, a note of despair in his voice. Reeve had met Hanlon several times before. They shook hands in an atmosphere charge with uncertainty, and all three sat down. Father O'Mahony's face was now a sombre grey and his voice was just above a whisper.

"I think Patrick has something to tell you. Go on Patrick," he said reassuringly.

Hanlon slumped into the vacant arm chair. In a low trembling voice he began "It's hard to know where to start.

"From the beginning!" his uncle prompted.

"In my teenage years and beyond, I supported "The Cause". Many of us did," It was said in the hope that Reeve might be something of a kindred spirit. In fact the Garda officer sat bolt upright, unmoved. He sensed that here was a man, about to admit something shameful and he needed to be on his game. Patrick Hanlon was unprepared for the lack of reaction. He put a trembling hand to his lips.

"I was involved in moving stuff across the border…mainly guns," Father O' Mahony winced and Reeve turned a page in his notebook and, without altering his gaze, wrote something down. Hanlon drew in a deep breath and continued.

"You know, I worked in my father's funeral business."

"Was your father was involved in this?" Reeve interjected. "No! No! He knew nothing about it!" Patrick Hanlon, stricken by panic, looked nervously at his uncle for support; who nodded gently in response.

"When a shipment was ready, I would take it in the hearse across the border. No one thought about stopping a hearse in those days. I knew where to cross; with my work."

He looked hard at Reeve, trying to gauge his response to what he had already said. All he could see was an unblinking mask. He put his hand to his mouth, as if to prevent further incrimination tumbling from his lips and took a series of short, shuddering breaths through his fingers, before his shoulders started to tremble uncontrollably and he burst into tears. His uncle moved forward and handed him a handkerchief.

"And what else?" said Reeve. Patrick Hanlon wiped the tears from his eyes and sucked gasps of air to reclaim his thoughts. Nervously he returned to his narrative,

In August nineteen eighty five a shipment of guns was due to be transported north. They'd been hidden for some time and two of our group went to pick them up. They saw a young boy watching them." Reeve's stomach turned somersaults, as he realised what was coming next.

"I suppose the boy must have panicked and he ran. They caught him and…,"

"The English boy?" Reeve challenged.

"Yes. But I had nothing to do with that," he said plaintively.

"What did you have nothing to do with?" Reeve strove to keep his mind focused, avoiding the temptation to take the man by the throat.

"The boy died. They hit him and he was dead." Hanlon bit his lip.

"They were supposed to turn up at my place to load the guns into a coffin. Instead they turned up with the boy's body in the car. They wanted me to help them get rid of It."

"It?" raged Reeve. "What the hell is "it"?" Hanlon leant back, fearing the Garda was about to hit him.

"He was dead!" Hanlon whined. "I wanted no part of murder, but what could I do?"

"Who are "they"? Reeve himself was struggling hard to control an all-consuming anger.

"There was Joe Riordon. He's the top man round here. He's ruthless. Mad! Nothing stands in his way. It was him who hit the lad with a rifle butt. There was no need to do that!" Hanlon shook his head violently.

"And Michael McMahon! It was him that got me into all this. He made coffins for my father from time to time, and I must have expressed my support for the movement. Before I knew it, I was drawn in. He adapted some of the guns and stored them in an old boathouse near his house. I would pick them up and take them across."

"Where to?" Reeve asked urgently.

"There were several places. They changed each time." Recognising that Hanlon was now in full flow and wanting to unburden himself of his guilt, Reeve held back his anger.

"What of the boy?"

"They said it was a foolproof plan to move the body."

"Were you there when all this happened?"

"No! I had nothing to do with it," Hanlon added desperately.

"Did you move the body?"

"I had to! You don't know what they're like."

"Tell me!" Reeve waived his hand in a beckoning motion

"Riordon told me if I didn't do what he wanted, my family would suffer," he looked at his uncle, who nodded, encouraging his nephew to tell all. There was a moment's hesitation, as he gathered his thought. He drew in a deep breath, as if preparing for a special announcement.

"He said he'd got friends in high places."

It took a moment to register. Finbar Reeve, his composure almost blown, stood up and moved menacingly towards him.

"What the hell does that mean?" he thundered. Patrick Hanlon recoiled at the threat.

"I don't know. He just seemed to know what was going on at all times."

"Did he give any names?" Reeve persisted.

"No … No names!"

"How did they know?" Reeve moved closer.

"I don't know! Just that they were top people."

"What kind of top people?"

"The Gardai?" Hanlon whispered desperately.

This shattering revelation was something Finbar Reeve could not have expected. Confidence drained from him as he took in the allegation. He eased himself back into the chair in an attempt to restore his equilibrium. All that he was hearing fitted in with the known facts, and might explain why the hunt for the boy had been so woefully unsuccessful. He despaired that his force, An Garda Siochana, "The Guardian of the People" might be implicated. If it was true, those responsible could still have been in office when the case was reviewed years later. Even now! It angered him to think that he might have been an unknowing tool in these deceptions.

"So what did you do?" he lent forward and pointed directly at Hanlon. Hanlon gripped the coffee table that sat in front of him, as if securing it as a barrier between himself and the angry inquisitor. He drew in a deep shuddering breath.

"We put the boy in the coffin that Michael had made for the guns, and set it in my Chapel of Rest until we moved it that night," Father O'Mahony crossed himself and muttered an invocation and Hanlon dropped his head, sobbing quietly.

"You moved it the same night, while the search was on?" Reeve was incredulous at the audacity, and yet was beginning to understand the fruitlessness of the search that had drained so much from all those who took part. The slow search at the lakeside had ensured that a wider search would be delayed. Reeve sat back again. The Father raised his eyes to the ceiling.

"How did you know when to move?" Reeve continued.

"Riordon just seemed to know!" And with a shake of his head and hands held out palm upwards in a sign of resignation, Hanlon snivelled "He just knew!"

"What next?"

"We took the coffin to the deserted chapel on the Cawdon Estate, and buried it in the little cemetery there. It was far enough away and it had not been used for years. We used an old grave and put the old stones back."

Patrick Hanlon, now in full confession mode, continued filling in the details. In his career, Detective Sergeant Finbar Reeve had never felt the way he felt now. The tragedy, sadness, cruelty and obscene banality of the tale, gripped him like a vice making it hard to continue, but the disdain he felt for this wretched excuse of a man needed to be put to one side for now. He must do his best to ensure that justice be done.

"Then what?" he urged.

"We just waited for things to die down."

"What do you know about a black mini?"

"That was Riordon's. He told me it's in a lake, somewhere round Cork." The features on Reeve's face screwed up into a mask of contempt, which Hanlon could not misinterpret.

"Since then, I've had no dealings with Riordon, I promise. For two years I was glad it was all in the past… Until now… He came into my shop yesterday. He wanted to know what I knew about the Englishman turning up. I told him I knew nothing. Only that my uncle said he had come to see Mary McMahon." Hanlon looked nervously in the direction of his uncle, who in turn exchanged knowing glances with Finbar Reeve.

"He was very edgy. He told me not to talk to anyone. Then he said "Remember what happened to Michael?" "I knew at once what he meant. Oh my god! He'd got rid of Michael. I never knew that. I promise! Then he said he might have to pay Mary a visit. Oh Jesus!"

Patrick Hanlon was visibly falling apart. Father O'Mahony could hold back no further. He rose from his chair, knelt down before his trembling nephew, and drew him close.

"It's alright, Patrick," he promised and drew the weeping man's hands down from his face. Looking eye to eye, he repeated quietly over and over "It's alright Patrick!" It was said with such simple compassion, that no other words were needed. Patrick Hanlon drew in deep gulps of air and scrubbed his face with his hands. When Reeve judged that he was sufficiently recovered he asked,

"Where does Riordon live?" knowing that he was not a Drumlasheen man.

"Roscommon! Somewhere there! He moves about. We usually met in a pub. He was well known there." he paused and then said triumphantly "The Falcon. That's the one. The Falcon Inn!"

"Daytime or night?" Reeve was quick to respond. These were crucial details.

"At night. Always! The place would be full for a darts match."

The Falcon Inn at Gailey was well known to Reeve and his Gardai colleagues. It drew drinkers in from the scattered rural area. He had been called in many times, as a fledgling Garda. It was usually about an altercation between drunks, but he knew it was a place where skulduggery and dark dealings likely had a home. But he had never come across Joseph Riordon. Reeve pressed harder.

"Do you know where he is now?"

"No! Sorry!"

"Do you think he intended to harm Mary McMahon?"

"I don't know why, but it seemed so. He's mad enough."

"What do you know about the attempt on the Englishman's life?" "Nothing!" "Was it you?"

"No! No! I know nothing about that!"

Garda Sergeant Reeve knew that Patrick Hanlon would need further in-depth questioning, but he was now satisfied that he had enough to move on. He went through the formality of arrest and Patrick Hanlon looked as if he was glad to have unburdened himself. His uncle stood by, reassuring him that it was the right thing to do. Finbar Reeve knew that after he'd locked up Patrick Hanlon, his mission was to find Joseph Riordon before he disappeared. His dilemma was just who could he tell about his plans? If Patrick Hanlon's accusation of high ranking involvement was true, who could he trust in An Garda Siochana? The source of leaked information might come from anywhere, at any level. Whatever else he might decide to do, whatever the outcome, Finbar Reeve knew his duty was to tell a superior officer the details of the nexus of the investigations so far. At least one major crime had been effectively resolved. It wasn't something he could hide, even if he wanted to.

Failure to do so, would find him guilty of dereliction of duty, or worse.

28

Tom Ellison was on the verge of nodding off in the comfortable armchair, when a knock on the front door interrupted his reverie. He heard Mrs Murtagh speaking to the young sentry. Another voice interlaced the conversation and Mrs Murtagh entered the room, followed by a small man of slight build, wearing a voluminous, ill fitting grey mackintosh. Tom could see that the base colour was near-white, but it was overlaid with earthy stains. It gave the figure a troll – like appearance.

"This is Tyrone Connahay," Mrs Murtagh said, waiving the figure closer.

"He says he wanted to speak to you," she added with a hint of distrust.

As the man came away from the door and into the stronger light from the window, Tom Ellison recognised him as the man who knocked on his car window the previous night. They nodded in recognition. Mrs Murtagh continued the introduction

"I've known Tyrone since he was a boy and he's a good lad really," she tilted her head and continued "Although he's got into a few scrapes from time to time." Tom was amused to hear him described as "a lad", for as he looked closer, it was clear that Tyrone Connahay was about his own age: but his drawn features and slight stoop gave an instant impression of more advanced years.

"What was it you wanted to say?" Elizabeth asked, taking ownership of the situation.

"I wanted yer man to find the truth," he said, pointing at Ellison.

"About what?" she retorted, before Tom could muster the words.

"About the missing boy and all that."

It was as if a searchlight had been turned on in the room, and it fell on the gnarled figure of Tyrone Connahay. Tom, struggling for composure, by gesture invited the visitor to sit down.

"What is it you wanted to tell me?" he asked with barely hidden excitement.

"I thought you should know that I'm sure the boy's death wasn't an accident. You deserve that." Tom was almost afraid to ask the question, as so much depended on whether he could trust the unknown man.

"What do you know?"

"I only know that Michael McMahon knew what happened to the the boy."

"How do you know that?"

"At the time of his accident - you heard about that? Tom nodded.

"I was working part time as a porter in the hospital when he was brought in. Battered up he was. He wasn't long for this world, you could see that. Mary arrived just after the ambulance, ya know. I set him in the emergency room and waited for the doctor. Poor Mary was beside herself and wouldn't leave his side. She talked to him. The usual things, ya know. I was sure he couldn't hear most of it, but for a brief time he seemed to come to. He looked at her, grabbed her by the shoulder and said "Promise you won't say anything about the boy!"

Tom Ellison sat bolt upright. "What?"

"Real loud it was. She just said "I promise," An' that was it! The doctor arrived and we left the room. Minutes later he came out to tell her that Michael was dead." Tom Ellison listened intently to the account.

"Are you sure about this?"

"Certain!"

"What else?"

"That's all… at the time," it was as if his mind was in a different time and space. He smiled a smile that momentarily transformed his weathered face and continued.

"I've known Mary since childhood. We used to play together. The truth is, as I got older, I fancied her. And we stepped out a few times," He looked at the ceiling in embarrassment and added "After Michael's death, I went to the house to pay my respects. She was a mess. She hardly spoke a word, but when I was leaving she just came out with it. "You won't say anything either she said.

"She said that to you?" Tom responded.

"Yes. Y'see she knew I'd heard what was said at the hospital, but it wasn't me who brought it up. It just came from nowhere, so to speak. I asked what she meant by it, but she wouldn't say. After that I tried several times to see her, but she shut the door on me, so I gave up."

"Are you sure that's what Michael said?" Ellison asked, backtracking. "You could have misheard."

"There was nothing wrong with my hearing then or now! It was loud and clear," he replied indignantly.

"Why haven't you said all this before? Told the police?" The small man squirmed in his chair and said in a low voice.

"I've bin away."

"And why would that be?" interrupted Mrs Murtagh. Without allowing time for an answer, she turned to Ellison and said with a knowing nod of the head "I told you. Tyrone's had a few scrapes. How long this time Tyrone?"

"Two years."

Elizabeth Murtagh shot a glance in Tom's direction and the truth suddenly dawned on him. The storyteller sitting across from him, and the author of the postcard, were one in the same.

"You sent the cards!" It was an announcement and Tom knew it needed no response.

"When I first saw you at the lake I thought you was guilty. We all did at the time. Then I shared a cell with a lad who said he knew who'd taken the boy."

Tom Ellison's heart rose to his throat, and he could hardly speak. He grasped the arms of the chair. His mouth suddenly dry, he croaked "Who was it?"

"He wouldn't say a name, for sake of a beatin'… or worse. But I knew,"

"Then who?" desperation welled up in Tom's voice.

Connahay drew in a deep breath. "It was "the boyo's.""

Tom looked anxiously at Mrs Murtagh for confirmation of his fears.

"He means the "Provos," she confirmed.

The room was bursting with a stunned silence.

Connahay continued "T'was a farce, y'know. The Gardai didn't find anything, because they didn't want to find anything. They were frit."

The immensity of the story now gripped Tom Ellison and Mrs Murtagh, and they looked at each other with a mixture of astonishment and despair. How could it be? A small boy and the most feared organisation in The British Isles. *Was it true?* Over time, Tom had been haunted by how badly he might have miscalculated the danger of the trip. This was a shocking reminder, and he covered his eyes with his hand as if to block out the truth. Mrs Murtagh jumped into the silence and questioned Connahay whether the story was a fantasy, with him seeking revenge on the Gardai?

"I'd swear on mi mother's grave," he answered with a frown and a truculent lip.

"Why get in touch with me?" Tom asked.

"I read something in an old magazine. It's all we got inside," he complained.

"I thought how diabolical it was. There's a lot of us get fitted up," as if inviting Tom to join an exclusive club.

"So I sent the card," Connahay continued.

"What did you expect me to do?" asked Ellison.

"I don't know," he replied openly.

"How did you find me?"

"Prison library. I read in the magazine where you come from and I looked you up. There was only three Ellison's, so I sent a card to all three when I got out." A smile crossed his lips at his own ingenuity.

"When I heard you'd come to Drum, I was glad. When someone told me about poor Mary's passin', and it all seemed too much of a coincidence. Last night was the final straw!"

"Last night?"

"The shootin'!"

Tom had learned, from recent experience, of the speed with which news was passed in this rural community. He also knew how snippets of news were transformed into ill-considered gossip. However, he was not surprised at the failure to contain the unfolding story, in the face of such powerful forces.

Connahay's eyes bulged as he said "I'm guessin' they'll want to get rid of all of us. They'll find out about me for sure. Nothing secret for long," he said mournfully.

"You'll have to tell the police what you know," Ellison urged.

"Where would I start?" an agitated Connahay responded. "Why would they listen to me? They fitted me up over some car parts y'know,"

With lips pursed tight, Mrs Murtagh gave him a withering look of disdain and Tom Ellison was left uncertain of the truth of the accusation. Could it be that all

Connahay's tale was a fabrication from his biased imaginings? Yet it all seemed to hang together,

"I'll tell you what," interrupted Elizabeth Murtagh "I'll go and make us a cup of tea, and you can talk it over."

"Thank you," Ellison said, as he mulled over the extraordinary situation he found himself in. He tried to absorb the magnitude of what had been revealed.

His own experience had told him that visitors were in no danger at the hands of those involved in Ireland's conflict. Had he been so wrong? Should he, could he have known then that the cancer of the conflict which plagued the minds of factions were so deeply engrained on both sides of the border and knew no line that could not be crossed. In the years that followed it would result in violence in mainland Britain too.

The cruel randomness of the boy's fate took it beyond the bounds of a planned activity. However, Connahay's testimony had energised hope within him. Tom realised that Tyrone's incarceration would explain the time gap between the boy's disappearance and the mysterious postcard. He decided to park his doubts for the time being and concentrate on the man's allegations. Any doubt that the story was a fabrication was fast fading.

The two men sat motionless, neither wanting to begin the next phase of the conversation. Ellison saw the need to test the veracity of the claims as soon as possible, in stark contrast to Connahay's distrust of authority. A compromise seemed the only option, if the informant was to bring about what he had decided was "the right thing," On that they could agree. Connahay broke the silence.

"Can't you tell 'em?" he pleaded. "They'd take notice of you. You and Fin Reeve seemed to be getting on well last night in Reynold's."

"I can't just give them a theory. I'd have to tell them about you to make any sense. You would be a key witness. We have to trust someone."

"You might!" was the Irishman's sardonic rejoinder.

Ellison felt a rising tide of irritation at this reluctance.

"It's better that you tell them first, rather than them having to come out and get you," It was tersely put and with a hint of threat, and seemed to be having the desired effect, as Connahay tugged nervously at his ill-fitting coat's lapel. Finally he said "You'll contact them and you'll come with me?"

"Of course," said the delighted Tom Ellison. He took Connahay's bony hand and shook it vigorously.

"You're doing the right thing," he said, encouragingly.

"Let's hope so," Connahay replied, firming up his own grip and responding in kind.

Mrs Murtagh re-entered the room carrying a tray.

"Here we are then," she said sizing up the pair with a prolonged stare. She began to pour the tea.

"I knew you'd sort it out," she added, like someone in the process of wrapping up a parcel.

29

Finbar Reeve had known his boss Inspector Eric Blane for the whole of his police career, and had never had any doubt about his commitment to the rule of law. However, his trust in the integrity of the Gardai had been shaken and his own effectiveness within it damaged. Nevertheless he could find no reason to hide his concern from his immediate boss, who had little to do with the original search for the boy and its subsequent review. Blane, though often gruff and harrying, was a good policeman and Reeve knew that the cases he was presenting would be investigated fully, if Blane was involved. Blane shared with him a pride in An Garda Siochana, and he too resented dents in its reputation. Having arrested Patrick Hanlon on an initial charge of Perverting the Course of Justice, they had locked him up without fuss; to fester unnoticed.

In his office he outlined the case for action to Blane, emphasising that he thought that they were slightly ahead of the current game, due to Patrick Hanlon's confession. Reeve had kept his incarceration discreet because, as Riordon had been in the locality the day before, the hope was that his circle of protection still knew nothing of Hanlon's confession. Added to that, his disdain of The Gardai might have kept him close by. If there was a mole in the force, the cases would soon become public knowledge and Joe Riordon would evaporate into the ether. *Could they use the tiny edge and act quickly?*

The early day sun was fading outside, as Finbar Reeve and Eric Blane sat at the desk in a deserted office. This suited Finbar Reeve. He spent some time bringing his superior up to speed on the cases of the missing boy, Mary McMahon's death, and the shooting. He recounted the Hanlon confession, and listed their evidence to support it. They discussed the logistics on how to further pursue the evidence involving all three potential murders. Their immediate imperative was to get Joseph Riordon under lock and key.

The only clue to his whereabouts was his association with the Falcon pub. Reeve's search of their internal records had failed to reveal anything. No address, no car registration, no tax records. *Joe Riordon was a non-person!* On one level the lack of information did not surprise the two detectives, as so many of their compatriots seemed to live in a twilight economy outside the norm. They were more disappointed that, on inspection, police records did not reveal any past demeanours.

"Coincidence?" Reeve asked, wondering if the records had been tampered with. Blane, who had at first been sceptical of the Gardai involvement, raised his hands in a gesture of despair.

They studied a large scale map that occupied the centre of the desk, considering the virtues of an observation operation at the pub, against a house to house search in the area. Reeve theorised that habit and a sense of invincibility might draw Joe Riordon back to his favourite waterhole. Blane started by putting the case for, and against, the classic approach, the tried and tested method of tracking somebody down.

"We could mount a house to house search in the area before he gets spirited away." Blane lent on the desk in deep thought.

He pursed his lips and growled, "But we've no idea where he might be and we'd need a bucketful of men. Bags of money and drains come to mind." He was thinking of public reaction if it didn't deliver results. "There's only one road in and out of Gailey. That could be an advantage," Reeve responded. "If he was there, we could close the village down."

"He could go cross country," Blane reacted brusquely, fingering the map in a circular motion. "And you know what that would mean!"

They both knew the complication of collaboration between their force and the RUC, when swift action was needed would prove vital. They would have to reveal their hand, and experience told them that it should be avoided, if possible.

"Problem is, he doesn't live in the village. We don't really know where he's based," Reeve pressed the point home with a sweeping gesture over the map. Blane rose from his seat and stalked round the desk.

"O.K! Let's look at your alternatives," he said decisively. He was now set in pugnacious mode.

"We need some bloody good intelligence. What have you got?" Reeve shook his head disconsolately in response.

"Well we need to get some, bloody quick. Have we got anyone who lives there that we can trust?" Blane asked, thinking of local police informants. Reeve shook his head and thought for a while.

"Student Sibohan Farraday lives near there," he responded finally. At first the Inspector didn't recognise the name and gave Reeve quizzical look.

"I saw her just now. She's on duty." He had made an unnecessary visit to the support team office, in the hope of seeing the young trainee. Recognition dawned on Blane

"Oh yes! Farraday. What can she do, and can we trust her?" Blane had fully taken on board Reeve's concern over internal security.

"I think we can. She's been a Student officer in the force for a year, and came here from County Cork. She's bright and keen," he said with suppressed enthusiasm.

"Get her in here!" Blane responded. Reeve picked up the phone, dialled an internal number and said "Sibohan? Finbar! Got a minute?" he put the phone down.

"She's on her way,"

"Let's have a look at this piece of scum Riordon," Blane instructed. Reeve shuffled amongst the papers on the desk and passed a sheet to Blane. He looked down on a face that would not easily be forgotten. The long dark hair, the distinctive Roman nose, the piercing eyes and narrow mouth reminded him at once of Laurence Olivier in the film of Richard III.

"Nasty looking bastard! Where did we get this from?" he said, pointing to the photograph.

"At Mary's house. I found a newspaper cutting of him and Michael McMahon." Reeve was pleased with this bit of detection and added "Hanlon confirmed who it was. That's the original," Blane studied the photograph in silence, and then Reeve prompted "There's an enlargement?"

Finbar Reeve rummaged through his paperwork and produced another sheet and handed it to Blane. It showed Riordan and McMahon, arms round each other in a triumphant pose, holding a trophy. Blane laid it on the desk and lent forward for close inspection. After a moment, he held the photograph out for Reeve to look at.

"Do you see what I see?" Casting his eye over the photograph, Reeve grimaced and shook his head.

"Above their heads in the background!" Blane prompted. "The sign... A.. L.. C.. O.. N. Falcon!" Reeve uttered a curse. In the tumultuous events of the last two days he had missed it. He was annoyed with himself for a moment; then acknowledged his boss' keen eye.

"Well spotted!"

"You rang sir," Sibohan said jokingly as she entered Reeve's office; then recognised the presence of Inspector Blane.

"Sorry Sir!" she mumbled deferentially.

"Sit down Farraday," said Blane. Reeve stood up and offered her his chair.

"Can I trust you Farraday?" Blane said slowly and with a weight of tone that left no doubt as to the seriousness of the question.

"'Course sir!" her resentment of the question was clear.

"I gather you live near Gailey?" She nodded in response. Stretching across the desk, he handed her the press cutting.

"Do you know either of these men?" She scrutinised the picture with eyes screwed up for better clarity, and then answered,

"The one on the right, I seem to know him. Not the other one." The one on the right was Riordon. Michael McMahon was on the left.

"Michael McMahon died before Student Farraday joined us," confirmed Reeve.

"Where do you think you know this man from," Blane persisted. She gazed fixedly at the picture for a long time.

Finally, she said "The hair. It's too long," she said, masking off parts of the image with her hand. "But the face is familiar."

"Familiar?"

"I know this one...I'm not sure...."

"Think woman!" Blane snapped impatiently.

Sibohan Farraday looked up from the desk, and very deliberately said "Thinking takes time...sir!"

Reeve smiled inside and Blane visibly melted at the rebuke. Resuming her scan of the clipping, trainee Farraday pursed her lips in thought.

Then suddenly she said "Got it! I've seen this one at the pub. Bit of a darts player."

Then she said "No! No!" It was more than that, something of a celebrity. He's a top player."

"You sure it's the same man?"

"Yes sir!" she replied without hesitation. "Hair's different though," she added as an afterthought.

"Go to the pub a lot do you?"

"No sir!" she said in mild indignation, assuming that an imagined rebuke from the starchy detective would follow.

"I've been half a dozen times with friends."

"Same day of the week? Same time?" Blane pressed.

"Tuesday. It's always been a Tuesday. Match night and sandwiches," she responded.

"When did you last see him there?" Blane urged.

"About a month ago. It was my friend's birthday. Can you tell me what this is about sir?" she asked respectfully.

Blane studied her carefully. Although he was not prepared to show it, he liked the way she had held her corner. Feisty! Although she was a woman, perhaps she might be a useful tool in the search for Joe Riordon. He looked quizzically at Reeve, seeking confirmation that the young trainee was to be trusted with knowledge of whatever was to be their next move. Reeve nodded. Blane began by making sure she understood the confidentiality of the information that he was about to share with her, but without revealing the extent of his concern over internal security. He filled in the history of the case of the missing boy. She listened intently to the gruff detective, as he drew together the links between that case and recent events. The enormity of the situation was now sinking in, and she gasped at the details that Blane was revealing. He emphasized the need to track down the man she had just identified.

"If we're to set up an observation," he continued "we would benefit from your local knowledge." Blane pre-empted her unspoken question.

"You come highly recommended," Blane said with a sideways glance in Reeve's direction. She too was looking at Reeve for a sign of his reaction. Her pulse quickened, as with a tilt of his head away from Blane, he winked at her.

"I'm yer man sir," she joked instinctively, feigning a salute. She knew at once, from his disapproving look, that Blane was not amused. On his part he wondered if this flippant young girl really was up to the job, but he knew that time for reflection was not a luxury they could afford.

"Let's get down to business!" he snapped. "Fin it's your case. How d'ya think we should play it?

Finbar Reeve nodded in appreciation of his boss' trust. He had become convinced that, if they were to get a resolution of the cases, and arrest Riordon, there might be a small window of opportunity in which to track him down, before he got wind of their activities. He was considering a plan in which Sibohan Farraday's credibility as a local girl would work to their advantage, without putting her in jeopardy. He crouched down beside her and looked at her intently.

"I think if we can get you into the pub on some pretext or other, you can tell us if Riordon is there. He's a canny sod, so he'd spot any of our vehicles close by, but if we stood a way off, you could radio in. What do you think?"

Sibohan was stirred with excitement. She had thought it would be a long time before she might get into such close contact with serious crime. The prospect was exhilarating beyond measure for the young hopeful. She looked at Reeve and Blane in turn. Even without answering, she assumed a more proactive role. "I collect for a local charity. That could be my "in", she offered. Blane looked quizzically at Reeve.

"You done that before?" Blane asked and added "It must look natural."

"Only once at The Falcon, but there's folk who know that I do it. It would work," she responded. It was full of a youthful confidence, alien to Blane and, to a lesser extent, Reeve.

They could no longer prevaricate. With their combined police experience, they both knew they had reached a tipping point. Was this fledgling plan worthy of the risks to the young woman and to their own careers?

"It's like something from a bad crime thriller," Blane said sarcastically, but Reeve sensed that the usually decisive Blane had not yet rejected the idea. Blane needed a push and his Detective Sergeant reminded him that, if successful, it would mean they had turned about a long term failure that had blighted the force, and for which they had both felt some culpability.

"I think it's worth the risk, if Sibohan agrees. What's the worst the bosses can do?" Reeve wasn't sure of his attempt at a joke, but it seemed to stir up Blane's long held membership of the Awkward Club.

"They could try and sack us!" It was a challenge to authority and was a response that Reeve had hoped for. The phone rang at his elbow, breaking the growing tension.

"Detective Sergeant Reeve." he announced on picking it up. He recognised the caller straight away. "Hello Tom," he answered.

"I know Tyrone well," Reeve said, without enthusiasm. On the other end, in a voice quivering with excitement, Tom Ellison re-told the arrival of the eccentric visitor. All that he had heard from the man, who confessed to sending the postcards, convinced him that they were on to something.

After listening for a while Reeve said "You believe him? He really overheard it?" Reeve listened intently to the long answer.

In an unruffled voice he said "Calm down Tom. Did he say who he thought was covering things up?" Reeve knew there would always be a large question mark against anything that Tyrone Connahay said. The answer to his question was clearly disappointing, and it was reflected in a twist of his lips.

"But no names?" he repeated. When the effusive story was complete, Reeve said "That's great news Tom. We're up and running, without, mentioning his own progress.

"You bring him over here and we'll get a statement." His delight for the Englishman's indefatigable perseverance knew no bounds, and he said "That's brilliant Tom. Well done! See you soon."

He put the phone down and repeated the details of the conversation to Eric Blane, who responded with his own compliment. Finbar Reeve knew this last evidence did not add substantially to his own discoveries, but it was reassuring that it gave verification to the expanding investigations. There were crucial decisions to be made.

"What do you say Chief?" He rarely used the soubriquet, but it felt right in that moment.

"We go for it, that's what we do! Eh Sibohan?" There was a "gung ho" resonance in what amounted to a call to arms, which surprised and delighted Finbar Reeve and excited his young friend.

"Let's get down to detail!" Inspector Eric Blane was fired up in a way Reeve had rarely seen before.

The next two hours were spent developing a plan for action. Reeve knew that first he had to formally question the priest's nephew, before he could detain him longer. He believed that Patrick Hanlon would willingly accept being held in Protected Custody to assuage the abject terror that he felt. Once the undertaker was legitimately taken out of circulation, they could concentrate on the search for Riordon.

Blane was confident that he could make a request for the necessary resources, but it should be done as late in the day as possible, to avoid their target being forewarned. Growing in confidence, Sibohan began to build up her own cover story for her assignment, which the two detectives could not fault. Reeve caught a glimpse of Blane's growing respect for the vivacious young woman, and he marvelled at it. Blane's misogyny had long been a byword in Gardai circles.

Taking a firm grip on the investigation, Blane warned "If we are going to be involved on the ground, I think that we should trust at least one other person with the facts. Just in case." They looked at each other quizzically.

"Sam Irons!" they said in unison.

When Finbar Reeve had deposited Patrick Hanlon in the single cell at the tiny station in Drumlasheen, it was Sam Irons, his former mentor that he asked to keep the arrest under wraps. Sergeant Samuel Irons, near to retirement, and rarely seen out in the field, was the desk officer at Drumlasheen. He was respected for his dependability and integrity. He was the public face of the Gardai in Drumlasheen. Everyone and everything went past Sam Irons. They both knew that he had a tried and trusted loyalty to the force. He could be relied upon to be discreet and judge the situation decisively as the strategy unfolded. Detective Inspector and Detective Constable were both content that they had engineered the fast moving investigation as well as could be expected. It all seemed to fit. They gave short shrift to any thought of failure.

Questioning Tyrone Connahay later was a frustration that Reeve could have done without, as the reluctant informant sought to apportion most of the troubles in his life to the police. But, when Reeve was able to separate the bile from his narrative, it contained subtle links to all of the three cases.

30

Finbar Reeve stirred from brief, shallow, sleep to the sound of the early birds practicing their tunes outside the bedroom window of his flat. He sat up in bed and looked out on wispy grey clouds scudding across a leaden sky. It didn't augur well for the day ahead. It was to be a defining day, one way or another, he thought. In the dark hours before, with sleep banished to the corners of his mind, he had gone through the day that he had mapped out with Blane. He knew that their decision to waylay Joe Riordon, if he was to appear at the Falcon Inn, was a chancy thing, but the rewards would be high. He had a lingering concern for Sibohan Farraday's safety, but he saw how credible her fund raising guise would be. He had a feeling that she would wear the mantle of their confidence in her, with consummate ease. She just needed to spot the man and get out. He fingered through the papers that were on his bedside table, a reminder of the work still to do.

Having dressed, he prepared a breakfast of egg, sausage and toast. He wasn't sure when he would get his next proper meal. He prepared a large flask of coffee, a pre-requisite for these occasions, and extra rounds of toast – just in case.

He decided to walk the short distance to the Police station.

He took in deep breaths of the damp, cold, Leitrim air, stirring body and brain into action.

Drumlasheen had not yet come to life, and he was a solitary figure on Main Street. Ghostly movements behind the windows of shops, not yet open, were the only hint of life. He passed the Post Office, one small light burning over the counter in the back, hinting that newspapers were being sorted. Outside, still in place from the previous day, a sandwich board announced "NEW MOVING STATUE. SENSATIONAL SIGHTINGS!"

Earlier that year, the first moving statues phenomena had occurred in Ballinspittle, County Cork, where statues of the Virgin Mary were reported to have moved spontaneously. It had caused a sensation throughout the country and world wide. Since then a number of phenomenon had been reported, sometimes involving mysterious stains on church walls. The footnote on the board read "Bishop declares the phenomenon 'an illusion'." Reeve smiled at the division that had split the whole community. He knew that there were many in Drumlasheen who believed that the happenings were signs from their God.

Having replaced the two one-man police houses in the district, policing in Drumlasheen was now housed in a converted saddlers shop half way up the High Street. Simply but effectively, it played home to the representatives of law and order and, on rare occasion, hosted petty criminals and drunks in the single cell in the basement. In the floor above, the old stock room had been made into accommodations for an officer. A large sign over the door announced "An Garda Síochána".

A tired bell tinkled as he pushed the door open. A large man with a moon like face, tiny sparkling eyes and hair the colour of broken biscuits sat at a desk, just settling in to his daily duties. He stood up as soon as he recognised Reeve and marched forward, hand held out in welcome.

"Well done son! You were right all along," he said, shaking Reeve's hand vigorously and slapping him on the shoulder. "Eric's filled me in." Inspector Eric Blane had left the previous night's meeting and gone straight to Sam Irons to fill him in on their basic plan and to establish his support. They had shared a glass or two and talked well into the night.

Reeve had spent the first two years of his service under the wing of Sam Irons, and owed the man, who was the district representative of the Police Federation, a great deal. He was a doughty advocate for "the men on the ground".

Sam Irons, Finbar Reeve and Eric Blane were bound together by a commitment to maintain justice. Each had his own way of working. Blane was brusque and blustery, Reeve was instinctive and caring, and Irons was the bucolic extravert with strong opinions and great powers of persuasion. But they were as one when it came to getting the job done.

"I knew Joe Riordon was scum," he muttered. "We've come close a few times, but he's a slippery sod. We need to get him on this one. Where do we start?" Reeve pointed in the direction of the cell.

"We need to persuade that bastard that he's best off here, for the time being."

"That won't be difficult. I've already had a word. He's scared shitless."

"Do you think Protective Custody will hold?" Reeve asked seeking the advice of the more experienced man.

"What's the difference – if he agrees," replied Irons with a wink. The conspiracy between the three was complete.

Reeve made his way through the desk area to the miniscule interview room beyond. Carefully placing a sheet of paper and a pen on the table in the centre of the room, he removed his jacket and put it on the back of one of the two chairs. He made his way along a narrow corridor and down steps to the cell below.

Taking the key from a hook on the wall, Reeve turned the lock and pulled hard on the heavy door. The cell was as basic as you could get. Its only furniture was a wooden plank crudely bracketed to the wall, serving the dual purpose as a seat and a bed. In the corner was a galvanised bucket.

Crouched forward, his hands to his head, Patrick Hanlon looked up as Reeve entered. His face was a near perfect match to the grey painted walls around him. In contrast his eyes were vivid red hollows. His hands trembled as he forced himself to sit up. He started to sob heavily. Was he crying through contrition or fear? Reeve felt no sympathy for his disintegrated state. Here was a man capable of taking a young child, and hiding him from his mother forever. Reeve could make no allowances.

"Come this way Mr Hanlon," he said formally.

The prisoner stopped crying at once, and slowly raised himself from his seat, and was ushered up the stairs and into interview room, where Finbar Reeve sat down. Hanlon stood, as if waiting for permission to do likewise. Reeve gestured in the direction of the chair opposite, and Hanlon slowly eased himself into place.

"I havn't got much time sir, so I'll cut to the chase. For now, I need a brief record of what you told me yesterday, and also your written request to remain in protective custody. We can go into more detail later, when we've caught Joe Riordon." Reeve thought that the mention of his prisoner's nemesis would inject a dash of urgency into the situation.

"Yes of course! Thank you!" Hanlon lent across the table and made a grab for the Garda's hand, which was removed quickly. "What do you want me to say?"

"Just tell the truth sir."

Reeve was careful not to lead his prisoner in any way, as he wrote out his statement, punctuated by expressions of remorse, which Reeve found obnoxious. He read it through, and he thought it met his needs. He asked Hanlon to read it through again and sign it. As he did, he looked at Reeve for a sign of approval. A disdainful look was the response. Nothing was said as Reeve returned his prisoner to the cell, pushing the door behind him hard, to ensure an earth trembling bang. Reeve felt better for that!

Sam Irons met him at the front desk, a newspaper held aloft.

"I thought I'd seen something," he said laying the paper flat on the desk and pointing to a small piece on the back Sports page of The Leitrim Observer.

Reeve read it out. "Roscommon Shield. The deciding match in the Roscommon Shield will take place at the Falcon in Gailey on Wednesday next, between the Falconers and The Bell Inn". Would they have a better chance for their man to be there? Reeve thought.

"You jammy bugger!" Irons exclaimed triumphantly. "That's tonight. He'll be there, you can bet. He's an arrogant sod! Go and get him!" They clasped palms in congratulation. Sam Irons joyfully agreed on his role in the plan and his support for it.

Despite wanting to limit the number of people possessing information, Finbar Reeve had felt all along that he owed it to Tom Ellison to keep him informed. He'd promised it! Without him, so may matters would have remained suppressed.

The house was close by, so he soon found himself outside of number three Weir Lane acknowledging the salute of the officer on guard. In response to his knock, the door was opened by Elizabeth Murtagh.

"Morning Mrs Murtagh," he said. "Can I speak to Mr

Ellison please?"

"Come in Finbar," she said with a welcoming sweep of her arm. "He's in the sitting room." She waited for an invitation to join them. It didn't come.

"Thank you," said Reeve, as he opened the door to the sitting room. He carefully closed the door behind him and Tom Ellison stood up from his chair, his face alight with expectation. Reeve sat down without speaking and Tom Ellison followed suit.

"I want you to understand that what is said here does not go any further. EVER!" he stressed. Ellison knew from the stony look on Reeve's face that this pact was non-negotiable and replied quickly "Of course!" After Reeve had outlined his plan to capture Joe Riordon, he said "I promise you we're gonna get him. You were right all along! It was never an accident! We know that now."

The pressure of frustration and soul searching that had built up in Tom Ellison over years, burst within him. Tears welled up from the darkest of places, and he sobbed uncontrollably. Finbar Reeve let the moment expire naturally, not saying a word. He understood that this was the teacher's moment.

Gaining some control, Tom Ellison, stared through tearful eyes at Garda Reeve; his friend Finbar. He drew in a gasp of air and, through trembling lips, he whispered "Thank you!"

Reeve felt himself on the verge of a tear at the man's joy.

"Mrs Murtagh will find out soon enough," he said, reaffirming the promise that had just passed between them.

"Is there anything I can do?" Ellison asked.

"I think you've done enough!" he said with a smile "Without you we'd have been nowhere." Tom Ellison was overcome by the accolade and moved round the table and took Reeve by the hand.

"Good Luck!"

It doesn't seem enough, Tom thought, but eloquence had deserted him.

Reeve nodded in return. He moved to the door and then turned towards the kitchen. He knocked gently on the kitchen door, hoping that Mrs Murtagh would not hear it, giving him an excuse to leave without cross examination, but she responded instantly and asked,

"You away Finbar?" He nodded, and her face sagged in disappointment. She was enjoying the excitement that had burst its way into her life.

"Yes…Things to do," he said feebly. He reached the safety of the front door, dipped his head in thanks, and was gone.

"Well!" she said, hands on her hips and arms akimbo.

Finbar Reeve left the Murtagh house, relieved at the outcome of his unofficial visit, but glad that had helped to take a great weight from Tom Ellison's shoulders. Now he had his own dragons to slay. Reeve picked up his car from home, and decided to do a detour to remind himself of the geography around The Falcon Inn at Gailey.

He drove up the Main Street of Drumlasheen, which, by now, had stirred into the same busy, but unhurried, pattern of life typical of small Irish towns. He crossed the river bridge and continued up past the Infant School and the sports field beyond, where he had played Gaelic football and rugby in his teens. The Dairy was the only building of industrial scale in that part of the town and provide the bulk of work for the local community. Rising out of the village, his car climbed to Fenan Hill, the highest point in the immediate area. At its summit, a flat featureless landscape presented itself, as far as the eye could see, made up of coarse grass and heathers. A scattering of small pools of standing water confirmed its identity as a blanket bog – so called because the grassy surface serves as a blanket for the rich, dark peat that lies beneath. Digging the peat had always been a vital part of the rural community. Commercial digging provided an income for some, and for many a free source of fuel.

In the distance, as the road dipped slightly below him, Finbar Reeve could see the scatter of white buildings of Gailey hamlet, set startlingly against the earthy colours of the surrounding landscape. The Falcon Inn sat in the middle of a tiny cluster of cottages and small holdings. It proudly announced itself as "The Best of The Best." It was a claim that, from the outside at least, could be justified by its carefully manicured lawn and freshly painted exterior. As he eased past it, Reeve remembered from his youth, that it had been a tiny cottage pub, small but cosy on the inside.

Now it had the addition a single story function room. It was a long shed-like structure that was disproportionate to the original, and without redeeming architectural details. Reeve reckoned it could seat about two hundred and fifty at a pinch It had become a venue for the show bands that had become so popular since the 1950's. Six to eight was the usual size of these ear splitting, crowd pleasing groups, who could be relied upon to make a room-bursting sound with their brass and wind sections.

Reeve made mental notes of the sizeable car parking area behind the function room, as well as the position of entrances and exits. His next concern was to find a concealed spot, far enough away not to attract attention, but near enough for his team to move in quickly on the target, should Riordon be there!

He took a moment to consider the implications of drawing a blank, and just as quickly thrust it to the back of his mind. He was now beyond the little scatter of dwellings that made up Gailey and caught a glimpse of a path which, as he remembered, lead to a derelict old cow shed, abandoned for as long as he could remember. He reversed down the rough, rutted path and checked through his rear window that the ramshackle building had not changed over years and still looked unused. He moved out back on to the road, now facing the direction from which he had just come. Confirming his first impressions as he passed The Falcon, Finbar Reeve felt he now had a grip on the logistics of the plan that he and Blane had conceived. He headed for District H.Q.

The watery sky of earlier had become a threatening mixture of puce tinged with green, which he knew bode for a wet night to come.

31

Finbar Reeve and Eric Blane had arranged to meet at noon to finalise their basic plan, as well as to put in place any contingency plans they might need, if their strategy failed. It was now ten thirty and Blane had not appeared or made contact. These were worrying moments for Finbar Reeve, as he sat on the corner of his desk, resisting the thought that their plan had been obstructed from above. Sibohan Farraday sat in the chair opposite, her excitement undaunted. Her presence caused knowing looks amongst the three detectives working at the desks nearby. Nothing was said, but Finbar Reeve knew he was in for full- on ribaldry, in time. He went over her role and made it clear that all he expected of her was that, if Joe Riordon appeared, she informed him. Nothing else was required, he insisted.

"You're the boss." she said with a smile that hinted at something more. For a moment, Reeve was consumed with a desire to enter the game that she had clearly initiated. His moment was gone, as Eric Blane entered, dripping from head to foot from the rain that had intensified into a torrent over the morning.

"What a feckin game!" he barked as he entered the office shaking off the rain and taking off his overcoat. On seeing Sibohan Farraday, he added a "Sorry!" that lacked conviction.

"I've just spent three hours trying to set up this job. It's like knitting bloody spaghetti. I've tried to called in favours."

At once Reeve began to fear that their need for secrecy had been compromised. Blane saw the look of disappointment that his colleague had failed to conceal, and added with a smirk "But we're on!"

Reeve bristled with excitement and in a reflex action made a grab for Sibohan's hand. A nervous smile passed between them as they quickly disengaged.

"I managed to convince my boss that this is a bit of a fishing trip and we don't need the full treatment. As far as he knows, we have an iffy lead on a suspect for yesterday's shooting and … nothing else."

Blane explained that his first job was to assemble a number of men to support the operation, should they have to move in to arrest Riordan. The pub was likely to be full, so crowd control might be needed to empty the building.

"And of course there's always the odd boyo about who's looking for a rumble," It was said with more than a hint of hidden anticipation.

"So," he said with untypical drama "we've been given that lot out there for the night." He pointed to the three young officers outside, now heads down, but ears straining.

"Before you complain, it was the best I could do without revealing our hand." Reeve was not even thinking of complaining, as he was amazed that his boss had managed such a coup. He was sure that Blane had picked out these young officers because they had no back history or connection with the earlier cases.

"Doing it that way, if it goes tits up, we settle back on the investigation in the usual way. What the hell happens if we catch him is another matter," Blane said ironically.

Leaving Reeve and Sibohan to take in these developments, Blane went to the door and shouted "You lot, in else."

The three young Garda sheepishly made their way to the office, uncertain of what the summons was about. They entered in file. First in was Herbert "Herby" Collins a tall athletic figure, his dark hair sliding into a fringe down his forehead, his open face expressing his willing and dependable nature.. At his shoulder was fair haired lady's man Daniel Smythe. His good looks did not flatter to deceive. A sharp mind lay behind those blue eyes. Last in the triumvirate was James Artherton, his stocky body, topped by a head that looked out of proportion and exaggerated by a mop of black curly hair. Atherton was a grafter, short on initiative but strong on perseverance. They gathered nervously inside the door.

Blane explained the unsolved case of the missing English schoolboy and its link with recent events.

"You three are mine for the rest of the day. Before it ends we might have put right a wrong that has besmirched the Gardai for years. We have a slight chance of capturing one Joseph Riordon of this parish, who has definitely committed one murder, possibly three, and goodness knows what else."

There was simultaneous intake of breath, which seemed as if they were about to break into unison song. Blane outlined the sequence of events that led to this point in the investigation.

"We believe he might appear at The Falcon Pub tonight."

He doesn't know we are on his tail. Up to now! That might give us a slight advantage. He's arrogant enough to carry on with his normal life. He has friends. He feels protected. We have to be smart enough to catch him on the hop."

Blane allowed the concept to sink in. An acknowledging look and a nod spread through the three men, then he added. "I'll let Detective Reeve fill you in on the details."

"If you've never met, this is Joseph Riordon!" Reeve moved to the blackboard and pinned the enlarged picture of their prey on the wooden edge.

"Not quite as we believe he looks now. Older. The hair is cut shorter, but it's a face to be remembered. Information tells us that he would not want to miss a darts match tonight. The problem is, if we have any chance, it'll depend on surprise. We need to be sure he's there before we go in. We need someone up close."

Reeve explained that Sibohan could get in to the pub without creating suspicion, and he explained her cover story. Degrees of scepticism showed on the faces of the three detectives, which clearly upset the young trainee.

"Can I say something Sir?" she asked. Reeve nodded consent.

"I've been in there before with my charity tin. It'll seem perfectly natural. They like children's charities. I know I can do it," she said, carelessly brushing her hair from her eyes.

Pointing in Blane's direction, Reeve said "We've weighed this up and it's as good a plan as we can come up with in the time. We want this bastard! We need him!" It was said with unbridled passion that could not be gainsaid, and the trio vigorously nodded their agreement.

Reeve moved towards the blackboard and, taking up the stick of yellow chalk, proceeded to draw a plan of the Falcon Inn and its surroundings. He included details that he had noted in his hurried reconnaissance trip earlier, and outlined the sequence of events he had envisioned, if the man was spotted. By now the three young detectives were absorbed in the strategy and Blane was clear that it was also necessary to consider in what circumstance things could go amiss; and that they all understood their role, if it did.

"It better not!" Blane emphasized, one side of his parting falling over his eyes.

"We leave here at six. We could be late back. You're all big boys. No need to ring yer mammy. Any questions?" Herby Collins asked the question they all wanted to know.

"Are we armed sir?

"Yes!" he replied at once. I don't need to tell you that I hope we can avoid using 'em; but be prepared. We must assume he will be armed. This shite-hawk is ruthless and won't think twice about shooting, so we must separate him from the crowd quickly. I want him!" It was the final note in a crescendo, and was delivered with mounting passion. Then in a deliberately subdued tone he said "Better alive than not!"

They all understood. They were as prepared as they could be. There was a tangible feeling of excitement in the room.

32

Five forty five, and the members of "Operation Elvis" (a name invented by Garda Daniel Smythe in memory of the king of Rock and Roll) gathered for a final briefing. Inspector Eric Blane stood in front of the blackboard, with the freshly drawn schematic of the operation showing a timeline and a ground plan of the Falcon Inn. Using a wooden ruler as a pointer, he emphasised the key points for the last time. When he had finished, he invited Finbar Reeve to have the last word. He stood grim-faced.

"We're all proud Irishmen I know. Some people have great sympathy for "The Cause" he said. "Whatever your view about the fenians and their friends, I believe no one here has any time for those who kill women and children. This man Riordon is one of those. Let's treat him as that," he puffed out his cheeks in relief, as preparation had come to an end, and the task was now live. "Good Luck!" he added.

Rain was falling heavily as the white unmarked van moved down the road into Gailey. They had planned to be in position before people gathered for the darts match. As they entered the village and passed the Falcon pub, the bad weather and their early arrival seemed to have worked in their favour, as there was not a soul about. With as little disturbance as possible, they secreted their vehicle behind the tumbled down barn, well out of sight from the road. Satisfied that they were well positioned, they settled down for what, at best, was a long wait for any action and, at worst, a total waste of time. Conversations were brief and spoken in muted tones. Support for the idea of the operation was unanimous, but they all shared a significant doubt as to its outcome, none more than Eric Blane and Finbar Reeve – its instigators.

Their doubts were answered by Jamie Atherton "We can always take 'em on at darts," he said. It broke the silence and released the growing tension.

"You alright?" Finbar said to Sibohan, with an encouraging smile.

"Fine!" she answered in return.

"Now don't forget, one long press and then get out of there," he insisted.

They had decided to use the transmit button on the radio that she was to carry in her handbag, to signal that their target was in place. His concern for her safety matched his desire to catch Riordon. Sibohan tried not to let her nervousness show. She was gripped by a mixture of fear and excitement. A fear, not for her personal safety, but at the thought that she might not carry off the deceit that was central to the plan. The excitement was in being asked to be involved.

She had picked up a collection tin from her friend Maire, and had to be at her most devious to reject her friend's offer to come along with her. She explained that it was really all a cunning ploy to see this gorgeous guy who she knew would be there.

"Wink! Wink!" she joked." "Who knows what might follow?" Maire accepted the story and offered the loan of her new faux-gold earrings, which Sibohan took to re-enforce the deception.

During the next half hour, from their hidden position, they had no idea how many people had arrived at The Falcon, but there had been a brief let up in the rain. At quarter to seven they all wished Sibohan "Good Luck." as she climbed out of the crowded van with as much elegance as she could.

She opened an umbrella, turned and gave a thumbs-up sign. She tilted herself against a gentle drizzle, protecting her collection tin under her coat, and made her way towards The Falcon Inn. A sudden burst of heavier rain hurried her to the porch over the front door. She shook her umbrella and opened the door to the cosy bar that was the entirety of the old Falcon pub. An old man, who might have been there since lunch time, sat in the corner next to an ingle nook fireplace. Slabs of dark chocolate coloured peat were piled inside, in early preparation for colder days.

"Hello darlin'," was the cheery greeting from the middle aged, heavily made up woman behind the bar. Sibohan knew her as Bernadette. The bar was her domain, and her gregarious personality was reflected in the bright curtains, matched slip- on seat covers and the weird collection of bric-a-brac, from tea pots and copper bed warmers to milk ladles and an old fashioned blunderbuss, decorating a high shelf running along three walls of the bar room. Sibohan took off her green coat with the fur collar and shook it, before putting it on a hook just inside the door. She hooked the collection tin over her arm.

"What'll it be," greeted her as she reached the bar.

"Cinzano and lemonade please Bernadette!" While the drink was being assembled, she held up the tin and asked "Bernadette, can I collect for the children's home tonight?"

"Of course you can darlin'," was the ready reply, as she placed the fizzing drink on the bar and popped a cherry on a stick into it.

"Not very busy tonight," Sibohan started the conversation that she hoped would get her the information she needed. The landlady confirmed that very soon a large crowd was expected to be in for the darts final.

"Biggest night of the year," she said proudly.

"Let's hope so," Sibohan said, struggling to hide her excitement.

Bernadette suggested that Sibohan take her collection tin round during the refreshment break in the match, and calculated that this would be about nine o'clock. It was now just before seven. Up to that moment she had felt very calm in her role, it having been minutely planned out for her. This was something they had not planned for. If she was to be authentic, she would have to agree to this arrangement. She had no way of letting Finbar and the others know the change of the timing.

A brief hesitation and "That's how it's got to be," she resolved.

Her poise restored, she remained seated on a stool at the end of the bar, as numbers grew slowly. It was usual practice to have the first drink in the cosy house bar and thereafter buy from the bar set up in the function room. From her position she could size up everyone who came in through the front door. A connecting door, that allowed entrance from the rear car park, was next to where she was sitting: so a quick look up would go unmarked. The atmosphere in the room became more and more excitable as opposing fans arrived. The pre match high jinks were good tempered, but it was seated in fierce rivalry. She wondered whether her memory of their quarry would stand up. It had been a month or so since she had seen him, although she'd spent some time closely scrutinising the photograph that Finbar had given her. She swivelled on the stool and, as she did, she scanned the room.

Her heart missed a beat. In the far corner of the bar, a man, whom she had not noticed before, sat in the middle of a group of friends. There was something about the face she recognised. Her memory was at full stretch. The dark hair, the piercing eyes and the slanting nose were all irrefutable, she thought. She fiddled inside he handbag and searched for the transmit button. It was a mind – numbing moment.

Suddenly the figures parted and, to her astonishment, it was clear that the man she had homed in on was in a wheelchair. She hadn't notice him before. He must have been wheeled in; and he and his wheelchair blocked from her view. She looked hard at the man and although the facial characteristics vaguely matched, as he turned his head the awful diagonal scar above his right eye was clear. She had allowed her judgement to be affected by her excitement. Everything she had learned about the man meant that this couldn't be Riordon!

On closer examination, she saw that the face lacked the impact that Joseph Riordon's had had on her. She was ashamed of her mistake, and was relieved that she had not set a disaster in motion. It was a sobering thought and, for a moment, she doubted her ability to match up to the task. She took in a deep breath and determined to be more judicious.

By now the noise in the tightly packed bar had become ear slitting. People came to the side door, looked in on the crowd and turned about. Slowly individuals and groups started to make their way to the side door, which also lead to the function room. Siobhan allowed the bar to empty, leaving a couple of non darts aficionados in conversation with the old man next to the fireplace. She moved towards them and shook her tin. They squeezed a few coins into the slot. Bernadette emptied in the contents of bar's collection jar "to set things off."

The passage through to the function room had toilet facilities to left and right and a double door that opened up to the back of the room. In this case, room was really a misnomer, as the space she entered was more like an aircraft hangar. A high ceiling and width about the same, gave it a square, box- like aspect.

At the far end was an elevated stage, bombarded in a harsh light from battens of spotlights hung from the ceiling. The centre piece was a small stage with a dart board and highlighted from the spotlight above. At the side, a man was giving a final wipe to the scoreboard. Round tables surrounded by chairs filled the floor area to capacity. Tables nearest to the stage area had already been taken, and the room was starting to look pretty full. Next to the double door was the bar. No temporary structure this, but purpose built and vandal-proof with a retractable grill. Sibohan decided to set herself up on one of the chairs at a table nearest the bar. At once a fresh face young man sidled into view, and sitting down on the chair opposite and without a whiff of self-doubt announced "I'm Shaun… and you are?"

"Engaged!" she said brutally. Deflation was total and he returned to a sniggering group of juveniles at a nearby table, and she moved to a single chair in an alcove next to the doors.

Sibohan cast an eye over the crowd. The man in the wheelchair was still the closest match to her prey. Had he failed to turn up? The combatants in the match were starting to gather next to the stage. Shouts of support and derision mingle, and somebody had brought in an old car horn that burst through the noise. Then, in the middle of a relative silence, the master of ceremonies for the night, announced over the PA system.

"Ladies and gentlemen! Here are the captains of the teams for tonight's decider. For The Bell Inn it's Colin Dyer." Fierce clapping and hoots of support and derision met the name. Before it faded he added "And captain for the Falcon… Joe Riordon!" The noise swelled at the name, as the man at the scoreboard turned and, with arms raised acknowledged the crowd.

"My God it's him!" She was knocked aback at the thought. Composure gone, for a moment she was transfixed. She lent forward and screwed her eyes up for better focus. There was no doubt. Even without the name she would recognise this man. It surely was a face to remember. Handsome to some! There was arrogance in the way he held himself, that spoke of unfettered self-confidence and ruthless chauvinism. She knew some women would find it exciting, and some men inspiring.

"Here is Finn MacCool, long mourned leader of The Brotherhood," she thought.

She guessed that Riordon must have been in the function room all the time. She upbraided herself for not checking earlier, before the crowd grew. She looked around to ensure she was not observed, before sliding her hand into her handbag and located the transmit button. Fingers trembling, she pressed on it hard, and silently counted up to twenty before releasing it. Her mission was complete and her instructions clear.

"Get out of there!" Finbar Reeve had said.

As she made to stand, she turned her head and saw landlady Bernadette standing by the door and joining in enthusiastically with the applause. Did it matter now whether she blew her cover and left? Instantly she determined to hold fast and maintain the pretence. She sat back, a false smile of approval disguising her anxiety.

Players started to assemble at the edge of the stage to a chorus of rallying calls.

"Ladies and gentlemen! The Falcon to throw first," announced the Master of Ceremonies.

The tall figure of Joe Riordon moved to face the dart board. He looked down at his feet to check the toe line. Sibohan's dad, who thought of himself as something of a darts player, had taught her that this pitch marker was called the ockey. Riordon's style was precise. He lent forward, holding the dart in a claw like grip. First with a short trial movement and then, with a more expansive one, he released the dart. Three darts were thrown in quick succession and retrieved. The routine was repeated. She wondered why no score was recorded. The MC announced "Match On!" As Riordon re-checked his mark, the door behind her opened and the five detectives sidled through one by one, unnoticed in the growing clamour.

The first set of three darts was greeted with the call "One hundred and forty!" and a roar of approval. Riordon reclaimed his darts and turned to make way for his opponent. He raised a hand to acknowledge the applause, and stared out in satisfaction at the audience. As he scanned the crowd, his eyes fell on the cluster of men by the door. Recognition was instant and the reaction instinctive. He knew the significance of the Gardai's presence at once. From the band in the back of his trousers, he drew a gun and in one leap jumped off the stage. Screams rang out as he grabbed a young woman from the nearest table. She was now his shield. He raised the automatic above his head and let off a shot. More screams and clatter as people scrambled to hide for cover. The building was a cauldron of confusion.

Inspector Eric Blane signalled to his men to remain calm. He shouted above the pandemonium. "Give it up Riordon!"

But even in those brief moments Joe Riordon had moved into military mode. Training trips in Libya had taught him that in these circumstances, he needed to create confusion and fear. Take the initiative and move fast.

"Move away from the door," he shouted, pointing the gun at the temple of the girl. She whimpered in terror. He moved carefully down the side of the tables, hoping to shepherd the Gardai away from his escape route.

"Stay where you are!" Blane muttered to his colleagues. Another shot boomed out.

"The next one's hers," yelled the gunman. A crescendo of screams filled the air. Eric Blane's instinct had been to hold fast, but now he feared for the safety of the young girl and others who might become victims of a shoot out.

"We've got to let him go sir," whispered Finbar Reeve at his side.

Riordon waived the gun in front of him, directing them to move away from the door.

"Do as he says lads!" Blane muttered contemptuously, fearing his plan was about to crumble around him.

The two groups moved slowly in a synchronous circle, until Riordon and his captive were next to the door. He inched them backwards, all the time with his gaze aimed at the Gardai. He turned his head to line up with the door handle and, as if from nowhere, an object crashed into his hand. It was the collection box which Siobhan had swung like a hammer thrower. It described a huge arc before smashing into his wrist. He screamed in pain and the gun fell to the floor and for a split second, his steely calm was gone. In that moment Garda "Herbie" Collins launched himself into a flying rugby tackle across the top of a table and crashed into the disorientated Riordon. In the midst of the panic that had exploded all around, the two thrashed about on the floor Finbar Reeve and the other two young detectives threw their combined weight on top of the struggling mass, and soon the three had Riordon pinned down. For good measure, Collins threw a final punch, "after the bell" which in later reports nobody saw. Reeve snapped on handcuffs, and Riordon was roughly raised to his feet.

"Get him out of here," ordered Blane.

Finbar Reeve carefully picked up the gun and placed it in a plastic evidence bag. There wasn't much struggle left in Riordon, as two detectives hauled him through the doors. All around pandemonium reigned, as men, women and children extricated themselves from beneath tables and behind chairs. Angry protests, and the sound of weeping, sustained the chaos. Eric Blane moved down to the stage area and grabbed a microphone.

"Ladies and Gentlemen! Ladies and gentlemen!" Even amplified, his voice failed to pierce the clamour. He turned to the control box and turned up the volume.

"I'm Detective Inspector Blane of the Gardai. Please keep calm!" However predictable the plea, the panic stricken assembly seemed to be beginning to regain its composure. Except for one young woman, whose hysterical screams from underneath a table, increased as others became more controlled. Friends tried to get her to come out of her bunker, but she refused and screamed all the more. Blane's focus was now on a group of men whom, he assumed, were members of the darts team. Friends of Riordon.

"Everybody sit down please!" Finbar Reeve shouted. Recognizing his boss' concern, he moved towards the stage.

Now in full view of the crowd, the two Gardai officers seemed to have a hold on the situation, however fragile. They counted on the fact that everyone had been traumatized by the incident, and it might take the edge off any long held antagonism to the forces of law. Meticulously Blane explained that theirs was a routine visit which, to their surprise, had escalated into a major event. He emphasized that the danger was now over and added that, after giving their name and address to his officers, they could go home. Landlord Liam Coyne, stone faced, nodded in agreement. His wife Bernadette moved among the crowd offering encouragement and a drink to "steady the nerves."

A few young men, emboldened by the change of atmosphere, began to make loud uncomplimentary comments about the Gardai. Blane had heard it all before. He pointed fiercely at the ringleaders and shouted "That's enough!"

The effect was dramatic, and the culprits sat down in glum silence.

Blane, Reeve and Danny Smythe set themselves up at tables near the exit doors and took down personal details as each person left. Reeve thought there might have been some mileage in questioning people there and then, but they were stretched, and had much to do before the arrest was complete. They spent some time interviewing the Coyles, to get a sense of their involvement with Riordon, who clearly was held in high esteem at The Falcon. Reeve was left unsure about Liam Coyle and made a mental note to check him out later.

The whole process took over an hour to complete and at the end Blane, Reeve, Smythe and Sibohan were left alone. The building was eerily quiet now. They looked at each other in a moment of assessment.

"We did it Fin! We bloody did it!" Blane's voice had a sharper, crisper resonance and a surprising gusto. They shook hands vigorously. Finbar moved to Sibohan, sitting by the door. He held her drawn face in his hands.

"What the hell did you think you were doing?"

"All in a day's work," she joked, as she lifted her head and shaped a kiss without making contact. Impulsively he responded and drew her face closer and kissed her on the lips. Blane coughed into his fist, Smythe smirked and Sibohan's face lit up with pleasure.

33

It had been a strange day for Tom Ellison. He was at the centre of a tumult of events on the one hand, but isolated from it on the other. He had accompanied Tyrone to make his statement at the police station in Drumlasheen, under the supervision of Sergeant Irons, who strove not to prompt the statement and allowed Tyrone to express himself in the vernacular, which Tom found amusing.

When completed, the sergeant said "For once in your life Tyrone, you've done the right thing." Feigning bruised injustice Tyrone turned to Tom Ellison and said "See what I mean?"

Under the protective custody of Mrs Murtagh and the Garda at the front door, Tom spent most of the rest of the day, at Finbar Reeve's suggestion, writing down his account of events going back to 1985 and, where relevant, more recent times. It was less a statement and more a rummaging about in the kit bag of his memories. Weird details came to mind. He remembered the name of the ferry boat that brought the group to Ireland, and then for a moment got stuck on the name of one of the boys. His own emotions were never far from the heart of the narrative. At first he felt he had to edit out any criticism of the investigation and links with the more current happenings.

"Sod it," he thought, and wrote a purple passage criticizing delays in the initial search. However, even if he remembered them, he was careful not to mention names.

"Feet on the ground are told where to walk." It was something his father had said, from his trade union days, and it seemed appropriate now. He had completed seven pages by the time Mrs Murtagh called him for lunch.

"Almost enough for a book!" she said.

"Who'd read it?" he joked.

Lunch was a Leitrim classic of boxty (a fried potato cake) bacon and scallions, followed by sweet home grown rhubarb tart and custard. All served proudly in Mrs Murtagh best blue and white.

"For special guests," she flattered. Afterwards, he settled himself into one of the arm chairs and was invited to watch racing from The Curragh on the television.

"It's not my thing," he said.

"You just watch Tommy Carmody in the three fifteen," Mrs Murtagh enthused.

It soon became clear that hers was not a passing interest, but an intimate knowledge of riders and runners, backed up by occasional reference to the Sporting Life.

Tom was drawn into her excitement and enjoyed picking his own horse by the "stick a pin" method. Two winners and a third place was Mrs Murtagh's record. His was one measly third place.

As if part of some plan to fill the day, tea followed hard on the heels of lunch, and reluctantly Tom accepted the proffered plate of sandwiches and valiantly consumed half of them. He nervously eyed the Victoria sponge that sat inside a glass dome on a pedestal stand in the middle of the table. Resistance was futile, and he agreed to a small piece when offered. He already knew that Mrs Murtagh didn't do small, and the slice that she delivered on to his plate was the size of half a house brick.

"Now it's you trying to kill me," he joked.

"Get away now. You're a growin' lad," she said, not quite getting his joke. His need to show that his respect for her effort was greater than his feeling of bloat, and he slowly ate his way through the giant slice.

"More?" she asked.

"No!" he replied, and added "I surrender!" They both laughed.

Throughout the day he wondered how Finbar Reeve's investigation was going, and as the evening wore on he felt a slight sense of disappointment that there had been no communication. Tiring of the Gay Byrne Show, he decided to turn in and start the book he'd bought on the ferry. He wished Mrs Murtagh goodnight.

"Goodnight Mr Ellison," she replied.

He turned and said "It's Tom!"

"Goodnight Tom,!" she said with a kindly smile.

34

Joe Riordon was safely locked away in the cells of County H.Q., and members of the "Operation Elvis" team were busy writing up their reports and checking out information. Inspector Eric Blane phoned his immediate superior, Superintendent Charles O'Dowd, a career administrator, to tell him of the evening's goings on. They had a good, sound relationship and O'Dowd had a sneaking regard for Blane's detective skills and for its no nonsense methods. In his turn Blane felt his boss had supported him, even at times when his approach had been somewhat irregular. As they spoke, Blane made the unsolved mystery of the missing boy the focus of his report. He knew that O'Dowd had also been embarrassed at the publicity over the review of the case, so he thought that this new development would please him. The rest was a bonus he would reveal in time. He had expected the roasting for the fact that he had gone without official backing.

"You bloody idiot!" O'Dowd barked. "You realise you put your career on the line!" Blane was prepared to eat a certain amount of humble pie, but he knew the kudos to be gained from the exercise far outstretched the misdemeanours on his part.

"You'd have been sunk if it went wrong," O'Dowd added.

"Why didn't you tell me?"

Without going into his fear of a leak, Blane justified the need for a quick response to their discoveries, by emphasising the fear of losing Riordon. Calming down, O'Dowd expressed his relief that the arrest had resolved a long running case. Then, briefly, hesitancy returned to his voice. He knew that the PR implications of the solving of the old case were bound to open up old wounds. He was long service Gardai, and although not personally involved in the original case, he had felt the weight of public opinion later towards the subsequent Case Review, in which he did have a role. Ever the pragmatist, he realized that he couldn't wipe out the criticism of the past. His job now would be to maximize the achievement of his officers, and make sure that he appeared to have been involved from the beginning. He would need his best skills in media management.

Blane added urgently "We need to make arrangement for this grave to be reopened. Best if we get over to the graveyard before someone beats us to it."

"Leave that to me," O'Dowd promised.

"Today?" Blane pushed.

"Difficult!"

"It's our strongest evidence. We need it!"

"I'll do what I can! You make a plan for now," O'Dowd answered, adding "And I want a full report on my desk. Forty eight hours!" His order contained all the implications that might follow, if Blane didn't do a thorough job.

"Thank you sir!" Blane said with a hint of sarcasm in his voice. He turned to Finbar Reeve, sitting opposite to him.

"Back and covering come to mind," he said, readjusting the phone that he had replaced the wrong way round in its carriage.

"Get a move on!" He looked at his watch. It was now almost midnight.

Notwithstanding the fact that they had all been on extra duty, Inspector Eric Blane insisted that, after a short rest, the members of the "Operation Elvis" team be back in the office by six a.m. to pick up the threads of the multi layered investigation, and follow up on clues that were already the basis of Finbar Reeve's clutch of cases..

To their credit all the young detectives were at their desk by the stipulated time and when Blane and Reeve satisfied themselves that their three deputies were up to speed with their tasks, they sat down to consider their needs in the search for the boy's body.

Its location was their most crucial piece of information so far, and they agreed that they needed to be at the graveyard, described by Patrick Hanlon, as soon as possible. If they were to get permission to open a grave, then they would need to have specialist support in place. The next two hours were taken pinning down the logistics of the operation and organizing the manpower they might need.

Much was based on the assumption that O'Dowd would come through with the necessary permissions of a court order, and the agreement of the church authorities.

Failing that, they needed to have the site mapped and protected. Once their plan was complete, Reeve remembered his promise to Tom Ellison.

"It might be a good idea to have the teacher present. He might be helpful." Before Blane could answer he added "I think we owe it to him."

"You serious?" Blane said doubtfully, remembering police protocol.

"He's had the burden of this on his shoulders two years," Reeve argued. Blane cupped his chin in his hand and recalled his one and only meeting with the teacher. He now regretted the ready judgment he had made, and which was clearly wrong. After a long pause, he nodded slowly. He looked intently at Reeve and said

"It's been your case from the start. If you think we should do it, O.K.!"

As a rider he added "But make sure he doesn't get in the way." The smile that lit up Finbar Reeve's face reflected his gratitude to Blane and his own empathy for Tom Ellison's guts.

"Thanks!" He picked up the phone and dialled Mrs Murtagh's number.

"Hello Mrs Murtagh. It's Finbar Reeve here. Is Mr Ellison about? Can I have a word?" Reeve could hear the old lady calling upstairs and very soon Ellison was on the other end of the line.

"Hello Tom. We got him! Yes! Last night. Can you be ready to be picked up at ten? We might need your help today." He smiled at the excited response he was hearing down the line.

"Ten it is then!" Reeve replaced the phone. Almost immediately the phone rang again. It was Superintendent O'Dowd and he asked to speak to Eric Blane.

"Blane, I've sorted everything out for you to go ahead" he announced, full of self-importance.

He continued "As this body is supposed to have been buried on consecrated ground without proper committal, we can consider it as a retrieval and not an exhumation. I've been given the nod that the church has no objections, but they want to have someone on site. When will you be ready?" he asked.

"Ready to go sir!" Blane replied with a wink to Reeve.

"I'll let them know. Keep me informed."

"Yessir!" Blane put the phone down and hammered the desk with his fist in triumph.

They looked at each other wide-eyed, amazed at the speed of events. The church could have been a difficult nut to crack. It was hard to believe that in forty eight hours, the resolution of the long lost case had reached this point. They were bound together in a way that neither had ever thought possible. Reeve took down a plan of the graveyard, drawn by Patrick Hanlon, which had been pinned to the wall. Blane checked off the list of "to do's". They were ready. All that was needed was to pick up their informant from his cell.

35

Tom Ellison had not been able to eat much of the breakfast that Mrs Murtagh had provided, despite her urging.

"It'll keep up your strength!"

Excitement, nerves and the uncertainty of where events were leading him, had shrunk his appetite. He spent much of his time wondering what Finbar Reeve had in store. He was relieved when a knock came to the front door. Finbar Reeve stood at the bottom of the garden steps by the side of a minibus, hand raised in welcome. Tom stepped down and Reeve slid the side door open and ushered him into a seat behind the driver. He nodded to the two man seated at the end of the long bench seat which ran down the side of the bus. Settling into the driver's seat, Reeve turned to him.

"You remember Inspector Blane?" A hand was thrust back from the front passenger side and Tom took it and shook it saying "Yes of course!" The face that turned towards him, despite wear and tear in the intervening years had been indelibly printed in his memory,

"How are ya?" Blane asked flatly.

"Fine thanks," Tom replied. It was an awkward moment and neither knew how to continue. Reeve pierced the silence.

"Your job's nearly done," he said to Ellison.

Their journey took them through the town, over the river bridge, and on through a maze of narrow lanes, testing the suspension of the ageing Transit. The grey dampness of the early morning had been burnt away and the sun caste an enriching warmth over the fields. The journey was made in total silence, until Blane shouted

"There! By the gate!"

It drew Ellison's attention to a derelict building that must once have been at the outer reaches of a large estate. Passing between the vestiges of columns, that must have supported impressive gates, the straight road that lay in front of them, and the large swathes of overgrown grassland on either side, would once have created a sense of grandeur. At the end of a gentle bend, the bus turned over a narrow bridge leading to a slight uphill climb. They passed into an avenue of rampant, overarching trees. Low hanging branches clattered the roof of the bus. They were in a dark tunnel, at the end of which was framed the levelled remains of a large country house.

Out in the light, they could see that long grass, unbridled trees and bushes had randomly taken hold where, experience told Tom Ellison, immaculate formal gardens had once prevailed. The after-image of gravel paths was revealed, where grass grew shorter. A once-grand set of steps, now limped its way up to the truncated pillars of the crumbled portico that guarded the main entrance. To either side of this central portion were the vestiges of two large three story wings. Ellison's native curiosity made him wonder when this derelict pile had last been the setting for a grand ball, when guest would have mounted these steps and their arrival announce by one of the staff. It certainly had been grand enough, but it was now a tragic sight. The roof had completely gone and only parts of the ground and first floor levels remained. Its elongated Georgian windows were now black holes, consumed by rampant ivy.

Finbar Reeve pulled up to the side of the building next to a gateway, which Ellison guessed had been the entrance to stables. According to Hanlon's roughly drawn map, the chapel and its cemetery was located on the other side of the house. Blane eased himself out of the vehicle and a young constable left through the rear door.

Right! Outside!" he shouted angrily to the man sitting by the back door

"Nothing's changed!" he said to himself, recollecting their only previous encounter.

The man inside seemed reluctant to move. Reeve climbed inside and helped him to stand. Hand under his elbow, he helped him to the door, where Blane waited. The man lent forward for support, and it was at that moment that Ellison noticed the handcuffs securing him from behind. In an instant his blood ran cold at the recognition that this pathetic looking man was his unknown adversary. This man who knew all the details that he had striven for so long to understand.

Blane bundled the man out of the bus and directed him to a block of stone and said "Sit!" It was like a command to a miscreant dog. His balance affected by the handcuffs behind his back, the man stumbled to his appointed place and slumped down.

"Let's have a look at that drawing," he said to Finbar Reeve. Blane was unrestrained in his eagerness to get going.

"According to him, he says the cemetery is round there," he added, pointing to the drawing and checking it against the reality before them. Reeve looked over his shoulder to study the map, and they agreed on their orientation.

Whilst this was going on, Tom Ellison sat in the bus, his gaze fixed on the huddled figure, head bowed and features concealed. Tom was struggling to suppress the bile he felt bubbling away in his stomach. When the man lifted up his head and looked in his direction, he could see vividly the haunted look of a man without hope; all salvation gone. He remembered, with bitterness, that feeling. Sympathy had little to say in his opinion of the man. He gagged, as the liquor of his anger filled his mouth. He lent forward hoping to project the vomit through the driver's window, but failed and the seat was covered in it. He grabbed at the sliding door, and tumbled out on to the grass. His head was spinning as he grabbed the handle of the door for support and drew himself on to his feet. He lent heavily on side of the bus, hoping the nausea would subside.

"You alright?" asked Finbar Reeve, coming round the back of the bus.

"Yea." he said "That ride shook me up." He spat out the remains from his mouth, as dizziness overcame him. He slumped to the ground. Reeve moved forward and put his hand on Ellison's shoulder.

"You sure?"

"Give me a minute," he said, easing himself to an upright sitting position against the side of the bus. Reeve offered a bottle of water from the holdall he had assembled for the search. Ellison drank some, rinsed it around in his mouth and spat it out.

"Get a move on Fin!" Inspector Eric Blane's agitation was clear and Finbar Reeve had no choice.

He whispered to Tom "We're going to have a look around. You can come if you want, but you must not interfere. Not a word!"

Tom Ellison had re-wound to the point where he first set eyes on the handcuffed man. A confusion of emotions needed to be resolved. The natural hatred and revulsion he felt towards the man conflicted with his need to find answers to questions that had wracked his brain to a pulp. He raised himself shakily to his feet.

"I'll be alright," he said, and followed Reeve round to the back of the bus. They were met by an Eric Blane, keen eyed and bristling with self-importance.

"Let's go!" he commanded like someone leading an expedition through darkest Africa. He grabbed the seated man by the elbow and thrust him ahead. Reeve and Ellison followed in file behind. Tom Ellison had not yet seen the details of the man's face.

They trudged through long Blue Eyed grass, with its sword shaped leaves and blue flowers, triggering the invigorating smell of wild mint, released from beneath their feet. The remains of a gate led them through to the south side of the building and the adjacent chapel. It had faired better than the rest of the main house, perhaps because of its protected position in the lee of the devastated remains and, Ellison guessed, because robbers of stone had respected its religious identity. Nevertheless its roof was gone and its walls consumed by the ubiquitous ivy. A wrought iron gate was the entrance to the cemetery, which sloped from the chapel and up to a large Yew tree with a bank of ferns at its feet. The tops of gravestones peered out at various angles through the long grass. Blane consulted Hanlon's map.

"Over there?" he asked pointing towards an area next to what might once have been a fountain. Hanlon nodded in silence. The grass clung to their feet, like walking through deep snow. Ellison was breathing hard and his heart rate increased as they got nearer to the spot that Blane had identified. He was now level with the handcuffed man and could see his white, strain-worn face.

"This it?" Blane asked brusquely, pointing to two flat stone slabs, surrounded by a low rectangular wrought iron railing, each vertical strut topped by elaborate fleur de leys finials; surprisingly un-corroded in the midst of such ruin.

"Yes," answered Hanlon weakly. "We removed the slabs to hide the coffin and then placed them back so that there was no evidence of digging." It seemed so matter of fact and Ellison, standing close enough to hear, felt the urge to smash the man with the spade that lay on the ground beside him. Fighting back the anger, he turned and took several steps away.

Leaning over the railing, Blane swept grass aside and read from the larger of the two stones.

"In memory of Albert Crighton Aged 57 died January 7. 1851." and then "Anna Aged 56, died May20. 1858. R.I.P.,"

Even in these bizarre circumstances, for a moment the group stood perfectly still and silent, each focused on his own thoughts. Blane broke the silence.

"You'd better be bloody sure!"

Instinctively Hanlon turned his head, as if struck by a heavy blow. At that moment several figures rounded the corner of the house. Reeve had ordered a scene of crime officer and he recognized the slim figure of James Cronin, accompanied by a pair of uniformed officers carrying spades balanced across lengths of timber. A man dressed all in black was obviously a representative of the church. The fourth figure, perhaps a driver, remained behind as the others trudged to the graveyard.

The priest introduced himself as Father Hague, and explained that he was there to represent the interest of the church. Blane made it clear that he had the right to retrieve evidence from consecrated ground and, in his turn, Father Hague emphasized *his* right to object to any desecration that might occur. Demarcation lines had been drawn. They both knew where they stood.

For all but Tom Ellison, Hanlon was forgotten for the moment, but Tom's gaze was fixed on the handcuffed man who stood beside the grave. *Glenn Wallace's grave?* There was no display of arrogance or pride of one committed to a cause. This was a man drained of all self- respect.

Finbar Reeve took charge of the first phase of the operation, which was to photograph the scene and do a search of the immediate surrounds of the grave. He doubted it would reveal anything after so long, but the grave and its contents were now secure. Satisfied that they had done all they could to survey the area, they considered the best way to go about lifting the stones. The railing presented a problem of access to the stone slabs, and after discussion, the priest agreed that the railing could be removed.

The four corners of the rectangle seemed to be points where the railing had been cemented in. After removing their jackets Blane, Reeve and the two young Garda set to digging, with Father Hague making sure that any grave material would not be disturbed. In the event, the corners of the railing were set shallow in very crumbling cement, and soon the whole of the railing lost its stability. They concluded it could be lifted whole. With Reeve at one end and Blane at the other, Garda James Cronin and his colleague took up position on the sides. They counted down their effort. "Three!Two!One! Heave!" They struggled to sustain their effort with grunts and groans, but all at once the corner started to yield and very soon the whole structure was free of the ground. Lurching sideways with the strain, they dropped the railing clumsily beside the grave. The long grass cushioned its fall, and no harm was done other than a loss of dignity, as all but James Cronin fell to the ground.

"Don't you bloody well smile!" snarled Blane to Hanlon. Tom Ellison knew a smile had not passed those tight, expressionless lips, but Blane felt better for it. Clearing grass and weeds from the slabs, and with the edge defined by the aid of a trowel, photographs were taken. Blane held out the spade in Reeve's direction.

"After you Jeeves," he said with unexpected humour.

Reeve took the spade and for a moment looked in Ellison's direction, who gently nodded his approval. He held the spade at a steep angle, feeling for the depth of the stone. Then he gently lowered the handle of the spade as it took hold of the softer earth beneath, and the stone began to lift.

"Try not to split the stone!" Father Hague urged.

Finbar Reeve halted for a moment, raised his gaze and, looking the priest in the eye, said with mock obeisance "Yes Father!" and then continued to lift the stone into a vertical position, revealing the dark earth beneath.

Tom Ellison watched the scene, his heart thumping in his chest. The hike through the long grass and the growing tension had caused him to sweat profusely and his scrambled mind brought on a dizzy spell that went unnoticed by the others – except Patrick Hanlon. The man that Tom had come to hate, made an involuntary step forward before realising his cuffed hands would be useless. Tom swallowed the acid phlegm that filled his mouth, and drew in deep breaths of air to clear his head.

The stone was now vertical and Finbar Reeve rolled it over and over on its edge until it was clear of the grave cut, and then he laid it gently down. The second half of the stone cover was moved in the same way, and Reeve stood back wiping his brow, allowing more photographs to be taken. Blane stepped forward for a closer look.

"O.K. so far," he said. Reeve and Father Hague nodded.

"How deep?" Blane demanded, looking at Hanlon.

"About three feet," he squirmed.

"Then you bloody dig it!" Blane said in a mood of retribution. He unlocked the cuffs and handed Hanlon a spade. Father Hague looked disapprovingly at Blane, but he was unrepentant at his decision, and Tom Ellison warmed to the gruff Inspector. The hard crust of the earth was now broken and Hanlon soon found softer ground. He had been digging for about five minutes when the spade clunked against something hard.

Blane pushed him aside, knelt down and scraped earth from the centre of the grave, until he revealed the unmistakable lid of a coffin, bleached grey by its time under-ground. He swept the length of the grave with the spade and soon the complete outline of the coffin lid was visible. Where lengths of wood had been jointed together, a crack had opened up.

"This it?" Blane asked, stony faced. Hanlon hobbled hesitatingly. He looked into the grave, turned his head away in a gesture of despair and whispered "Yes!"

"Sorry?" Blane said, wishing to extract further discomfort.

"Yes!" This time it was shouted hysterically and it turned into uncontrolled sobbing, as he sank to his knees.

Tom Ellison felt he was observing a bizarre Victorian melodrama unfolding, as the priest stepped forward and put a sympathetic arm around the wretched figure. He surveyed the derelict house, the wild cemetery, the policemen, the miscreant criminal, the priest and an open grave. Added to which, he felt an integral part of it in his role as chief mourner.

He could find no sympathy for the man's anguished state, which seemed to him to be at best, a sign of deferred shame, and at worst cynical fakery. Tom knew his judgement was seated in his own growing desire for revenge: revenge for the abuse and imposed guilt that had been forced upon him. It was, he knew full well, a base instinct. He failed to quell it now, and felt no shame in it. When the perpetrators were unknown, revenge had not figured in his thoughts. Now that he was face to face with one of them, it was different. If there was blame for what had happened to the boy, this man must accept his share. There was nothing to mitigate his part in it. Blane and Reeve stood over the trench and discussed their next move.

"I think we're done for now," said Blane. "The Examiner needs to supervise things, so we'll put a canvas over this for now, and get him down here."

Tom Ellison had been prepared, reluctantly, to identify the body of Glenn Wallace, should it be found, but he now felt a huge sense of relief that it was not to happen before he had regained his composure. For now he was fixated on the man called Hanlon.

Finbar Reeve had revealed to Tom as much as he felt he should know about the man's background. Ellison wondered how a man regarded as a pillar of society could be involved in such a despicable deed. Tom had a degree of sympathy for republican ideals, and he understood that "The Union" had a strong appeal for many to become involved in protest. What he found difficult was the next step, which took them into crime and murder. However, this pathetic story was not even that. The boy was not a victim of a noble cause. It was too easy a defence. That a boy should meet his death by a *blunder* relegated the validity of the cause they espoused. That was Tom Ellison's opinion. It was the boy's death, separated from all other considerations, on which he judged the man called Hanlon.

Finbar Reeve came over to where Ellison was standing and explained the next stage in the procedure. The coroner had been pre-warned and would be there quite soon. In the meantime he suggested that Ellison, who he could see still looked unwell, remove himself to the shade of the nearby tree. Blane took the opportunity to quiz Hanlon. With the pace of developments, it was the first chance he had to question the prisoner. He adopted his official, no nonsense approach, despite the informality of the setting.

"Whose idea was this?" he asked, indicating the grave.

"Not mine!" Hanlon pleaded. "It was Riordon!"

"Had he used this place before?" Blane was quick to press the point to see if the spot held other secrets.

"I don't know!" Hanlon threw his hands up in despair.

"Mr Hanlon. Did you kill the boy? And did you plan to bury the body here?"

"No! It was Riordon! He killed the boy and he planned the rest."

"And you agreed?"

"I had no choice!"

"No choice!" Blane exploded. He was now in his stride and his reddened face expressed the anger he felt towards his prisoner.

"You had every choice. Not to get involved in the first place."

"I was young," moaned Hanlon.

"So was the boy!" Blane persisted remorselessly. Hanlon fell into a blubbering heap at his feet. Blane stepped back, resisting an urge to exact further physical pain. Finbar Reeve put his hand on the inspector's shoulder and said "I think we should find Mr Hanlon some shade."

It was a gentle warning to his boss not to put his career on the line; and the case in jeopardy. Blane realised at once that he had come close to making a serious mistake and he tapped Reeve's warning hand twice, in recognition. Reeve knew from his own reaction that this case was having a profound affect on all involved in it – even the case-hardened Inspector Eric Blane.

For the next hour work on the grave was suspended as Blane, Reeve and Cronin made a closer inspection of those parts of the graveyard that were still accessible, in search of further evidence. It was no surprised that there was none after eight years. The coffin held the key. Looking over to the house Finbar Reeve saw the arrival of two more police vehicles. One was unmistakably a hearse. Three of four men trudged their way to the cemetery. Introductions were unnecessary, as Blane and Reeve knew Coroner Andrew Kerr and the two Garda accompanying him. Andrew Kerr was a tall figure, drain-pipe- thin, with a walk not dissimilar to a wading bird. His pale, gaunt face with features sharply drawn, had a melancholy look that denied his fiendish sense of humour.

"Afternoon Eric," he said, dropping down an enormous leather bag that had seen years of wear and tear.

"Andrew!" Bane responded courteously.

"Let's have a look at what we've got," Kerr said, signalling to his companions to remove the canvas. Kerr, never one to waste time, tied on a white face mask, snapped on plastic gloves and gingerly knelt down beside the exposed coffin.

"I've heard of economy," he said on seeing the shallowness of the grave. He eased his glasses up on to his forehead, lay flat on his stomach and peered closely at the exposed coffin lid.

"How long has he been here?" he asked. "A couple of years at a guess." Blane replied.

Kerr cleared away the remaining earth from the lid. He turned to Blane.

"You want a look see?"

"If we can. I've somebody here who might be able to identify," Blane replied.

"Should be alright to have a peep. It looks in good order. Pass me a screwdriver Fin!"

Reeve was surprised at the request for a non-medical tool. He opened the cavernous bag and took out a large screwdriver and passed it to Kerr. He easily removed two large screws from one side of the lid, and placed them in a small plastic bag he took from his pocket. The reaming screws were too corroded and he said

"That should be enough," he said sitting back on his haunches.

"I reckon this will come away in one," he said, examining the cracked lid.

He squeezed his fingers into the widest part of the split and gently pulled. At first the crack opened a little. Then, with maintained pressure, one half of the lid separated from the other. He placed the split plank on the opposite side of the grave cut. Now he could see one exposed half of the contents of the coffin.

"Looks like a child," he whispered. Blane and Reeve looked at each other, their expressions a confusion of dismay and subdued satisfaction. They moved closer.

"That's close enough," Kerr said, holding his arm out as a barrier. They peered into the opened space. Nothing was said. Their heads dropped in a silent token of respect.

Finbar Reeve knew that the responsibility for bringing Tom Ellison to the graveside was his. He made his way slowly up towards the trees, from where Ellison had been watching proceedings. As he came closer, Reeve looked into the face of his friend and found unseeing eyes. It was as if Tom Ellison wasn't there.

"This can wait," Finbar whispered, putting his hand on his shoulder. Then, as if taken by an electric shock, Ellison's wilted body flexed, and his expressionless face was jolted into life. "It's alright," Ellison said, acknowledging Reeve's concern. Together they walked down to the graveside. Reeve stood aside as Ellison shuffled forward to the edge. He looked straight ahead, gathering his resolve, and then took a tiny step backwards to reset his balance. He looked down into the coffin and with his expression unchanged, took several seconds to take in what he saw. The hood of a green one-piece fishing suit was drawn forward, concealing what lay beneath, but the tiny bones of a decomposed hand protruded from the sleeve that lay across the chest. Sewn on to the chest was the blue badge of Everton – Glenn's favourite team.

He looked up, drew in a giant breath and turned round to face Reeve, Blane and Kerr. His head dropped and he nodded.

"The boy?" asked Blane quietly.

Without answering, Tom Ellison put his hand in his back pocket, removed his wallet and opened it carefully. He took out a photograph folded in two. It was the picture of a young boy sitting on a fishing box, leaning forward in concentration. He had had it in his wallet for eight years.

"I took this the day he went missing," he said haltingly and handed the photograph to Reeve, who looked at it and wondered about its significance. They had other photographs of the boy.

"The fishing suit!" Ellison prompted. "They're the same!" The suit that the boy was wearing in the photograph, was an unmistakable match to those that shrouded the small skeleton. There could be no doubt that this was the body of Glenn Wallace that lay in the fractured coffin. Blane leaned over Reeve's shoulder and whispered "Good enough for me!"

Father Hague made a sign of the cross over the coffin and uttered a prayer.

Sensing that Ellison's role was complete, Finbar Reeve suggested that he returned to the bus, while they made necessary arrangements for the removal of the body. With a positive shake of the head Ellison said "I'd like to see him out of there first." He turned and walked away, putting distance between him and the grave.

More photographs were taken and, on Kerr's instruction, the two young Gardai removed their jackets and set to the task of removing earth from around the coffin. Great care was taken not to damage it.

Soon sufficient soil was removed and the whole of the coffin was revealed, sitting above the surrounding earth. Apart from the crack to the lid, it seemed in a solid state and there was a discussion about the best way to transfer it to the waiting hearse. A trolley across the overgrown field seemed an unlikely option, so it was decided to ease the coffin on to planks to carry it out. The spades were used to lever it up sufficiently to slide the timbers underneath. Grasping what had become the handles of a stretcher; the young Gardai lifted the light coffin and set off on the journey to the hearse. Father Hague walked ahead and the others followed in crocodile style, retracing the path through the grass that they had made earlier. Tom Ellison was touched by the respect the Gardai had shown to the proceedings. Patrick Hanlon stumbled unsteadily between Blane and Reeve.

Tom Ellison knew an even greater blame lay with the man called Riordon.

Later as they made their way back to police headquarters, he began to savour the thought of the day when they would come face to face.

36

Tom Ellison had been called in to Police H.Q to make what, he hoped, was a final statement. Two hours of brain ferreting left him exhausted. In fact it was several statements dealing, in turn, with the original disappearance of the boy; the mysterious message; his return to Drumlasheen; the attempt on his life and the identification of the body. Riordon and Hanlon had been charged and were being held in custody for further questioning prior to their initial appearance in court. Tom understood that the main charge of Murder had been made against them. They were also accused of attempting to conceal a death as well as other gun running charges. Having finished his statement, Tom sat back in relief.

"We need to talk about protection," said Inspector Blane.

"Protection?" Ellison responded, confused. Riordon was under arrest, and surely did not represent a threat.

"You don't realise how important this case is," continued Blane.

"Your evidence is crucial. Who knows what interests will be exposed?"

Nothing, following Riordon's arrest, had allayed their suspicion that the case had been impeded, even by elements from within their own organisation.

"The threat could come from anywhere," he continued.

"It could be retribution from Hanlon's immediate family or from his larger family." With both hands he drew an imaginary globe in the air.

"I won't go into hiding!" Ellison was adamant.

The argument that followed went backwards and forward between Blane's official concern and Ellison's obdurate determination. Tom Ellison was resolved to be in full control of his life from now on. His mission in Ireland would not be complete until he had met his tormentor face to face in court. Hiding away did not figure in his need to rehabilitate himself with those who had judged him so unfairly. He would not give them the chance to set up a hunt for him in hiding. He needed to meet them full on, and on his terms. If there was risk involved, so be it.

"The least we can do while you're here is to keep you under close observation for now," Blane argued.

"I get to go wherever I want!" Ellison stipulated.

"Only if you keep us informed as to your intended movement," bargained Blane.

"Fair enough!" Ellison replied as a signature to a contract.

"This is Garda Daniel Leahy," announced Blane quickly, indicated the young Garda who had been standing at the door of the interview room. He was a solid lump of a man, with close cropped hair, hardened features and a wide-based, crouching stance that spoke of hours spent in the middle of a steaming rugby scrum.

"Sir!" He nodded in Ellison's direction. Blane added "He'll be on hand at all times," and then as an after-thought. "You'll need accommodation for you both."

"I'll ask Mrs Murtagh. If she'll have me." He knew that the feisty old lady would be upset had he chosen anywhere else.

"Send us the bill," Blane prompted. Ellison was relieved at the offer, as his funds had almost run out, plus it also meant a bit of extra cash for Mrs Murtagh.

Tom left Police Headquarters, with his protector tagging a short distance behind. He was pleased when he walked through a gathering group of reporters, without being recognised.

Tom Ellison decided to spend some time in the Leitrim countryside that day, motoring between villages – always punctuated by stretches of running water or the glimpse of a lake. Garda Dan Leahy was an admirable tour guide and an effortless rapport was set up between them. Ellison had read over the years, of the location of giant catches of roach and bream. Drumshambo, Ballinamore, Roosky. All names for the English angler to conjure with. He stopped near Ballinamore and came across three anglers from Sheffield fishing in Lake Bolganard. With his guard watching from the car, Tom got into easy conversation with them and was soon exchanging fishermen's tales. It gave him simple pleasure and he lay on the bank for over an hour watching, with growing envy, as the Yorkshiremen showed their considerable skills.

"Tight Lines!" he shouted as he mounted the bank and walked back towards the car. The fisherman's greeting was repeated back at him. It left him knowing that he was still a member of that fraternity at least. It brought a fleeting normality to a time when insanity had reigned.

As he pulled up outside Mrs Murtagh's house feeling relaxed and refreshed, he thanked Garda Daniel Leahy for his company. Ellison was glad that arrangements had been made for Leahy to stay at Mrs Murtagh's. Coffee and a sandwich in a tiny cafe on the shore of Lough Allen was all they had to eat, so they both looked forward to the fayre she would produce for their evening meal. Ellison was amazed at the huge amount of Shepherd's Pie that Leahy consumed, but Elizabeth Murtagh could not disguise her pleasure at what she called "a healthy appetite," and gave a sideways look at Ellison's relatively meagre effort.

37

The following day Tom decided to visit the gorgeous Rhiannon – on the pretext of further research. Without revealing his motive to his guardian, he insisted that Leahy remained in the car outside the library. He rang the bell for attention. The window slid open and, to Ellison's disappointment, the face that greeted him was the same pasty, slack-faced youth he had seen before.

"Is Rhiannon in?" he asked nonchalantly.

"Go through," the youth said, his expression unchanging. The window slid shut. As he entered the library Tom was confronted with the sight of his target standing on the top step of a metamorphic chair, rearranging books. He coughed.

"Oh hello again," she said turning to face him.

She was wearing a pink turtle neck sweater and a red skirt that met her leather boots just above the knee.

She began to climb down and held out her hand for assistance, and he took it. As he held her hand in his for the briefest of moments, he saw the unmistakable glint of a diamond ring – an engagement ring! His mind raced, as he realised that his next move, which he had rehearsed in his mind, had now become a massive error of judgement.

"Just to say thank you," he blurted out as, at the same time, he thrust the bunch of flowers that he had concealed behind his back. They exchanged embarrassed smiles: his for his childish naivety and hers out of confusion.

"I'll let you get on," he said pointing to the books she still held across her chest.

"Thank you for these. They're lovely, but you shouldn't have," she said.

It was all she could say as, for her, their meetings had been part of her daily routine. After an awkward moment, when neither knew what to say next, he mimicked tipping an imaginary top hat and turned about, pushing hard on the swing doors, leaving the library behind him. As the doors hushed shut, he heard her shout

"Goodbye!"

Outside on the street, his equilibrium restored, he looked around at the every-day scene that confronted him and when normality seemed to have crept unnoticed back into his life. Talking about fishing! Making a pathetic attempt at chatting up a beautiful woman!

"It happens every day doesn't it," he mused.

He was savouring again a sense of the mundane. Far removed from the tumultuous events of the last few days and he was enjoying it. He wandered up the street avoiding prams and knots of people deep in conversation, and looked in at the variety of shops. As he turned to retrace his steps, the sight of Leahy, who had been following close behind throughout, brought him back momentarily to another world. The world of fear, prejudice, cruelty and distorted values. He determined to put them from his mind and he invited his watchdog into a café for a cup of coffee. They talked the aimless sort of talk of strangers thrown together, and took in the busying scene on Drumlasheen's main street.

38

At Police H.Q. things had moved on at frantic pace. Eric Blane and Finbar Reeve had agreed, from the moment Riordon had been arrested, that the cases needed to be tied up as quickly as possible before outside hands had the opportunity of compromising them in any way. Inspector Eric Blane took responsibility for liaison with the legal professionals; to construct the charge sheet that would face Joseph Riordon and Patrick Hanlon. At the same time he needed to leave flexibility to prosecute other crimes, because he was convinced their future investigations might reveal other matters.

Finbar Reeve's task was to gather the established details of the cases, and put together the statemented evidence and forensics details to support them. The home of Mary Mc Mahon needed more forensic investigation, now that they had a potential killer. They needed to place Riordon at the scene, if they were to nail him on that charge. One piece of good new evidence that quickly came to light was that the gun that they had taken from Riordon, was the same one used in an attempted robbery on a bank in Carrick-on-Shannon months before.

The questioning of Riordon and Hanlon had begun and Blane realised that he would have to ask for more time, because of the complexity of their cases. They all knew that there was much more to be revealed.

Questioning Hanlon was a simple affair. The story poured from the penitent prisoner in a torrent. Reeve and Blane felt no compassion for him, despite the fact that he was prepared to answer all their questions, and it was he who could give them vital information that would set up the case against Riordon. Patrick Hanlon's was a debt no amount of confession could assuage, and they pressed him relentlessly. His detailed disclosures would become the main plank in their case, despite the fact that his co-conspirator Michael McMahon was dead.

They might never know the true cause of Michael's death, but Garda James Atherton was charged with looking into the coroner's records and into Michael's background. Reeve's instinct was that it might lead them deeper into the grass roots of the struggle that obsessed some of his countrymen. That might be for another day: for another team?

The fruitless questioning of Joseph Riordon was a different affair. Eric Blane sat in the chair opposite him and his Dublin based solicitor Gordon Naismith. Neither Blane nor Reeve knew anything about Naismith, other than that his fees would be astronomical, and there was no way Riordon could pay them himself. Sitting back in his chair, Riordon looked directly ahead with icy eyes, as if Blane and Reeve didn't exist. Blane opened his folder.

"You are Joseph Patrick Riordon?" The silver haired lawyer nodded, confirming he could answer the question. He also acknowledged, with a smirk, that he had no fixed abode. Formalities over Blane asked "Did you kill Glenn Robert Wallace in August 1985?"

In the two hours that followed, Blane tried every approach that he knew to wheedle out any acknowledgement of his part in the boy's death, or anything else for that matter. At first Blane's tactic was to claim that he knew everything about the case, and just wanted Riordon to confirm it. His prisoner's blanket reply was "No comment!" to all of Blane's questions. Then he adopted a more conciliatory manner, hinting at empathy for Riordon's chosen cause. It was a transparent deceit and Riordon leaned forward, answering each question with an emphatic "No comment!" He was not going to be softened up by this line of questioning and Blane's composure was starting to be ruffled. He made a final stab at Riordon's conscience.

"Don't you have any feelings for the boy's mother?"

A flicker in the piercing eyes was gone in a flash. "No comment!" Blane's exasperation exploded and he stood up, leaned over the table, eyes narrowing, and said sarcastically "Thank you Mr Riordon!" Riordon sat back in his chair and said mockingly "Thank you Inspector!" Blane fought his base instinct, turned about, and left the room.

Blane and Reeve came together at the end of an exhausting day with remaining suspicions about interference from unknown quarters, but they felt that their case was solid.

39

Tom Ellison had spent a mostly peaceful night, but as light glanced through a gap in the bedroom curtains, he awoke suddenly and at once felt the tension that the day held. He had no role to play in the court proceedings that Finbar Reeve had told him were about to happen that morning. He doubted his ability to remain a silent bystander at proceedings that mattered so much to him. Men who had had a devastating impact on his life would stand before him, and he would want to ask "Why?" Immediately he felt ashamed, as he realised he was thinking of retribution for himself and all the wasted years, not for justice for the boy and his family.

A call from Finbar Reeve indicated that the preliminary court appearance would take place later that morning instead.

"What time?" he asked.

"Eleven!" It was now eight thirty.

"Plenty of time," he said.

"You don't have to come."

"You'd have to lock me up," was Ellison's unyielding answer. In the face of Ellison's determination to be present, Reeve insisted on additional police protection.

"What does that mean?"

"You don't need to know. Pick you up at ten."

The Courthouse was a large square, grey stone building built in the Palladian style. The traces of large windows in the front façade had been bricked up, giving it a seriously dour impression. Tom Ellison thought there could be no more a stern, severe looking setting for the arraignment of Joseph Riordon and Patrick Hanlon. At this first stage, they would be expected to answer the charges, and bail would be set or denied. Next at the Preliminary hearing the Gardai would expect them to be held on remand until the next stage, known as Disclosure, when the prosecution gives all its evidentiary information to the defence. Reeve had warned Tom that, due to the complexity of the cases, this would take many months, and in the end would almost certainly go to the SCC (the special court that dealt with acts of terrorism).

"You really mean a trial could be years away?" Tom had said, and Reeve held his hands upwards and replied "It's the game we play!"

Small groups of people were gathered on the steps outside the court as Tom Ellison, with Garda Leahy in close attendance, made his way towards the entrance. Finbar Reeve had warned him about the interest of the press. However for now their interest was centred on a young man holding a placard proclaiming loudly "Stop Police Discrimination!"

Tom's presence seemed to have gone unnoticed; and he impishly held back the door with an extravagant gesture, inviting an embarrassed Garda Leahy to enter.

Tom was struck immediately by the immaculate cleanliness of the place; its marble floor polished spotless, and the high wooden panelling displaying a patina more akin to polished glass. He was impressed by the unadorned simplicity. Imposing, but essentially functional. Then with a physical sensation, as if an internal gear had changed within him, his attention was hauled back to the significance of the event ahead.

He entered the courtroom through a door at the back of a raked balcony, looking down on the dock, with its polished brass handrail. He calculated that a seat at the far end of the balcony would give a better view of the accused.

After settling in to his seat, he surveyed the room before him. At ground level, officers of court scurried about amongst tables, making sure that the room was ready for the proceedings to begin. Looking like the top layer of a giant chocolate cake, the platform containing the judge's high chair and above it an elaborate shield, overlooked the cramped arena below. To the right, slightly elevated above floor level, was the witness box. He pictured himself sitting there, cheek by jowl with jurors in the adjacent jury box, but which now stood empty.

Surveying the courtroom, his overall impression was that it was smaller than he had expected, based only on watching "Crown Court" the Granada TV courtroom drama. But there was no TV glamour here. It was business-like and un-cluttered; a place to administer justice, pure and simple. Lawyers entered, followed by legal minions who helped them arranged documents on the tables, before sitting down languidly, as if they were about to order a cup of coffee.

The quiet banter of court officials and members of the public was broken by a loud shout of encouragement as Joseph Riordon entered the court from somewhere below the dock. From his position slightly above, Tom Ellison watched intently as the tall figure stepped forward. He was wearing a white T shirt and Levi jeans. A murmur of approval greeted him from the seats in the balcony, which was now full. Ellison sucked in a deep breath and focused on the man in the dock. Immediately he was surprised at his striking appearance, even more than in the photograph that he had seen His heavily sculptured face with its prominent equine nose, handsome in a rugged way, was set like concrete in a look of total distain. The forty year-old stood bolt upright, in military style. Ellison thought, at first, that it might be a pose to cover up true feelings of fear of what lay ahead, but the eyes did not lie. They were set beneath bushy eyebrows.

The dark brown pupils against the white sclera made them unnervingly piercing.

As Riordon slowly scanned the room, his eyes fell on Ellison. His eyebrows raised in recognition of a man he'd never met. A shiver shot through Ellison's body as he was held in that hypnotic gaze. Then, his face unchanging, Riordon lifted his hand above the wall of the dock and with two fingers drew them across his throat. He blinked extravagantly, as if in his mind the deed was done. The message was unmistakable and Ellison sagged back in his seat, his heart racing fit to burst through his chest. He forced himself to look back at Riordon and tried to restore some calm. Riordon lent forward to speak to his brief.

As he did, Tom noticed the figure that had been standing slightly behind him and blocked from view. It was Patrick Hanlon, dressed in a dark suit and white shirt open at the neck. The tortured, fearful face that he had come to despise at the graveside, in contrast to Riordon's, was one of open shame and remorse. For a moment, Ellison felt a pang of pity for him, as he recognised that the influence of men like Riordon over men like Hanlon had long been a tool in the struggle for power. It passed in a flash, as he remembered the catalogue of what the man had been part of. He was a perpetrator, not a victim! Tom Ellison's hatred of the two was equal.

Movement and chatter was brought to a dramatic halt by a large bearded clerk, who announced, in stentorian fashion.

"All stand!"

The Judge entered and bowed to all sides.

The preliminaries were dealt with stark simplicity and great speed. The two defendants were asked to acknowledge their names, and answer to the charges of which they were accused. Both men acknowledged their name, pleaded "Not guilty!" and they were remanded without bail. Defence lawyers succumbed to the inevitability of the decision, and voiced no objection.

Throughout the short hearing, Riordon maintained a demeanour of aloof disdain. Ellison had wondered if he would hear him take responsibility for the boy's death. But he really knew he was going to get it here, and he wondered if it would ever happen.

Over the years Tom had held a sneaking regard for all those who argued for change; wherever in the world. These people should be heard, he had argued. But at some time they were forced to answer the question "at what price?" The sad, simple story of this lost child was the country's tragedy in microcosm. The unbridled fervour of the extremist should not always prevail, and certainly not with a boy just wanting to go fishing. There were misguided principles at work here, and nothing was beyond reproach to the zealots. Would humanity, compromise and negotiation ever infiltrate the tangled world of "the cause" he wondered.

The hearing was over in a few minutes. Tom Ellison watched fixedly as the two men were shepherded out of the dock. Briefly Riordon was now facing him directly and Tom mustered every vestige of composure within him, as their eyes met. He manufactured a defiant smile in response to Riordon's glowering stare. Hanlon, head down shuffled behind and they disappeared into the labyrinth beneath the court.

Garda Leahy, signified to Tom that proceedings were over and it was time to go. They moved from the courtroom into the foyer which was now full of clusters of people in animated conversation. Tom noticed Finbar Reeve standing by the main door and raised his hand in recognition and made his way towards him through a knot of people. He excused himself to a woman who had her back to him. She turned in surprise and Tom stepped back in utter shock as he recognised the boy's mother. Elaine Wallace.

She must have been in the court and Tom had not seen her. The strain of the build up to the brief court hearing was imprinted on her face, where tears had etched into her makeup. Her eyes narrowed as realisation dawned, and her face was transformed in an instant, from deep sadness, to utter loathing. Tom Ellison mouthed a silent hello and made to offer his hand. She turned away and clung to the man beside her. Stunned by her response to his clumsy gesture, there was a moment when anything he might say or do would seem inappropriate. Self-consciously he moved through the gap that had opened and, as he passed the couple, he saw her ravaged face resting on the shoulder of her companion.

At the door, Tom Ellison turned to look back at the tragic figure. She returned his gaze briefly, but a hint of reconciliation was no more there, than it was in the conflict between rival men of Ireland. He understood that the hunt for the boy and the tracking down of his killers was almost over, but Elaine Wallace's loathing of him was unyielding. However he knew that the story would not end there in the courthouse; or in The Special Criminal Court – in however many months. Those who fight for "the cause" would not go away. His own burden had been lightened for the time being, but he knew it would be a permanent thread through the rest of his own life, and as long as the struggle would last. Would an end to the madness come in his lifetime, he wondered?

Finbar Reeve directed him through the front door. Immediately a small phalanx of out of uniform police officers stepped in front and became a protective shield to deflect eager Press photographers and reporters. Protected from the clamouring pack, Tom, Reeve and Leahy jumped into an unmarked police car and Garda Leahy put his foot to the floor and tore off, leaving galloping photographers in their wake. Breathless with excitement Tom felt a sudden burst of euphoria at having at last seen the face of his tormentor.

On the journey back to Drumlasheen, Finbar Reeve showed his delight in the morning's events, and at the way their investigations had gone in such a short time. Joseph Reardon's fingerprints had been matched with one on the bullet casing found near Mrs Murtagh's house, as well as several on the coffin. Tracking back through Hanlon's account of the day of the boy's disappearance, they had found residual traces of explosive material on timbers in the old boathouse. All of these strands coming together made their case undeniable, he enthused. However he doubted that Joseph Riordon and his supporters would make their job easy. For their part, the Gardai needed to be meticulous in the compilation of the evidence and leave no loopholes that Riordon's lawyers would surely try to exploit. Reeve reiterated his warning that all this would take a long time.

So that they might have a certain amount of control of the press output, if Ellison and Mrs Wallace agreed, they would arrange a press conference at Gardai HQ for the following morning, when carefully prepared statements could be presented, so that the press would know just as much as the Gardai wanted them to know.

"We can't lose control of this while we're still in the early stages."

Reeve's determination to put right the shortcomings of the past was clear. Tom Ellison's natural instinct would be to use the occasion to unburden himself of the unfairness meted out to him over time, but his respect for Reeve, Blane and the rest of their team, persuaded him that their restricted ploy was in the best interest of the investigation. The outcome of his return to Drumlasheen had given him a sense of vindication and was not something to help sell newspapers. He had determined that he would never again be the property of the press, but agreed to the Press Conference. He was to hear that Elaine Wallace also agreed.

Was reconciliation still possible?

40

Sitting in Mrs Murtagh's lounge, Tom Ellison placed the remainders of his breakfast to one side, and studied the hand written statement for the press that he had spent the whole of the previous night composing. He had taken Reeve's advice and set out not to mention information crucial to the case and to concentrate on the outcome of his search for justice for Glenn Wallace. As he had started to write it, clarity of thought eluded him, and the opening lines required rewriting several times. He had been looking for an opening with impact. It was the teacher in him coming through. In each attempt, he came across as being too pompous, too self-important, too self-righteous. It was a real test of authorship, the sort of task that he had set countless pupils before. Then he remembered the quote from Confucius, which he invariably gave them.

"Life is actually really simple, but we insist on making it complicated."

Quickly he wrote down a list of facts on the back of a discarded sheet of paper, and then set out to bring them together in as coherent an account as he could, without straying from Finbar Reeve's brief. He read it through for a final time, and was satisfied that journalists would have to work hard to earn their keep. He wasn't going to write their story for them. It was a minor revenge, but it pleased him.

A police car arrived to take him to Police HQ where the Press Conference was due to take place. He was ushered in through the main door and into the reception area.

A lone photographer appeared from nowhere and moved in to take a picture, but two burly officers placed themselves strategically between him and Tom, and the opportunity was gone, as they steered him into a side room.

Eric Blane was surrounded by a group of senior officers, epaulets and cap bands glistening, in sharp contrast to his care- worn suite. Tom Ellison was greeted formally by one and all. Finbar Reeve was setting up a microphone in the middle of a long table. Tom moved forward and they shook hands. Reeve took great care to explain the procedure due to take place. It had been decided that Eric Blane would make an opening statement on behalf of the Gardai. They were unsure of how Elaine Wallace would cope with the tensions, so Tom agreed with the plan that he should follow Blane.

"Did you put something down?" Reeve asked and Ellison nodded in reply.

"Can I see it?" Reeve had been given instructions to check the statement in advance, but he wanted to avoid any hint of lack of trust.

"We need to make copies."

Tom handed over the single sheet of A4 on which he had struggled to limit his remarks. Reeve took it, and drew Tom to a corner of the room, where a photo copying machine was housed. Reeve read through the statement and nodded with satisfaction.

"Great," he said "Just what's wanted!" He slid the sheet into the machine and made a copy.

The room started to fill, and a palpable sense of excitement and expectation pervaded the tiny space. From his corner, Tom watched as reporters and cameramen set themselves up opposite the long table. Nods of acknowledgement were exchanged between them, but business was in hand and their performance would be judged by what they could make of the occasion. Tom counted fourteen cameramen and a huge posse of reporters by the time Eric Blane sat down in his place next to the microphone. Tom's name was printed on a piece of card placed in front of a chair at one end of the long table, and Reeve motioned him into place, setting off a fusillade of clicks and flashes.

Through blinking eyes, Tom Ellison struggled to focus on the gallery in front of him. Featureless faces that were diagnosing and dissecting him instantly, and black eyed cameras, ready to record the moment that would set him into one category or another. He tried to be open faced, giving nothing of any of the stereotypes that they were looking for.

The commotion died down and a strange silence, full of expectation, descended on the room. The knot of senior officers split apart and Elaine Wallace, her bald-headed companion from the Magistrate's Court at her side, entered the room. Commander Charles O'Dowd directed them both to chairs at the opposite end of the table to Ellison, as another barrage of sound and light flooded the space.

Elaine Wallace was dressed in a black two pieced suit with a black shawl draped over her shoulders. An open hand to her face indicated the tension that she was enduring, as the piercing scrutiny continued. Slowly at first, her shoulders trembled as she began to cry. Her companion put his arms around her and gently kissed her on the forehead and she seemed reassured. Looking down the table, Tom Ellison's heart bled for the grieving mother and strengthened his doubt that she should be put through this circus. He tried to imagine the extra pressure it put her under, so soon after the court hearing.

When the pandemonium faded, and silent expectation filled the gap, Commander Charles O'Dowd stood at the end of the table and, in his official capacity, welcomed those present and introduced Inspector Eric Blane, who was to take charge of proceedings. Blane lent forward, unnecessarily close to the microphone, and his voice boomed out from speakers on the floor in front of the table. His embarrassment lightened the atmosphere briefly. He sat back in his chair and started again. He was at pains to point out that investigations were at an early stage and he would not be able to reveal operational details. He read from his prepared statement and finished by saying "When I can, you will be informed. Thank you."

A collective mutter of dissatisfaction filled the room as the brief statement sank in. Then a deafening clamour of questions was aimed at Eric Blane. In response, he raised both hands and waited for the furore to dampen down. Begrudged order restored, he lent forward and said "It's no good gentlemen." And he quickly added "and ladies. I am not going to answer questions today."

Uproar broke as out reporters, previously sitting down, rose to their feet in a tirade of frustration. It carried on until Commander O'Dowd moved in front of the table and stood in open-stance until the protests died away. Seniority seemed to have had an effect, and he announced sternly "I will call all this to an end if you cannot accept Inspector Blane's directive."

The thought that they might go away empty handed, brought about a collective retreat, despite the rancour and resentment that was widely felt.

Eric Blane continued calmly, as if nothing had happened.

"I'd like to introduce Mr Tom Ellison, who was the boy's teacher and he might be able to fill in some gaps."

Tom Ellison was still recovering from the cumulative anger of the crowd, as he nervously accepted the microphone which Blane passed to him. He looked around the gallery of faces before him, and was surprised to see some that he recognised from his previous encounters with The Fourth Estate. He remembered the dictionary definition. *"hacks(n): Worn out horses for hire,"*

He unfolded his sheet of notes and enjoyed the moment of silence.

"Good morning everyone. My name is Tom Ellison," he said. Simply, and as matter of fact as he could. He explained his presence in Drumlasheen in August 1985 and the details of the boy's disappearance. Then, in a moment he could not explain later, and completely ignoring his notes, he said. "I thought I had taken all the necessary precautions that I could to ensure the boy's safety. It didn't seem to satisfy anyone, especially your colleagues, who made my life a misery." His dig at The Press did not go unnoticed and one or two at least moved uncomfortably in their seats.

"In the minds of many people, from that day to this I was a murder suspect." His blood pressure was now off the scale. To help ease it, he took a drink from the glass provided and returned to his written statement. Deep breath.

"I have cooperated with the Gardai at all times. Two weeks ago I received a strange message, saying that I should come to Drumlasheen if I wanted to know about Glenn Wallace's death. As soon as I arrived, my life was threatened." He knew it was not his place to go any further along that line.

"I am grateful that this dreadful matter has been brought to a successful conclusion and I hope those responsible get their true desserts."

He looked to his right and extemporising said "Finally I would like to express to Mrs Elaine Wallace, my heartfelt sympathy for her loss and for the suffering she has undergone over such a long period of time." Head bowed, he sat down, all emotion and energy spent.

In the hiatus that followed, Eric Blane reacted quickly and took the microphone.

"I'd like to introduce Elaine Wallace. You will understand that this is a very sad time for her and her family, and I ask that you respect this and, for now, accept her Statement."

His emphasis on "for now" made his intentions his clear. He passed the microphone to his left. Prefaced by another fusillade of flashes, a respectful silence descended on the room: but pens were poised, ready to record the any morsel of detail.

Elaine Wallace, her head having rested on her companion's shoulder throughout, straightened up and looked through glazed eyes at her interrogators, pausing for a moment on each expectant face. Slowly a tremulous quivering overtook her whole body. She grabbed the table to sustain herself, stood up on faltering legs and announced to the room

"I can't do this! Sorry!" In the stunned silence, she turned to her companion and added plaintively, "Get me out of here!"

He stood up, put his arm round her and she sobbed into his shoulder. A female officer, allocated to her, moved forward and whispered in her ear. A short murmuring conversation took place between them. With a shake of the head in silent communication with her superiors, the officer signalled that Elaine Wallace would take no further part in proceedings. The mood in the room crackled silently, as the expectation of a dramatic story fought with respect for the tragic woman's plight.

As cameras flashed and well rehearsed questions burst out. Elaine Wallace left the room and Tom Ellison was ushered out behind her. In a frenetic exchange of glances Eric Blane sought direction from his superiors. He stretched to take control of the microphone.

"Ladies and gentlemen," he began, "I'm sure you understand Mrs Wallace's distress. Our Press Release will give you information on our investigation so far. Thank you!" Blane made a deliberate show of turning off the microphone and stood to leave. Protests mounted, as the senior officers made their getaway, leaving Finbar Reeve and a constable to issue copies of the prepared statements amongst a furore of protest.

The side room, to which the witnesses had been shepherded, was in sharp contrast and gripped by a silent air of desolation. The final resolution of Glenn Wallace's fate made no difference to the chasm that still separated his mother and Tom Ellison. He stood by the door and she sat at a table by the window, the loathing for him, that she had often expressed, still etched on her face. It was a naked hate that showed no room for reconciliation. Deep down he understood it, but over the years he had longed for it to be put to an end. He would give anything to be able to look into her eyes and see that he had been forgiven. It was not to be, and Tom knew that now.

After what seemed an interminable length of time, the Family Liaison officer entered and knelt down beside Elaine Wallace, and after a short conversation motioned her to the door. Instinctively Tom moved to one side, unsure of how to react. Supported by her companion Elaine Wallace, head down, left the room without looking up. Tom was left alone in a confusion of relief that the Press Conference was done with, and the gnawing anguish that reconciliation had failed.

Finbar Reeve entered the room "You alright?" he asked sympathetically.

"Fine!" Tom answered without conviction. However, despite the irresolvable differences and his misgivings, he was satisfied that at least one load was being lifted from his shoulders.

Riordon and Hanlon must go down.

41

Eric Blane, Finbar Reeve and the rest of the "Operation Elvis" team gathered in Reeve's cramped office. The young detectives were there to bring together the results of the lines of enquiry allocated to them. Blane spoke first.

"You've done a great job...so far. What we've got to do now, is to tie up the loose ends of what we already know, and get to the bottom of the rest of what we suspect, before the anti-terrorist boys step in. I'd like to have the current status of the Mary McMahon investigation. I want it sorted as quickly as possible. Who's dealing with that?" Garda Detective Daniel Smythe slid off the corner of the desk and stood upright, his notes in his hand.

"As far as Mary McMahon's death is concerned, the forensic evidence is pretty clear. Blood on the door lock and skirting board is all Mary's. The only complete fingerprints we found were Mary's and Father O'Mahony's, but all the handles of doors downstairs had been wiped clean. Looking at the state of the house, I reckon these were wiped at the time of her death. No sign of the missing rug. We've also taken away some machined bits and pieces from the shed. I thought perhaps one of our technical boys could work out what they were made for. The white crystals that Detective Reeve found in the shed area is Ammonium Nitrate.

Mixed with fuel oil, it's commonly called ANFO and used originally in coal mining, quarrying, civil construction and such. The full content of the bag would have made several bombs."

Quiet mutterings passed round the room at this last piece of information. He continued "We went through the documents in the house, found very little except...,"

He let it hang in the air for affect.

"We found a letter dated November 1983 from Michael's brother Liam, which gave us an address in Belfast to follow up. The guys in the North tracked down the address, but Michael's brother hadn't lived there recently. Liam is known to them and they would like us to share information with them." Daniel Smythe put his paper work on the desk and stood waiting as if a performer at the end of a show anticipating applause.

Instead Blane snapped "Status?"

"Ongoing!" was the prompt reply.

"What do we know about Michael McMahon's death?" Blane pressed.

"Er. That's me," said James Artherton, nervously clearing his throat.

"I've gone through the Coroner's Report and the statements made by the timber company, and there's nothing there to question the coroner's finding of Accidental Death. The site was inspected by safety officers and they found nothing to suggest negligence either. They did find a notice stating that no one should move timbers single handed. The same sign was still up yesterday when I went round. On the face of it, they assumed Michael must have just been careless. On the other hand, our information casting doubt on this is what Patrick Hanlon says Joseph Riordon said to him. We've questioned Hanlon about it, and he is has no doubt whatsoever that it was an admission on Riordon's part that he had had something to do with McMahon's death, and that *he* could be next. Then there's Connahay's story."

"Oink! Oink!" The sound came from a shielded mouth and, as one, fingers pointed to the heavens.

"We are going to need more than that, if we're to mount a safe prosecution," he added, lost in his exposition.

"Hear! Hear! Yer honour," someone muttered from the back of the tightly packed room. Blane frowned at the frivolity, his lips pursed, to join his eyebrows in a mask of disapproval.

"That'll do!" he snapped.

James Artherton continued "I have spoken to the director of the timber yard and, as I expected, he could think of no explanation other than Michel McMahon had ignored the company rule about working single handed. He seemed nervous to me. That's about it! All we can do is hope that somewhere down the line, Riordon will cough up," he concluded and there was a stifled group guffaw at the prospect.

"Have we got anything more on the shooting of Mr Ellison?" Blane said, bringing the room back to its purpose.

Herbert "Herby" Collins squeezed past Artherton into a space where he could be seen. "As far as forensic evidence is concerned, the link with Joe Riordon is pretty solid. His fingerprints match marks found on the field gate. Needless to say the gun is not registered, but I have managed to link it with a bullet found after a robbery in Kilkenny two years ago."

A murmur of approval went round the room. Herby Collins' thoroughness had drawn in new elements to the investigation, and they all knew that these connections would open wide, what was now becoming, the Gardai's major case in many years.

Collins continued "I have found evidence that Riordon was in Drumlasheen that night and was seen leaving Flannigan's Bar around about the time of the incident. We've got three witnesses who verify that. Also a man who was night fishing on the river, below the bridge, says that he saw someone move past him on the bank. He couldn't give me any details other than it was a man."

There were nods of approval all round at Collins' account and he responded with a modest smile. Eric Blane fought his desire to add to the warm glow which had engulfed the room and said formally,

"Now Fin perhaps you can bring us up to date with the case of the missing boy?"

Finbar Reeve rose from his chair and inched his way towards the blackboard, which now displayed graphically their combined investigations, with arrows crossing from one case to another and showing the complexity of their efforts.

"You all know how dodgy our sources of information were in this case. Looking at the records from the initial investigation and the recent review, it's difficult to see what went wrong. But it's pretty clear that we let ourselves down badly in the past. But that can't be said of you lot. We have bust this case wide open."

There was a mutually triumphant smile amongst the group in response.

"I won't dwell on the initial searches for the boy," he said, knowing they all understood where that would eventually lead.

"In addition to the little "adventure" we shared at The Falcon, we have managed to make a case that the boy was killed by Joe Riordon with a blow to the head from a rifle butt when the boy came across him and McMahon preparing a shipment of guns. We can only surmise that, perhaps, the boy needed to go to the toilet and came across the old boathouse. We don't know where the guns went, but we know from Hanlon's evidence that the transfer to the hearse took place near the house. Did Mary see something, and sometime later put two and two together and questioned her husband about it? This fits in with what Michael was overheard to say at the hospital. Tyrone Connahay's information is our weakest piece of information."

There was general agreement about Connahay's probity.

"But it backs up our case about Michael's connection with the boy's disappearance," Reeve added.

"A lot of what we discovered has already been mentioned. Tom Ellison asking around in the village obviously prompted Joe Riordon to pay Mary McMahon a visit, and then try to see Ellison out of the way too. From that point, all of this (he swept the schematic with his hand) came together. Patrick Hanlon's confession is crucial, and he continues to give us more useful information. He's given us name of Lorna Keene, Riordon's old girlfriend and helper. She might be able to tell us about things from the early 1980's. We continued to question Hanlon, and Riordon, though in his case it's been a waste of time. He's saying nothing. Hanlon has given us more details of the way the group worked and we've added two names to our list of "persons of interest".

Reeve's eyes twinkled as he announced a dramatic new development.

"This morning, I was informed that a mini had been found in a lake near Cork. Details and forensic evidence will follow." The room burst into unfettered approval..

When the uproar had died down, Reeve summarised the situation.

"All the statements of witness tie up with each other, but there's plenty more digging to do before these cases are done. As Inspector Blane says, we must tie up this complicated set of incidents as tightly as possible, so that when the time comes to hand it all over, it is as water-tight as possible. I'm pretty sure it will go to the SCC. We may never know of all the goings- on there. It'll probably be held in secret, but we'll know that we have kitted them out with all the information they need." There was as silence as the idea penetrated.

Reeve concluded "And we have been able to give back a son to his mother, so she can now give him a dignified burial." There was a respectful "Here! Here!"

Without further comment Blane ordered "Go and get it finished!"

42

The meadows on the far shore were clear, and reflected in the flat calm water as he looked out across the lake. Tom Ellison had stayed on for a few days, complete with bodyguard, to help the Gardai fill in any gaps in their investigation. The hierarchy now had control of the process which everyone agreed, to his disappointment, would take many months or longer to complete. However, the truth about Glenn Wallace was out there. Reeve said there would be another internal enquiry into the conduct of the original enquiry. Who knew what that might reveal? Malpractice, subversion or even treason might be uncovered, and Reeve still had doubt about how high any conspiracy might be revealed.

As far as Tom Ellison was concerned, he knew that sometimes Justice becomes blurred in the need for expediency, and he worried that low level scapegoats might be offered up, if the real responsibility lay higher up the establishment chain. He was sure that good men like Finbar Reeve and Eric Blane would do everything in their power to ensure that it did not happen. All that Tom could hope for was that the underlying truths of the matter would be revealed, and those who lead young men down dark paths and stand aloof from the consequences, should be exposed too.

But the dark spectre of politics would have its say, he was convinced. Surely the public must be told?

In his meanderings over the last few days, Tom's mind had inexorably been drawn back to his teaching days. Over the years, seen through embittered eyes, he had observed what had been happening to schooling. Teaching for him had been a vocation, borne only of a desire to enrich the lives of the young and prepare them for life. Although, as a single man, teaching had given him an adequate standard of living, many of his married colleagues had found life in the early 1980's hard going.

Since his dismissal, he had observed the fight over pay and conditions which had affected (adversely he thought) a lessening in how the profession was valued.

In the early 1980's teachers had been involved into a drawn out battle to safeguard their working conditions and salary. Margaret Thatcher had taken on the miners and the print workers unions with anti-union legislation; and won. Teaching, embroiled in a salary dispute at national level, was characterised by inter-union rivalry and division within unions themselves. Tensions, he had heard, developed within schools between individuals supporting a call for withdrawal of labour, and those steadfastly opposed to it. He would have been in the latter camp, but he understood the desperation in the other. The ensuing squabbles had broken up long term friendships and had left some schools with activities curtailed, as teachers worked to rule.

Even from his disconnected position, Tom had worried that those things that he had accepted as a natural part of the teacher's job, consumed in a dispute, might be lost forever. Politics had now got a stranglehold hold on schools, and tinkering from the outside had increased. His kind of maverick teacher seemed to be more and more a rarity. Had he still been teaching, he doubted that he could have accepted the sort of changes that had been forced through. He hoped that it would not leave his profession and their schools discouraged and divided. He felt his beloved job was in crisis. He breathed a deep sigh at the prospect, but at once the reality struck. He was no longer part of all that!

Despite his roaming thoughts, he had felt more content than he had for years. Invigorated, re-energised and, in a childish way, light headed. Perhaps he could look forward to the future. For now, he was here for a last look at a place that had lingered in his consciousness for so long. Would he ever come back to Lake Descarr?

As he stood looking across the waters of the lake, he could still conjure warmth within, from the memory of shinning faces after a day's fishing here. Then one lone face crossed his imagining, and he whispered sadly "Sorry Glenn!"

He began taking a series of photographs to record views that circumstances had denied him doing before. He came to the log in the water and placed it in the centre of his viewfinder. It contrasted sharply, almost in silhouette, with the flat calm water beyond. He put his finger on the button, waiting for a sudden wind to expire. Then, in an instinct, he dropped the camera down to his side. This was a picture he did not need.

At that moment, he heard the clink of stones, as someone approached along the shore. It was Finbar Reeve.

"Mrs Murtagh told me I'd find you here," he said. "When do you leave?"

"Three O'clock! From Dun Laoghaire," Finbar Reeve moved about uneasily, as if preparing to make an important announcement. Ellison had caught the hesitation.

"What is it Fin?" he asked.

"I thought I should let you know that a Chief Superintendent in Security was found dead this morning. They're saying it was suicide. It may have nothing to do with our arrests, but I've heard that he was involved in the original search in some way, but I never saw him myself. We're not sure how, or why, but he was there. One of the photographs you gave me shows him in the background." The tall man in the long black coat came instantly to Tom Ellison's mind. Another piece in the jigsaw perhaps! Reeve added with a triumphant smile. "This business won't go away now, I'm sure. There's a feeling around the Force that we've stirred up more than a hornet's nest, you and me."

"I did nothing," replied Ellison modestly. "You took all the risks."

"Go on! You've borne the blame for years," reassured Reeve. "It's us that let things get away. We have some paying back to do!"

There was a silent moment, which they were glad to share, as they looked across the flat calm waters of the lake, deep in thought. This new development only served to make Tom wonder where events would lead him next. Perhaps it was the vital piece that made the jigsaw complete. For Finbar Reeve, if his worse thoughts were true, it brought things much clearer into focus, the magnitude of which the Gardai and the whole country would have to confront. Reeve was determined that justice be done, whatever the cost to his beloved Garda Síochána

Reeve broke the silence.

"You know we can arrange for someone from UK Special Branch to meet you at Liverpool to discuss protection."

The consequences of the statement, which they had discussed before, held the silence; neither wanting to develop it further. Tom Ellison had thought long and hard about the prospect that might lead to a clandestine life, of someone else's creation, and under another name. Finally he responded.

"I just can't do that Fin. I lost my reputation years ago. I won't lose my name. Especially now."

Reeve nodded in acceptance of the reaction that he had anticipated. He had to make the offer.

"Tom. Can I say something?"

"Of course!"

"When this thing plays out, and you have given your evidence to the court, you will have nothing to be ashamed of. So, for what it's worth, when the time comes, I think you should confront the press head on. Don't hide away from speaking out. It'll be your turn."

Finbar Reeve cared about the way his friend had been treated, and how he might rid himself of the burden he had carried.

For his part, Tom Ellison was taken aback by Finbar's advice, turning on its head his own mindset in dealing with the press. But it came from a source he trusted. Perhaps Finbar was right. His own sense of injustice had been mellowed somewhat by the solution of the boy's disappearance. Perhaps he owed it to all those teachers who daily took on "in loco parentis"," to speak up in support of the responsibility they had always accepted so readily – even in the face of the press' speed to judgement.

"You may be right. We'll see," Tom replied.

They wandered along the water's edge in animated conversation, filled with best wishes and hoped-for reunions. "I must go Tom. I was just passing," Reeve said, knowing full well that he had set aside time for the encounter.

"But you'll be back?" he added.

"Whenever I'm needed, if not before," Tom replied, expressing the bond of their friendship.

"One day you should write a book about it all."

"I don't think so," Ellison chuckled at the thought.

"Well somebody might," Reeve concluded.

They shook hands and clasped each other at the shoulders. Finbar Reeve turned and made his way back towards the tree line. As he disappeared from sight, he started to sing; as if in a rallying call. Before the first line was complete, Tom Ellison joined in lustily.

"Once more I had the finest dream. It came to me today. I dreamed that I was back again, down dear old Leitrim way.

I've travelled far by land and sea for fortune and for fame, But I cannot wait until I see dear old Leitrim's land again."

Book Reviews

Two years after the mysterious disappearance of one of his pupils, discredited teacher Tom Ellison returns to Ireland after receiving a cryptic postcard that might help to solve the mystery and restore his reputation. His return to the scene of his worst nightmare triggers a series of events, which include an attempt on his own life and the death of Mary McMahon, the woman who may hold the key to his search. Events take a dramatic turn as Tom uncovers links with terrorism.

At the heart of this novel lies the story of a teacher's position "In loco parentis".

Good story, well told

By ROBIN R. on 23 Feb. 2016

Received as a gift. This is a well structured novel that moves the reader through both time and place smoothly. All of the characters are expertly portrayed, so that it is easy to remember each one of them, and their role in the story, both the good guys and the bad guys! The gradual exposure of events past and present is well handled to keep the reader's attention, and the book is increasingly hard to put down as more is revealed. The story reflects the author's in depth knowledge of teaching and fishing. These topics may seem an unlikely pairing, but they work well together as linked threads throughout the story. The twist in the tail left me hoping for more - a thoroughly enjoyable read.

5.0 out of 5 stars Well worth a read

By WM on 16 Feb. 2016

It's a shame but I had to go to bed sometime so couldn't finish this book in one sitting. I found it fascinating and the twist, when it came, was truly surprising. Well written and completely absorbing, I can only hope that the author decides to follow up this, his first novel, with another. Well worth a read.

A very engaging book

By David Senior

A very engaging book, fast paced, short chapters and with a reflective style that was both endearing and profound in moral message. For any teacher, Priest, Police hierarchy, politician, youth worker, parent and young person this is a compelling read. Many issues are raised in a culture that has changed dramatically since the 1980's which sees community life challenged in the arena of friendship, appropriateness, safeguarding and vulnerability.

An entertaining and challenging book.

By Gwyneth Annie Johns

What a really interesting story. It grips you straight away so that you have to keep turning the page. Interesting at the end and I hope Mr Jones writes a sequel. I read this book in 24 hrs. Brilliant read.

Well written. A must read.

By Mrs A P Logan on 1 Mar. 2016

This is a story about a depressed alcoholic teacher whose life was turned upside own through no fault of his own. He's very likeable, and at times completely out of his depth. He returns to Ireland to try and find out what happened to a boy who went missing on a school trip years earlier. The teacher Tom Ellison who organised the trip was held responsible by the boys mother. The mystery slowly unfolds with surprising consequences. There's a twist in the tale that leaves the reader wanting more. (hurry up with the sequel)

Alan Jones

About the Author

I was born and in Earlestown in Lancashire, and I went to Newton-le-Willows Grammar School where I discovered my love of Art, singing and cricket. I attended Bath Academy of Art and Birmingham School of Art for my teacher training. After leaving college I taught in Warrington and then moved to Leamington, where I taught in Warwickshire Schools in charge of Art and as a Year Tutor until I retired after 35 years.

I have had a life-long passion for the all the Arts. This led me to writing plays and musicals, initially for school performances, and later for adult groups. I have enjoyed recording talking books and doing voiceovers for my own and others' films.

My love of fishing and its value as a teaching medium has been important to me. As Angling Education Officer for The National Federation of Anglers I co-wrote the National Kingfisher Award Scheme for beginners and I wrote and produced the DVD "Start Fishing" both for national distribution.

I wrote, voiced and produced a DVD telling the 900 year history of St. Nicholas Church, victim of an arsonist attack in 2008.

For further information on the author visit : ajpublishing.uk

Watch out for the Sequel

The Final Peace

Available in the New Year

Lightning Source UK Ltd.
Milton Keynes UK
UKHW020628291222
414373UK00012B/155